FYI, I CHEAT BACK!

B.M. Hardin

Hardin Book Co.
www.authorbmhardin.com
ISBN: 978-1-7350902-5-2

Author Email: bmhardinbooks@gmail.com
Printed in the United States of America

This book is a work of fiction. Any similarities of people, places, instances, and locals are coincidental and solely a work of the author's imagination.

In Memory of Uncle Fray

FYI, I CHEAT BACK!

CHAPTER ONE

He's one brave son of a bitch!

I'll give him that much.

I decided to circle the block one more time to give Emory enough time to get that bitch away from my house!

I let out a low growl as I caught a glimpse of Emory shutting the passenger side door of the green Nissan just as I passed by the street.

Emory knows that his bright yellow, old school Chevy Caprice, with chrome wheels, and his custom *King Auto* tag would be easily spotted by me or someone who knows me, while he was out doing his dirty deeds. So, I can only assume that Emory thinks he's being slick by having the woman he's cheating on me with, pick him up and drop him off, at our house, while I'm supposed to be at work.

I'm sure this isn't the first time she's been to our house. And because I'm currently hiding the fact that I know about her, I'm sure it won't be the last.

I've known for over a month that Emory is cheating on me. At first, I was ready to set it off; simply put, I wanted to stab him and that bitch!

But I said and did nothing.

Let me explain why.

Emory was supposed to be the love of my life.

I thought what we had was special.

We've been together for six years. And we've accomplished so much.

We bought a house together over two years ago. We've traveled all over the country together, hand and hand. And we're planning to have a baby. At least we were.

Marriage…maybe.

One day.

Though I already wear the three-carat diamond ring that Emory gave me for my birthday three years ago. Unlike most women, I've never been in a rush to walk down the aisle. As long as we were together, that's all that mattered to me.

For six years, I've put in the work.

I've put time into molding Emory into the man he is today. A man with his own business, goals, dreams and ambition. He is everything that he is because of me. And I know that for a fact! Emory is well on his way to becoming the first millionaire in his family. I just didn't expect unfaithfulness to come along with his success.

I've always been faithful to Emory.

No matter what, I had his back when no one else did. I poured into him. I spoke life into him. I lifted him up, and I'll admit it; he has done the same for me. I can depend on Emory for anything. He made me better in a way; at least he made me want to be better.

And for that, I love him.

Yes, although he's cheating on me, I *still* love him.

But…fuck him!

You see, sometimes you get mad.

And other times, baby, you just get even!

And that's exactly what I plan to do!

Sure, I could just call Emory out on the cheating and leave him. But where's the fun in that?

FYI…I cheat back!

And Emory is about to see just how low-down and dirty I can get when someone takes my love for granted! I'm a firm believer that you don't hurt people that's good to you. And once I'm done with Emory, he'll never do something like this to someone who loves him again!

There's a lot of things that Emory doesn't know about me. I haven't always been the nice, loving, supportive woman that he knows me to be. I haven't always been so cool, calm and collected. No. I was born and raised in pain and with issues. And let's just say…Emory has flipped the wrong switch!

Now, Emory is going to get a taste of the old me. The side of me that I thought was gone forever. The side that I'd tried to hide from him for all these years. The side of me where the saying "she gets it from her mama," truly applies.

Emory is about to see the monster in me.

Well, more or less.

And if I'm being honest, cheating isn't the worst thing that has ever happened to me. I've been through worse. I've seen worse. And honestly, I've done worse things too. I've done some things in my past that though I'm not proud of them, I don't regret doing them. Not one bit.

But cheating…cheating just does something to me. It hits a whole different nerve deep down inside of me. It's one of those things that I take very personal. Cheating on me is one of the worst things a man can ever do to me. I despise it. It reminds me of my father, and it takes me to a dark and angry place that's hard for me to come back from.

Honestly, I'm disappointed in Emory.

As stupid as I may sound, I never thought Emory would cheat on me. And I never thought I would be in this situation again.

I guess I thought wrong.

A part of me almost wishes I could just let it go.

I've worked hard over the years to change my life, and my ways. And doing what I *want* to do to Emory, just to get even with him, is going to set me and my personal growth back a few years.

And believe me, it was a lot of work to get to where I am today. I was damaged. Broken. Thanks to my awful parents and the unbelievable childhood I had to endure.

Both of my parents are, well, they were the definition of pain. Evil might be a better word to describe my mother.

My mother was raised by a horrible, evil mother, and she very well became a horrible mother too. She was mean for no reason at all. Honestly, I think she had some mental issues that she would never admit to, let alone seek the help that she so desperately needed.

Anyway, if my siblings and I weren't getting beat for no reason, my two brothers and I were running around the neighborhood looking for food. Not because we didn't have any. Oh no, we had plenty thanks to my father owning a very well-known car dealership back in those days.

But on random days, my mother would decide that we couldn't eat for the day. She would chain the refrigerator door shut. Then, she would take the cabinet food and lock it in her bedroom. No real reason. She would simply tell us to figure out where our next meal was coming from.

And she meant just what she'd said too.

I can remember her doing things like this as early as the age of eight. I would play at friend's houses all day, just so they would invite me to stay for dinner. I would eat as much as I could and praise the mother about her cooking in order to ask for a doggy bag to take home, so that I could feed my brothers. And check this out, my mother would then get upset because I actually found a way for us to eat.

How sick is that?

Sometimes, mama would make me do these little skits with her. She would make me be one of her enemies. Or someone that she envied or hated. Hell, sometimes she made me pretend to be one of her sisters. And then, she would say to me everything she wished she'd said to them about numerous of random situations. Sometimes she would hit me too, pretending as though I was whomever she had me pretending to be at the time. She would call me by their names and everything. And once it was all over with, she would act as though it never even happened.

And my father, he never said a word.

He never tried to stop her.

He was weak. He was a coward. He always let mama do whatever she wanted to do to us---just as long as she was out of his way so that he could cheat with every woman in our neighborhood.

My father, Geo Duane Parks, always cared more about cheating, than the welfare of his children. He cared more about cheating than making sure we were clean or fed. He cared more about cheating than saving us from the lunatic that we called mama.

And this is why cheating on me stirs up anger and pain inside of me. It reminds me of how selfish a person can be.

Cheating disgusts me. It makes me so angry that I can't even put it into words. So, I let my actions do the talking.

I caught my father cheating on my mother several times; twice in the actual act, once in their bed.

Strangely, he never asked me not to tell on him. In a way, I think he hoped I would. He wanted my mother to find out and divorce him. It was obvious that he wanted to leave her, but he didn't have the guts to. He wanted me to tell her what I'm sure she already knew, but I never said a word.

If I had to be stuck with her, so did he.

And then, my first year in high school, both of my shitty parents decided to find God. And that started a whole new level of crazy in our house.

My mother and father became so obsessed with being righteous and better people, that they actually ended up being worse than they were before.

Plenty of school nights, my mother would wake us up in the middle of the night and make us pray, chant, or meditate in the backyard. Butt ass naked, in the rain, sleet or snow. And if we fell asleep, we paid one hell of a price for it. She would beat us and say she was doing it because God loves us. She never once said it was because *she* loved us. Truthfully, I don't really think she did. I don't think she could.

Once, my mother, Evil Evette, forced me into a bathtub and poured oil all over me. She threatened to drop a match on me if I tried to get out. She made me stay in that bathtub for twelve long hours, while she read scriptures to me half the time, and dropped hot candle wax all over me. I remember asking her why she was doing it, and she said it was her duty as my mother to teach me lessons in pain, endurance and sacrifice.

My mother was a nutcase!

There were times that she would cut my hair if it grew longer than hers. And she wouldn't buy me any deodorant, for some odd reason, no matter how much I smelled or begged for it. I ended up stealing some from the store and keeping it in my locker at school.

Needless to say, as a child, as a teen, and as an adult…I couldn't stand my mother. Yet, somehow I loved her and felt sorry for her and whatever she endured to make her become the monster that she was.

Being the oldest, I tried my best to stay in the house as long as I could to look after my brothers, but by the age of seventeen, I'd had enough of my parents.

I left home and moved in with a friend who at the time, hated her parents just as much as I did.

Yana is still my best-friend to this day.

She was rich. Well, her parents were. As a senior in high school, Yana had her own condo, being paid for by her parents as they traveled all over the world.

She hated her life; until she got a whiff of mine.

I ended up living with her my entire senior year of high school. I rarely saw my parents but being that one of my brother's was in high school with me, as a freshman, Yana would give me money to give to him just in case mama had one of her spells.

That year changed my life.

If I'd stayed at home with my parents, I'm not sure what would've happened to me, or what I would've become.

Once I graduated high school, I enrolled into a community college, got a job, and finally, I got my first real boyfriend. But after dating him for a few months, he started to show his true colors.

At first, he pretended to be nice, and sweet, but the real him was controlling and abusive. He would yell and scream at me for no reason at all, causing me to have horrible flashbacks of my mother.

Then, one day, something in me snapped.

I was tired of people hurting me and causing me pain.

It was time for me to start doing the same.

One night, after he slapped me, I set his shirt on fire while he was still wearing it. He nearly broke his neck trying to get out of it. He suffered a few burns. But he didn't die though. He did call me a crazy bitch and said that he never wanted to see me again. I was okay with that.

And every man after him, I made it clear that I could get on whatever level they wanted to get on. And whatever they did to me, I did right back to them; most of the time, I did worse.

I always got even.

Always.

I've done some pretty crazy things in most of my past relationships.

Once, I flushed one of my exes mother's ashes down the toilet. Another ex, I pissed in his cornflakes…literally. I sat there and watched him eat every, single bite. And I encouraged him to drink the milk at the end. I remember laughing when he made a comment about the milk tasting a little spoiled.

I caught an ex in the beginning stages of cheating once. He hadn't cheated on me yet, but he was making plans to.

So, I told him I wanted to have hot, nasty, kinky sex that night. He was a sexaholic, so I knew he would be down. Later that night, I tied him up, face down, and then…I superglued his ass cheeks together. And the best part about it was that he couldn't do a damn thing to stop me! He screamed, as I laughed. And then, I got dressed and left him there, all tied up. I'm not sure how long he stayed tied up that night, because I changed my number. But he did show up at my apartment two days later threatening to whoop my ass.

I chuckled a little at my thoughts as I headed back towards my street.

My ex, Benji, crossed my mind. He's an ex from a long, long time ago.

One night, I found out that Benji was cheating on me. He was asleep when some woman that apparently he'd been seeing, for over a year, at the time, called his cell phone. She had no idea he was in a relationship with me and she told me that they were in love. She also told me that Benji asked her to marry him. She said he gave her a ring, and everything, all while in a relationship with me.

I was hurt.

Heartbroken.

Benji was the guy of my dreams, at the time, and I really thought he was the one.

I guess I'm just not that lucky.

Nevertheless, as he slept, I went into his roommate's bedroom down the hall. It'd been obvious for quite some time that his roommate wanted me. I could see it in his eyes whenever he looked at me. He would even make inappropriate comments whenever Benji wasn't around.

That night, I nearly sucked the skin off Benji's roommate's dick, let him cum in my mouth, and then I brushed my teeth with Benji's toothbrush. After that, I got dressed, packed up whatever belongings I had there, picked up Benji's dog, and put it in the oven. I turned the oven on three-fifty and walked out of the apartment.

I hated that damn dog anyway.

I didn't let it bake to death though. Unfortunately, after about three minutes, I called Benji's roommate's cell phone and told him to get the dog out of the oven. And a few minutes after that, Benji called me over and over again, leaving message after message calling my crazy and acting as though he hadn't done anything wrong.

I never answered any of his calls.

I never spoke to him again.

There was nothing left to say.

I got what I wanted.

I got even.

Although, that night did make me realize that I might have more of my mother in me than I wanted to admit. It made me realize that I needed to change. Just a little bit.

And so, I did.

After two years at a community college in Houston, after taking a lengthy break in between because I was too busy chasing behind men, finally, I headed to finish up my degree at the University of Mississippi.

A new state. New people.

Away from everything and everyone I've ever known.

I finished college, with a degree in marketing, and in a new place, every day, I worked on being a better person.

Better than the mother and father who raised me.

Both of them are dead now.

Six years ago, my mother died from a stroke and a few years later, my father went to bed one night, and simply didn't wake up the next morning.

I met Emory six months after my mother died. I was in in a pretty good place when I met him.

I had a good job at a marketing and advertising agency and a nice apartment. My stomach was flat and my booty was phat. Life for the most part, was good.

And I'll admit that my life got just a little bit better with Emory in it. It found a new purpose with Emory.

Emory was just starting out with his own business, but together, we took his business to the next level.

We hustled together. We made big moves and plans together. Everything was great between us.

Why did he have to go and mess it all up?

I learned early that what one woman won't do, another woman will, so I made it my business to keep Emory satisfied. If it was within my power to do it, I did it for him or to him, with no questions asked.

So, if you ask me, he had absolutely no reason to cheat on me; not a single reason. Not that men need a reason to cheat anyway.

And because I know that cheating on me was for his own selfish reasons, now, in my mind, he's no better than my father was. And no matter how much I've changed over the years; I can't let him get away with it.

I just can't.

Emory has been my longest relationship, and I've loved him with everything in me. And trust me, never really feeling loved, yet managing to give someone your entire heart was hard to do, but I did it.

For Emory. I did it all.

But just like everyone else, he hurt me.

So, now he has to pay. It's the only way.

I grinned, evilly, as I thought about my revenge.

Right under Emory's nose, I plan to do the unthinkable to him. Not only am I going to get him back by cheating on him, but if I'm lucky, I'll get pregnant by the other guy too.

You see, Emory wants a baby so bad. And I mean more than anything else in the world. Partly because for years, he was told he would never be able to have kids, but after a few different opinions and treatments, his soldiers started to do what they were supposed to do, and his fiancée, at the time, got pregnant with their child. Unfortunately, both she and their son died during labor.

And though Emory still gets emotional about it, sometimes, he wants to have another child like yesterday! He begs me, almost weekly, to stop taking my birth control pills so we can try to get pregnant. He always talks about baby names, and things that he wants to do whenever we finally have a baby.

So, my plan is, to cheat, get pregnant, get Emory all excited about having the baby that he's always wanted, and then on the day I go into labor…BOOM! I'll tell him that the baby isn't his. And while his heart shatters into a million little pieces, I'll smile bigger and brighter than I ever have before.

It'll serve him right.

It'll hurt Emory just as much as he has hurt me.

Sure, getting even with Emory, the way that I want to do it, is going to take months and dedication, but I don't have nothing but time. And the good thing is that I actually do want a child, so, it's a win-win situation for me.

Nova Revae Parks always wins in the end.

Emory has no idea how evil I can be.

But he's about to find out.

And I already know who I'm going to cheat on him with too.

Emory's new mechanic, Kojo, is a tall glass of chocolate milk, with a body hand sculpted by God.

I've caught him undressing me with his eyes a few times. Not to mention that he and Emory have become quite close these days. Almost like best friends.

Yes. He's perfect.

I'm going to let Kojo fuck me into a coma, over and over again, until he gets me pregnant with his baby. I'm getting excited just thinking about it!

Seeing that the Nissan belonging to the other woman was now out of my driveway, I pulled in and opened the garage. The bitch has to know that Emory has a woman. Just looking at our house; the landscape and front porch screams that a woman with style and flare lives here. She has to know that he's in a relationship.

She just doesn't care.

But that's okay. I have a little something up my sleeve for her disrespectful ass too!

As soon as I entered our lavish, yet cozy bedroom, I stepped out of my shoes. I rolled my eyes at the sound of the shower running. Emory knew I would be on my way home around this time, so, I'm not surprised that he rushed to take a shower. He wouldn't want me to smell her on him. He really does think that he's two steps ahead of me.

I work for the same marketing agency that I was working for when I met Emory. Only now, I make a double-digit base pay, plus I bring home four or five figure commissions every month.

I've been working on a big marketing campaign for a new client for the past three months. So, there's been a lot of late nights and early mornings that I've been spending at work.

Still, I would make time for Emory. Most nights, I would come home, completely exhausted, and still entertain and fuck him.

But those days are over.

The next time Emory touches me it'll be time for me to pull off my pregnancy stunt. I'll have to screw him, at least once, so that he thinks the baby is his.

As I undressed, I stared at myself in the mirror.

I've always been short and fairly slim, but for the past few years, my thighs have started to thicken up and finally, they match this juicy booty that I've always carried around.

My skin is coffee-colored, with two shots of cream, and my high-cheek bones are the best things I got from my mother. My head full of curly hair came from my father, and so did my eyes and nose. I'm as cute as I wanna' be. In my opinion, I'm a man's wet dream, and his worst nightmare all rolled up into one. So, I don't have a clue as to why men keep cheating on me!

"Hey, baby. When did you get here?"

Emory came out the bathroom with a towel around his waist.

"A few minutes ago."

Emory kissed my lips. I felt sick to my stomach.

Playing as though I don't know about his cheating is one of the hardest things I've ever had to do. In the past, I got straight to my revenge, and then, I walked away.

But not with Emory.

Pretending to be dumb is the only way I can hurt him the way that I want to. I've never wanted to hurt anyone so badly before. I'm trying to break his heart and give him suicidal thoughts, all at the same damn time.

So, a girls' gotta' do what a girls' gotta' do.

It'll all be worth it in the end.

"How was work today? I'm tired of them making my baby work these late hours," Emory pretended to be concerned.

"It was fine. How are things at the shop?"

Emory owns not one, not two, but three auto shops, thanks to me. When I met him, he was just getting started with the first one. It was in a little building right off Georgetown street. But with my help, and my marketing and advertising skills, I helped him get tons of business, a new building, and enough money to open two more locations within the state. With the marketing plan I put together for him, within the next five years, I predict that he'll have locations in at least three more states and generating millions of dollars a year.

"Things are good. I worked on a 1978 Monte Carlo today," Emory smiled.

That smile of his is what caught my attention.

The day I met Emory I was standing in line at the post office. He was three people behind me. I happened to turn around and he smiled at me.

I was instantly attracted to him.

Aside from his nice smile, Emory has some of the darkest skin I've ever seen. He's so dark-skinned that the only thing you can in the dark is his pearly white teeth.

He isn't all that tall, only maybe an inch or two taller than I am with heels on, but he has broad shoulders with big arms and legs. His calf muscles make my mouth water and he has big strong hands and thick dick too.

"Um, baby, you want me to run you a bath?"

"No. I'm just going to hop in the shower."

"Okay. I'll be waiting for you when you get out. I'll go warm up your food. I got your favorite from that Italian restaurant uptown," Emory beamed at me.

"Thank you."

These days, it's getting harder and harder to keep my cool, especially when Emory wants brownie points for doing little things for me that normally I would have thanked him beyond the moon and stars for.

Pretending is hard.

But somehow, cheaters do it so easily.

After finding something cool and sexy to sleep in, I headed to shower. The thumping sound the water made as it pounded against the shower floor, reminded me of a day a long time ago.

All I've ever wanted is to love and be loved.

I couldn't get it from home, so, I looked for it everywhere else. And not just from men. In my friendships too. The summer I turned fourteen, a new girl and her parents moved next door to us.

Missy.

Little Ms. Missy is what her parents called her.

She was always dressed in the latest styles, and she always smelled like candy. Missy would knock on our front door and ask if I could come over to her house to hang out. Surprisingly, most days, my mother would allow it.

On hot summer days, we would drink lemonade, while she put French braids in my hair and told me stories about all the places she'd been. Missy told the stories so well that I felt as though I'd gone there too.

Growing up, my parents took us to the beach every now and then, but that's about it. That reason alone is part of why Emory and I traveled the way we did together. I told him I wanted to visit all fifty states. So far, I've been to twenty-six of them. And on a few international trips too.

Anyway, Missy and I spent a lot of time together that summer.

She was my friend.

And I loved her.

I think.

But when school started, Missy became someone else. Someone horrible and mean. Someone like my mother.

We were both freshman in high school, and though I thought we were going to be the best of friends, Missy found other girls who I assume she thought were more her speed and on her level. She made it clear that she no longer wanted to be my friend. She started to tease me and talk about my hair and clothes. And then, one day, she told everyone in our gym class that my mother beat me. I never told her what went on inside my house, but I'm sure that a few times she probably noticed the bruises on my arms. She just never said anything about them until that day, in front of all those people.

Missy laughed and a few others laughed at me too.

She was supposed to be my friend.

After gym class, Missy always took a long shower. She was just anal that way, and she hated to sweat. Once everyone left the locker room, I stood outside the shower, listening to the water hit the floor and to Missy singing off key. And just as she started to sing the bridge, I pulled the cheap shower curtain back and pushed her from behind. Missy yelled, and tried to keep her balance, but she went tumbling down, hitting her head on the shower bench along the way.

I remember watching her lie there, with her eye closed, water hitting her face, and blood flowing from her head, painting the shower floor crimson red.

And I felt nothing.

Other than she'd gotten what she deserved.

She shouldn't have been talking shit.

I headed to my next class as though nothing happened.

Missy suffered a concussion and was out of school for a whole week. She told her parents and the teachers that someone pushed her. Of course, she told them that she thought it was me, but I denied it. And being that it all happened so fast and Missy didn't actually see me, she couldn't prove it.

But because she thought it was me, after that, Missy stayed far away from me. She never spoke to me again.

And she never teased me again either.

"Your food is hot and on the table," Emory said once I was out of the shower. "Um, I see something that I would love to eat," he eyed me greedily.

"Not tonight. I would probably fall asleep," I used as an excuse. I'm sure Emory has noticed all the excuses I have when it comes to having sex lately. But I don't care.

"I know, baby. At least eat something."

After putting lotion all over my body, I made my way to eat my food. I picked up my plate from the table and took it to the sofa, where I planned on sleeping.

I didn't want to be anywhere near Emory's lying, cheating ass; especially not in bed next to him.

Besides, the further away I am from him...

The safer Emory will be.

~***~

"Um, um, um," Ox followed me towards my office.

"What do you want, Ox?" I smiled at him as I took a seat.

"You."

"Other than me," I grinned.

Ox is actually one of my bosses, but he doesn't act like it. He's laid back, cool, inappropriate, and I can say with confidence that over the years, despite him wanting to have sex with me, we've become pretty good friends.

"How did the conference call go last night?"

Ox unbuttoned his jacket and sat down in the leather chair in front of my desk.

Ox is a character, to say the least. His sense of humor is something I look forward to on most days. He's a whole vibe, some would say. And I would have to agree. Ox's presence is somewhat invigorating.

Ox is in his late thirties. He's single, and fairly attractive. He isn't like jaw-dropping handsome, or anything like that, but his style, swag, and intelligence could help him snag any woman, in any room, on any given day…well, except for me.

He's been after me for years, but I've always turned him down. Mostly, I used not wanting to mix business with pleasure as my professional response to his flirting; which in a way is the truth. But really, I was just so in love with Emory, and cheating on him was always out of the question. But now that my faithful days are over…

I filled Ox in on the conference call. He gave his input and then got right back to flirting with me.

"Why are you playing with my emotions, Nova? You know I want you," Ox smiled. "You friend-zoned me for that little mechanic of yours. And it's not fair," he pouted like a five-year old.

We both laughed.

"That little mechanic has three locations now and headed towards millionaire status."

"And I'm already there…so what's up?" Ox smirked as he stood up and buttoned his blazer. "When you ready to stop playing with me, I'll be ready."

"Bye, Ox," I smiled at him, wiggling my fingers.

"Bye, *my* Nova."

Though my plans are to cheat with Emory's friend…maybe I can take Ox's dick for a test drive too. I mean, he has been trying to give it to me for years. I might as well see if it's as good as I think it is.

Cheating on Emory with Ox will be for my pleasure. Cheating on Emory with his friend is for a purpose.

Pleasure.

Purpose.

Hmmm…I think I'll have a scoop of both!

I opened my laptop and headed to my fake social media profile. I posted in one of the nasty sex groups I'd recently joined.

"I'm looking for a tall, dark and handsome man, that currently has gonorrhea or chlamydia. Inbox me if that's you. Payment involved. Serious inquires only!"

I typed.

Hopefully, I'll find just what I'm looking for.

I let out an evil chuckle. I've got something up my sleeve and trust me…it isn't pretty.

Actually, it's quite itchy.

~***~

"Okay, so what's really up, Nova? Every time I try to touch you, it's a problem," Emory complained. "Come on, now, it's been weeks. I'm a man. I'm your man. And I have needs and shit. And you're not taking care of them."

I wanted to tell him to go to hell.

Actually, I wanted to tell him to get that bitch to take care of his needs, but I swallowed my words and smiled.

"Emory, I'm just so stressed out at work. I haven't really been in the mood for sex. But I'm close to closing out this project and I promise you I'm going to fuck you so good that you'll be speaking in tongues when all of this is over." I kissed his lips. "I promise. I just need to focus. That's all. I have so much pressure on me already. I don't need pressure from you too."

Emory's face softened as I kissed his lips again.

"I'm sorry, baby. You're right. I know you're under a lot of stress. Come here," Emory pulled me closer to him. Once I was in his arms, he kissed the side of my face over and over again, until finally, he fell asleep.

For a second, warm and safe, I almost forgot how much I hate him. I remember the long days from work where we would both rush home just to be in each other's arms. I remember the days where business was slow for Emory, so, I would go out of my way just to make his day. And some days, I would be drawing a blank to come up with catchy, or unique, marketing ideas, but Emory would be right there with me, feeding me inspiration and talking out my ideas with me.

We made on hell of a team.

I'm disappointed in him.

Slowly, I slid out from under his embrace, and scooted over to my side of the bed.

He had no reason at all.

He had no right to mess things up.

I thought about forgiveness.

I haven't been to church since I left my parent's house. Once they found religion, they forced us to go so much that I never had the desire to go again once I was older.

Do I believe in the Man above?

I do.

But I also believe in karma---and his cute little side chick named *payback*.

And I like them a hell of a lot more than that forgiveness mess.

Emory woke up the next morning in a good mood.

It's Saturday.

And every third and fourth Saturday of each month, we spend the entire day together.

"Get dressed. Breakfast on me, baby," Emory smiled.

It amazes me how he acts as though he isn't doing anything wrong. He still acts like the perfect man. Hell, sometimes, he almost makes me second guess what I already know.

But I know what I know.

I'll never forget the time I followed him on my lunch break and saw him kissing her. Or the nudes she sent to his phone one night while he was in the shower. Or the text messages I read between the two of them, and not to mention, recently, seeing her drop him off at our house.

Emory is definitely cheating on me.

He just doesn't care.

He doesn't care that he's hurting me and tearing us apart. He doesn't care how his actions will affect everything that we've worked so hard to build.

All he cares about is himself.

No matter how much he pretends to care about me.

I got dressed for breakfast.

I dressed in a sexy, strapless, flower print dress, wedges, big hoop earrings, and I pulled my hair up in a bun at the top of my head.

"Shit! I just wanna' bend you over and…"

"Come on, I'm hungry," I interrupted Emory.

He exhaled loudly and followed me towards the front door. I walked slowly, so that he could get an eyeful of every, single, booty-jiggle, since I wasn't wearing any panties.

"Nova?" Emory said behind me.

"Yes?"

I faced him.

There was something on his mind. He looked as though he wanted to ask me something. Or tell me something. The way he looked at me was as though it finally hit him. As though he suddenly had the gut feeling that I knew he was cheating on me.

But he isn't one-hundred percent sure.

"Never mind," Emory said.

We decided to drive my new midnight blue Jeep Wrangler. Emory drove with the music loud, and all the windows down, and though it made my hair messy, the weather was warm and I was loving every minute of it.

Emory reached for my hand. I allowed him to hold it.

The part about trying to wrap up a big deal at work is actually the truth. I have about a week and a half left on the project I've been working on, but once it's all done, and once the $60,000 commission check that I'll be receiving is in my bank account, I'll be able to fully focus on the whole getting pregnant by Emory's friend thing.

I glanced down at the notification on my cell phone.

Yes! Finally!

I clicked on the icon, hoping to see the response I've been looking for.

"What's up? So, I'm STD free right now, but for the right price...I know where I can get one. I can put something in motion today. Just say the word. Let me know."

His response was like music to my ears.

I took a quick glance at his photos.

Damn! My mouth watered, a little bit, as I continued to scroll through his photos. He definitely gives me "Emory" vibes. And he's perfect for what I have in mind!

I messaged him back, asking him if we could talk more later and hopefully meet for lunch soon.

Emory grinned at me, just as I placed my cell phone face down on my lap.

I grinned back.

It's showtime, baby!

*****

CHAPTER TWO

"What's up, Nova. Emory isn't here," Kojo said, trying hard not to eye-fuck me.

I already knew Emory wasn't at the shop.

He's at one of his other locations about an hour away.

"I just came by to pick up some things from his office."

I smiled at Kojo, before sashaying away from him. I didn't have to look back. I already knew he was watching me walk away.

Kojo is a big six-foot-five chocolate-covered giant.

He's massive. He wears a bald head with a big scruffy beard. His eyes are a green and light brown mix. And don't even get me started on his lips.

The first time I saw him, I had to force myself not to stare. I found him overwhelmingly attractive, and though I've never fantasized about being with him, hopefully, I'll be able to get the real *thing* soon.

I entered Emory's office and closed the door behind me. I wasn't actually looking for anything, so I took a seat behind his desk.

Emory hasn't changed a thing in his office since I decorated it. He had the cutest picture of us on his desk.

I remember that day.

The day he gave me this ring.

Emory booked us a couple's photoshoot at the park.

That day, he made me feel so damn good.

He made me feel special. Beautiful. And as though I was the most important person in the world.

On that day, I was wearing a strapless yellow sundress. My skin glowed as a result of being kissed by the sun. I wore the brightest, most beautiful smile on my face. I felt complete happiness for the first time in my life.

A few minutes into the photoshoot, the photographer instructed me to turn around. And then, he told me to glance back over my shoulder.

Once I did, that's when I saw Emory on his knee.

He asked me to be his wife that day. And though, in the moment, I screamed yes, once reality set in, I made it clear to Emory that I wasn't in a rush to get married.

From the marriages I've seen, marriage isn't exactly goals for me. Most of the married people I know are either unhappy, cheating, or a mixture of both.

Hmm…

I wonder if Emory would've cheated on me if I was already his wife. He wanted to get married a long time ago. I wonder if it would've made a difference.

I started to rummage through his desk.

My heart stopped beating for what seemed like forever once I came across the box of condoms.

Hurriedly, I poured them on his desk and started to count.

Six condoms were missing.

Emory and I have never, and I do mean never used a condom. Not even the first night we had sex.

It happened so fast. One minute, we were having a lovely dinner. And the next, I was butt naked, on my knees, on top of the kitchen table.

Fury stirred around in my belly and I knew if I didn't get out of Emory's office, right then and there, I was going to break everything I could get my hands on.

I put everything back just as I'd found them, and I rushed out of the office more ready than ever to get back at Emory.

"Are you good?" Kojo asked.

"Yes. I'm good. I've never been better."

I smiled at him. And as I walked by Kojo, I allowed my hand to brush up against the dick print that was showing through the tight navy-blue work pants he was wearing. I didn't bother to look back to see what his reaction was.

Kojo…I'm coming for you.

And I'm not coming to play!

~***~

"I never doubted you!" My other boss, Ox's co-owner of the company, Don, complimented me, as Ox popped open bottles of champagne.

"You're a fucking rockstar!"

All of my co-workers cheered as I beamed with success.

I'd just finished my long marketing project for a billion-dollar company. My biggest project to date, and they absolutely loved it!

"I believe this belongs to you."

Ox reached me a check.

"$75,000?"

"They thought you deserved a bonus," Don smiled.

"Well, I wasn't going to mention it or anything," I smirked.

I was expecting the $60,000, but $75,000…

Oh, hell yeah!

This upcoming "planned" pregnancy might take me through hell, so, I need as much money as possible in my savings account, just in case I'm unable to work. And just in case my little plan somehow blows up in my face and Emory finds out the truth, and leaves me while pregnant, leaving everything to fall on me.

I'll be well prepared for whatever comes my way.

Getting pregnant by another man, on purpose, just to hurt Emory is fucked up on so many levels. It really is pretty evil. But on the other side of things, I actually *do* want to be a mother.

So, it's a win-win for me.

Emory and I have talked about having a baby for so long, that not too long ago, I finally agreed that I would consider getting pregnant at the end of the year.

I want to be a mother because I want to give a child everything I never had. I want to love them and I want to have someone who will truly love me back.

I'd wanted so badly to share parenthood with Emory someday. But now, I just can't wait to break his little lying, cheating ass heart!

I've already been trying to figure everything out.

Once my period comes on this month, I plan to stop taking my birth control pills without telling him.

And then…

"All I'm saying is…can I get a loan?" Ox laughed, pulling me away from my thoughts.

"Stop it," I took the glass of champagne from his hand. "I'm just glad it's done. Y'all worked me to death on this one!"

"Because we knew you could do it. There's nowhere to go but up from here, baby," Ox tapped my glass with his. "Let me take you out to dinner."

"Sorry. Emory wants to celebrate."

Ox rolled his eyes, as I thanked everyone before grabbing my purse and walking out of the building like a boss.

I'd lied to Ox.

I haven't even told Emory that the big project is officially complete. I did have a brief date with someone else though.

My first stop was at the bank to deposit my check and to take out what I needed for my upcoming transaction.

A few minutes later, I walked into the bistro where I'd asked *him* to meet me.

"Damn, you look even better in person," I eyed him.

"Thank you," he stared at me until I took a seat. "So do you."

I smiled at him. "Thank you."

He sat back in his chair.

I eyed his muscular frame, brown skin, and good hair.

"So, what in the hell did this lady do to you to make you want to get her back like this? This is some fucked up shit," he laughed.

Alan, that's his name, has been messaging back and forth with me for over a week now about what I wanted him to do for me.

"Are you down or not?"

"Oh, I'm down. As a matter of fact, I'm already burning. I'm ready. I'm just saying, damn, she must've really pissed you off."

I pulled out the $3,000 that I'd gotten out of the bank.

"Did you just say, you're already burning?" I questioned him. "So, now you do have an STD? How did you know? And where did you get one so fast?"

"Oh, shit, it was easy. My baby mama is trifling as hell. She stay at the health department with something. I can't count the number of times she burned me while we were together, until I finally left her ass. I just called her up and told her I wanted to fuck. I figured it was a fifty-fifty chance. My shit started tingling yesterday. I guess I got lucky." He moved around in his seat.

"Or unlucky," I frowned. "And you've been following *her*?"

"The chick you told me about? Oh, yeah, that's in the bag. You were right about where she worked. And I'm meeting up with her tonight. I followed her inside a bar the other night. We've been talking on the phone ever since. Tonight, she invited me over to her place. She's going to cook for me and shit," Alan smiled.

This is perfect!

Yes, Emory is my man.

And yes, he's the one who is supposed to be loyal to me. The cheating is his fault. I understand that. But I also want to get even with the bitch he's been cheating on me with. And that's exactly what I'm going to do!

If everything goes according to plan, Alan is going to sleep with Mimi, the woman Emory has been cheating on me with, and give her an STD.

This is exactly what she deserves for sleeping with men who don't belong to her.

I know that she knows Emory is in a relationship. If I felt like she didn't, I would give her a pass. But I know that she knows, so, I'm stepping in to teach her ass a lesson!

That little pussy of hers is about to be on fire!

And I hope she gives the STD to Emory too.

"Half now. Half when it's done."

"Cool," Alan took one of the stacks out of my hand. "You're too pretty to be this twisted. But I like it. I would hate to be on your bad side though," Alan stood up. "I'll send you pictures after I've fucked her real good and while she's sleeping like a newborn baby with her thumb in her mouth."

"Nice doing business with you," I grinned.

Alan shook the stack of money at me and walked away.

I cackled loudly as I walked out of the bistro.

Today has been a good day!

Finally, I decided to call Emory and tell him my good news.

"That's my baby!" Emory praised me once I told him my big project was complete. "We gotta' celebrate tonight. Everything is on me!"

Sure. I'll let Emory take me to dinner.

But that's it.

I'm sure he's going to want to have sex tonight, but I already have a way of getting out of it.

At dinner, I'll mix tequila and vodka. That should do the trick. It'll have everything I ate from the past week coming out of me from the front or the back, or maybe even both, so, that'll keep Emory's hands off of me, at least for tonight. I'll figure out tomorrow when it comes.

It won't be long before Emory goes to hook up with Mimi again. From what he's told me, he's never had an STD before. I can't wait to see how he pretends to not be interested in sex all of a sudden because his dick is itching or burning. I doubt he'll confess, but it sure as hell will be fun to watch.

"I'll see you when I get to the house."

I hung up with Emory and answered my other line.

"Well, damn, hey, how are you doing? I'm fine. I'm still alive. It's nice to see that you are too," my best-friend, Yana said in my ear as soon as I pulled out of the parking lot.

"Hey, Yana."

Yana and I have been as close as sisters since high school. I love me some Yana! She's one of the few people that I genuinely love. She's one of my absolute favorite people and there's nothing I wouldn't do for her.

And I'm sure the feelings are mutual.

Yana is stupid, crazy, ridiculously rich.

She comes from a family who made their money from computer software a long, long time ago. It was her parents money, but now, it's all hers.

Yana's parents have been missing for about two and a half, almost three years. Eventually, they were declared dead. And as a result of that, she got everything.

Millions.

Years ago, her parents traveled to some exotic island on the other side of the world, and never came back.

No one ever saw them again. No one knows what happened to them. They simply vanished without a trace.

Some think they got drunk on the beach, wandered into the water and drowned. Some speculate that maybe natives captured and killed them. Or even that there's a possibility that they're still out there, alive, somewhere.

Despite Yana's hatred for her folks, she spent an entire year and so much money, traveling back and forth trying to find them, before finally accepting that they're gone; which is something she was already quite used to.

She didn't cry; at least if she did, not to me or in front of me. Her parents were never around. Most of the time, she called them by their first names. She was just as unloved as a child as I was. And her heart can be just as cold as mine can be too.

Sometimes.

"Are you back from Brazil?"

Yana followed me to Mississippi a few years ago, though she's never in town or home. She's always on the go, in some other place, trying something new. I guess she got that part from her parents.

"Yep, I'm back...and...I brought a husband back with me!"

"What!"

"Yes! I'm married, girl!"

Out of the blue, one day, Yana decided that she wanted to spend six-months in Brazil. I never expected her to come back with a husband.

"Please, explain!"

I listened to Yana talk as I drove towards home.

My mouth was hanging wide open the entire time. Not only because she'd gotten married, but because the man she married isn't black.

Yana has always been adamant about only dating black men. She isn't racist or anything, but she just said that black men are gifts from God and that she couldn't wait to have some little cute chocolate babies.

Yet, she married a Brazilian man named Hanz.

I glanced down at my phone to look at the picture of her new husband she'd just sent me.

Shit, my preferences would've gone straight out the window too! Hanz reminded me of a lightly toasted, fluffy buttermilk biscuit. He had just enough scruff on his face, and jet-black curly hair. He's absolutely delicious!

Glancing at another picture of the two of them together, I smiled. They look so damn good together!

Yana is short, bow-legged, and the definition of a brown-skinned girl. Her skin matches the shade of a brown crayon. It's so smooth and perfect. No scars. No blemishes. Completely flawless. Yana has breasts the size of cantaloupes and God could've given her just one more scoop of ass, but she's absolutely gorgeous. Her face is perfectly round, her nose looks as though it was hand-drawn and then placed on her face, her eyes are the same shade of brown as her skin, and her natural hair is long and thick like a horse's tail.

"You're next!" Yana interrupted my thoughts.

Though she's my best friend, I haven't told her that Emory is cheating on me. I didn't want her to try and talk me out of all the foolishness that I was about to do.

Yana has been telling me for years to go to therapy, but hell, she went, and sometimes, I still have to reel her back in. Obviously, therapy doesn't work as well as she says it does. So, there's no point in me wasting my money too.

I'm fine. Or at least I will be.

"Let me call you back."

Pulling into the driveway, I spotted Emory sitting on the front porch waiting for me. He was holding roses and wearing a smile.

"Congratulations, baby."

"Thank you."

Emory reached me the roses and kissed me.

He didn't say anything else.

He simply opened the front door.

Roses and balloons were all over the place.

"Wow. You did all this in twenty minutes?"

"What can I say…I'm a man with many connections."

"Boy, whatever."

Emory followed me all the way to the bedroom.

A new red dress and black shoes were waiting for me on the bed.

"Oh, and let me guess, you found this in twenty minutes too?"

"Oh, nah, I've been riding this around in my trunk for a while. Waiting on the day that you closed that big project at work."

See! He's trying to suck me in with his little thoughtful gestures, but it's not going to work!

"That's so sweet, Emory."

"You're my baby. I knew the day would come! My baby always gets the job done!"

Emory had that look in his eyes.

The one where he's about ninety-nine percent sure that he's going to get some pussy tonight.

He's in for a surprise.

"Now, get dressed so I can show you the night of your life! I guess I'll let you spend some of my hard-earned money," Emory grabbed his clothes off the dresser and headed to shower in the guest bathroom.

I showered quickly, so that I could be completely dressed before Emory came back to peek in on me.

The dress and the shoes were a perfect fit, and exactly something I would've picked out myself.

It reminded me of how well Emory knows me.

Well, of how well he knows the side of me that I've allowed him to see.

"Damn, I thought you would still be getting dressed," Emory said all of twenty minutes later.

"Nope. All dressed. I'm just finishing up my makeup. I'll be ready in about ten minutes."

I finished up my face and looking like a match made in Heaven, Emory and I headed to dinner.

"I'll have two shots of your house tequila, with lime. Oh, and bring me a vodka-tonic too."

"Damn, okay, baby. I see you. You're trying to *celebrate-celebrate*, tonight, huh? Well, you just go ahead. Get everything you want. Get as drunk as you want. I'll take good care of you."

Emory continued to small talk. I smiled at him as I checked the notification on my cell phone.

Alan.

He sent me a picture of Mimi sitting in front of him with the caption: "It's about to go down!"

I grinned.

"Why are you smiling?"

"Huh?" I asked Emory just as the waiter placed the drinks on the table.

"You're smiling at your phone. What has you smiling so big?"

I picked up one of the shot glasses. "Yana, got married!" I held the glass in the air before gulping it down.

"What?" Emory smiled. "Wow. I'm surprised," he laughed, picking up his glass.

I deleted the message from Alan, before picking up my second shot of tequila.

"I know. I'm surprised too. But she came back married to this fine ass…"

"Ay, now, watch yourself," Emory smirked.

I grinned slyly, and together we took a drink.

For the next hour or two, we drank, ate, talked and laughed. After a drink too many, I caught myself making comments to Emory that were clear indications that I knew he was cheating on me, but luckily, he was just as wasted as I was and he didn't seem to catch on.

"Do you love me?"

"That's a stupid question. Of course I love you," Emory responded.

"No. Do you really, really, really, love me?" I slurred.

Emory hissed as he swallowed the last of his glass of Hennessey. "Yes. I really, really, love you."

I exhaled loudly. "Waiter!"

"Oh, no. We're done for the night."

Emory wobbled as he stood to his feet. "Shit. There's no way I can drive us home. I'm going to the bathroom, and then I'll call us a ride." Emory slurred as he wobbled away.

"Psst," I hissed at the waiter. "Can you bring me one more shot, please? And the check for him. Thank you."

Through watery eyes, I struggled to put my lock code into my cell phone. I stared at the email and social media notifications on my screen. After taking a selfie, as best as I could, I turned my phone off for the rest of the night.

I guzzled down the drink, and after staring into space for a few minutes, I realized that Emory was taking way too long to just be using the bathroom.

I stood up, with hopes of going to see what he was up to, but immediately, the alcohol sat my ass right back down.

"Whew," I started to giggle.

I haven't been this drunk in a long, long time.

The last time I got this drunk…

Emory appeared in the distance. He looked around as though he couldn't remember where we were seated. After spotting me, he skipped in my direction.

"Why the fuck are you skipping?" I howled in laughter once Emory reached the table.

"I'm sorry, baby. I'm fucked up," he laughed, spotting the check. "Cece and Rick are on the way to get us. They should be here in about ten minutes," he slurred.

Cece and Rick is by far one of our favorite couples. They're our neighbors. They're older than we are, but they're funny, entertaining, unique and dependable.

We have to keep a healthy distance from them though. They're swingers. And they've tried to swap partners with us on several occasions. And we just don't get down like that. We've declined several times, but it doesn't stop them from trying.

The husband, Rick, is in his forties, and as handsome as they come. But his breath smells like a skunk farted in his mouth. He laughed in my face once, and I couldn't breathe for about two minutes. I thought I was going to need CPR.

And Cece doesn't look a day older than twenty-five. She's absolutely gorgeous, with the perfect body, even after having four kids. If you ask me, I think she's a little more into women than her husband knows. On one drunk night, the last time I got super drunk, Cece asked me if she could eat my pussy through my pants. I laughed it off, and practically ran away from her. I was so drunk that I tripped over my own feet and ended up with a busted lip and bloody nose.

"Of all people, you called the swingers?" I laughed. "We're too drunk to be dealing with their nonsense tonight."

"Oh, shit. I wasn't even thinking about that," Emory chuckled.

"Would you do it? Would you have sex with Cece? Or any other woman?"

I'm drunk, but I reminded myself to choose my words carefully.

"Hell no! I don't want another woman. Just you. We don't need swingers or threesomes. We make enough magic in the bedroom with just the two of us," Emory lied.

I guess he isn't as drunk as I thought.

Just as I was about to make a comment, the Freaky Wilsons, as we called them, spotted us and headed our way.

Minutes later, Cece helped me inside their car, while Rick and Emory got inside of Emory's car.

Cece's Range Rover is all black, and though she's had it for a while, it still has that new car smell.

Rick makes a lot of money, but he's a cheap bastard! He only wants to spend his money on things like investing and things of that nature.

Cece cried like a baby, completely surprised, when Rick showed up with this car as her anniversary gift.

"Are you drunk enough for a threesome?" Cece asked as we drove down the street.

"Nope."

"Damn it," she laughed. Cece started to talk about random things. I listened to only about five percent of what she was saying. After a while, I closed my eyes, pretending to be passed out, hoping that she would get the hint and shut up.

"Nova?" Cece whispered as though someone else was in the car. I continued to pretend as though I was asleep. I thought she was about to come on to me again, but the next thing she said surprised me.

"Nova, Emory is cheating on you."

My heart started skipped a beat, but I kept my eyes closed.

How does she know?

"He's cheating with a woman in my yoga class. Her name is Christina."

Christina?

Wait a minute…

Who the fuck is Christina?

I've done my research and Mimi's real name is Moriah Nicole Adams.

So, you mean to tell me, that Emory is cheating on me with another woman too?

Oh, hell no!

"As far as I know, they've been fooling around for a couple of weeks," Cece paused. "I didn't know how to tell you. Or if I should. Nova? Nova?" She called out to me again, but still, I kept my eyes close.

Mad is an understatement!

I could kill Emory right now!

And I mean, literally kill him!

How did I miss that there was another woman in the mix? Once I found out about Mimi, I practically stalked her on social media and found out where she worked. I didn't see anything about a Christina in Emory's phone.

"Nova?" Cece called out again. "Well, God, I tried," Cece mumbled to herself. "I tried," she repeated again.

For the rest of the ride, she didn't say anything else.

I laid there, thinking about setting Emory on fire.

"Come on, baby," Emory pulled me out of the car, once we pulled up at home. I cringed as he touched me.

"She's been passed out for most of the ride," Cece said.

"Thank y'all for coming to get us," Emory said to them.

"You need some help?"

"Nah. I got her."

It took us a while, but Emory got us both inside the house. He sat me on the couch. I continued to pretend as though I was completely out of it, but the news of Emory cheating on me with yet another woman had almost completely sobered me up.

I was just sitting there, trying not to do something crazy. I just kept reminding myself of the things I already have in store for him, but in that moment, I wanted to do more!

After stumbling through the house for a while, Emory came back to me and took off my shoes.

"I really hope you enjoyed your night, baby. You deserve it. You deserve the world," Emory drooled. "Damn, I'm drunk."

Emory laid right there on the floor in front of me and continued to mumble. My stomach started to turn and I was starting to feel that familiar feeling I get from mixing tequila and vodka together.

"You work so hard. You love me so much. You just love me so much. And I love you," Emory slurred. At the completion of his sentence I couldn't hold it in anymore. Purposely, I leaned over and threw up all over Emory.

Love that, you cheating ass bitch!

~***~

"Hey, girl, what are you doing?"

"Cutting all the toe-tops off Emory's socks."

"What?"

I picked up another pair of socks and snipped the top of them off with the scissors, rolled them back together, and put them back in the drawer. Then, I grabbed another pair.

"What did you say you're doing?"

"I'm cutting the tops of his socks off…the part where the toes go. "

"For what?" Yana laughed. "That is the pettiest thing I've ever heard!"

"Girl, fuck him!"

Emory and I have been arguing like cats and dogs the past couple of days. He's arguing about sex. I'm arguing about shit that I can't actually say.

This morning, after I refused to have sex with him, again, he accused me of cheating on him.

And that sent me flying off the handle!

I cursed him out like a dog and I threw a hot coffee pot at him. I even let out a few speculations of him cheating on me, just to see if he would finally admit it, but he denied it, which only pissed me off even more!

"What did he do?"

Yana knows that I can be a little crazy, but even she doesn't know about all the crazy things I've done. I debated on whether or not I wanted to tell her what I was up to.

"Emory is cheating on me; with at least two different women, as far as I know."

"No! Are you serious? Tell me you're lying."

"Nope. And you know me…"

"Aw, hell, what are you going to do? I know how you feel about cheating. I know that it reminds you of your dad. And I know you're not going to just let him get away with it. Are you?"

"Nope."

"Oh, God. What do you have up your sleeve, Nova?"

"Just sit back and enjoy the show."

"Please, don't do something that's going to put you in jail. I mean, I'll pay off whoever I have to in order to try to get you out, but I'd rather you not end up there in a first place, okay?" Yana waited for my response.

"He hurt me, Yana. And for that, he has to pay," was all I could say.

"I thought you were taking this week off," Ox said following me into my office, later that day.

"I am. I just needed to come by and do a few things."

"Whatever it is, it can wait. Get out of here. Go take a trip or something, Ms. New Money?"

"A trip sure does sound nice. I definitely need one. Hmm, maybe I will."

"You taking ole' boy with you?"

"If I go…I'm sure he'll want to tag along."

"Or you could leave the lame at home and let me fly you somewhere exotic. I'll take you anywhere you want to go."

"Ox…if we're going to be friends you gotta' stop…"

"I don't wanna' be your goddamn friend," he pouted.

I chuckled.

"One day, I'm gonna' have you, girl," Ox prepared to walk out of my office.

One day…

Shoot, why not today?

"Ox?" I stared at him.

I mean, Emory is cheating on me, with two different women, right?

So, let's really get this party started!

"Lock the door."

"What?" Ox asked.

I stood up and started to close the blinds in my office.

"You talk a lot, Ox," I started. "Always saying this. Always saying that." Slowly, I lifted my skirt above my hips and then sat on the edge of my desk. "So...let's see what else that mouth of yours can do, you know, besides talking."

Ox's eyes lit up like the star on the top of a Christmas tree.

"Are you fucking with me right now?"

"No. Boss. This is your interview. If you pass...you just might get this ass."

Ox inched closer to me.

"Don't fuck with me like this, Nova."

Ox stared down at my thighs.

"I'm serious. Now, in my professional opinion, we should remain just friends. But the choice is yours..." I opened my legs.

Ox smirked. "Like I've been telling you for years...I don't want to be your damn friend!"

Ox made his choice as he slowly rolled my panties down past my thighs. And without hesitating, Ox put his mouth on me.

Oh, my!

******

CHAPTER THREE

"You've been begging me for ass for weeks, but now you're telling me no?"

Emory wiggled.

I saw the pharmacy reminder when I checked his email account this morning. Over these past two weeks, at some point, Emory recently had sex with Mimi and now he has gonorrhea.

"I'm just not in the mood."

"You said that yesterday."

"Well, you haven't been in the mood for weeks. So, now I'm not in the mood," Emory growled.

I didn't really want to have sex with him. I just wanted to see if he would break down and tell me the truth.

"Why are you walking like that?"

"Like what?"

"Like something is wrong with your dick or something?"

"Nah. I just need to take a shower. Sweat makes my nuts itch and I worked hard at the shop today."

Emory closed the bathroom door behind him.

I shivered in laughter and disgust.

If I had my way, I would never let him touch me again, but since it's almost time for me to seduce Kojo, soon, I'll have to give Emory the *goods*, eventually, at least once, to pull off my plan.

I stopped taking my birth control pills.

My period should be here soon, and after that, whenever my ovulation comes around, I need to be bouncing up and down on Kojo's dick like a pogo stick.

A part of me almost wanted to switch my plans and use Ox as my sperm donor.

With a father like Ox, my child will be well taken care of, forever, I'll tell you that much. But getting pregnant by Ox won't hurt Emory as much as getting pregnant by Kojo will. So, I have to stick to the plan.

Ox ate my pussy to the bone that day in my office. That was over a week ago. We met up the next day to have sex.

And it was everything I always knew it would be.

We had sex in his backyard, on a bed of about fifty pillows, underneath the stars, surrounded by lights, beautiful plants and a pool.

I'd gotten mad at Emory, again, because he wasn't answering his phone that night. That's probably the night he was screwing Mimi. I figured he was out cheating on me. So, I went out and did the same.

I called Ox, and he told me to come over.

Ox met me at the door butt naked and carried me all the way to his backyard. And then, he had his way with me. Actually, it was almost like he made love to me. Ox took his time with me, and for the first time, I could really see and feel how deep his feelings are for me. Ox showed me with every kiss, every touch, and every single stroke what he's been telling me for years.

He wants me.

I almost felt bad for having "Mad at Emory" sex with him. But it was so damn good. And I don't regret it.

The icing on the cake is that I didn't bother coming home that night.

And needless to say, Emory lost his shit!

The next morning, I was every name in the book.

Emory threatened to leave me. And he tried to make me have sex with him to prove that I hadn't been out having sex with another man all night.

Men make me sick!

They can do whatever the hell they want to do, but when you do it to them, all hell breaks loose!

I just smiled at Emory that day as he fussed and yelled in my face. I didn't say one word. I didn't try to defend myself, no matter what he said.

He started this mess.

And I'm going to finish it.

Emory singing in the shower reminded me of something I needed to do. I got dressed in a hurry. Heading out the front door, I walked three houses down to Cece and Rick's house.

"Hey, is everything okay?" Cece said as soon as she opened the door.

"Yep. Take an evening stroll with me."

A few days ago, I drove by the yoga studio where Cece takes classes. It has been driving me crazy not knowing who this Christina woman is or what she looks like. I was hoping to pretend not to know about her, but my curiosity these past few days has gotten the best of me.

"That night…the night that I was drunk…I heard what you said," I said to Cece as we started to talk.

"Which part?"

"All of it. Emory is cheating on me with some woman named Christina."

Cece exhaled loudly. "I shouldn't have said anything. I hate to get in other people's business; especially relationship business."

"You're my friend. You were supposed to tell me."

"I'm Emory's friend too," Cece said.

Honestly, I don't give a crap about anything that she's saying or how she feels. I just need to know how to spot Christina the next time I'm stalking their yoga class.

"Maybe you're wrong. Maybe they're just friends," I tried to play the naïve chick, who thinks her man is the exception.

"Nope. They're definitely having sex. She and I aren't super close or anything, but we've had quite a few casual and not so casual conversations before. He's cheating on you with her."

"Is she prettier than me?"

"No. Not really." Cece started to explain Christina's appearance to me. That's all I'd wanted to know in the first place.

"Just get him back."

Cece's comment pulled me away from my thoughts.

"He cheated on you. Go out, and cheat on him. Problem solved," she shrugged. "Shoot, you can start with…"

"Don't start your shit, Cece!"

"What?" she giggled. "You don't even know what I was going to say."

"Oh, I have a pretty good idea," I managed to chuckle. "I just might take your advice and get him back, just like you said. But as my friend, I do want you to do something for me. I want you to tell this Christina that Emory has a fiancée. Don't tell her that I know about her but tell her that she needs to leave Emory alone."

Cece nodded. "I can do that for you. And please don't mention that I told you. Rick will have a fit if he knew that I was meddling in your relationship."

"Oh, you don't have to worry about me saying a word. As far as I'm concerned, this conversation never happened. Agreed?"

"Agreed."

~***~

"Oh, my God! Josiah? What are you doing here?"

"I'm just passing through, sis."

Josiah is one of my brothers.

Jacob, the middle child, somehow turned out to be amazing. He went off to college, graduated top of his class, scored big with a position in IT, married a beautiful woman and now has two amazing kids. They live out in San Francisco.

Josiah, my baby brother, didn't get so lucky.

He's been in and out of trouble, in and out of jail, and he always seems to be two steps behind. Josiah made it through high school, but that's pretty much it. He can never keep a job, or a woman. He has a horrible temper, and major anger issues. And honestly, I believe that whatever mama had…he has a little touch of it too.

Mentally.

We all hated our parents, but I think Josiah hated them the most. He blames them for everything wrong in his life.

"I've missed you. I haven't heard from you in forever! I was starting to get worried, but I know how you disappear sometimes. But seriously, this time, was way too long."

"I've been getting myself together, "Josiah said. "Jacob got me a job out there in California. I start next week. I need a new start, so, I'm going out there with him. I decided to just come and see you before I head out that way. Is that okay?"

"Sure. Come on in," I moved aside so that Josiah could enter my house.

He looks better. He smells better than the last time I saw him. His energy feels a lot better too.

"You seem…"

"Better? Most days, I am. I take a shot once a month."

"A shot? For what?"

"Let's just say mama fucked me up in more ways than one. I know I told you I was going to change that last time I did six months in jail. I tried for a while. But you know how that goes. Anyway, I got caught up in a bad situation almost a year ago. I didn't tell you about it because I didn't want you to worry. I could've ended up doing some serious prison time. But the judge ordered that I have a psych evaluation. It changed my life. They diagnosed me with a couple of things. I was put on medication and ordered to go to therapy. I still have my moments, and my days, but unlike our darling dead mother, I got the help I needed. And now, most days, I'm a lot better."

"Oh, my god! I'm so glad to hear that! Not the diagnoses part or that you're on medicine, but that you feel better. I guess that explains why you've been off the grid for so long. I must've called that number I had for you a thousand times. I called it at least twice a week, but no one ever answers. I knew you weren't dead; I always check. I call the jail, hospital and morgue, once a month, and they never have you. So, I knew you were out there somewhere. I figured you would call me, one day, whenever you needed me."

"I don't need you anymore. And I'm glad to be able to say that. I don't need money or anything. I just wanted to see my sister."

I hugged him.

"This crib is nice," Josiah smiled. "You and Emory selling drugs?"

"Hell, no, boy."

Josiah chuckled. "Where is ole' Emory, anyway?"

"He's at the shop. I would be at work right now, but I've been having really bad period cramps for the past few days and decided to work from home."

"Damn, I thought you would be pregnant by now."

"I'm working on it," I admitted.

Josiah took a seat on the couch.

"My flight leaves in two days. I can get a hotel…"

"Boy, you're staying here, shut up."

I've always played this motherly role with Josiah being that I'm almost six years older than him.

My phone started to ring.

I declined Ox's call.

"Uh oh. Let me find out you dipping out on Emory."

"Uh, no, that's my boss."

"Oh. Well, why didn't you answer the phone?"

"Because I'm talking to you," I lied.

I didn't answer the phone because Ox most likely didn't want to talk about work. Since the night we had sex, all he's wants to talk about is when we'll do it again.

I told him it was a one-time thing.

But Ox could care less about the words that come out of my mouth. Hell, he didn't care about them before I had sex with him.

"Actually, I'm going to text him right now, and tell him I need the next two days off to hang with my baby brother. Is that okay with you?"

Josiah shrugged.

I texted Ox, and then I got myself together to spend some long overdue time with one of the few people in the world that I truly love.

~***~

So, that's Christina.

I was sitting across the street from the yoga studio watching Cece have a conversation with a tall, pretty dark-skinned chick with dreadlocks down to her butt.

I could tell by the woman's body language that Cece was telling her what I told her to tell her. She was telling Christina about me and Emory. Christina seemed upset. As though she didn't know Emory had a woman.

Finally, she stormed off in one direction while Cece headed in another.

Hmm...

I guess I'll leave Christina alone, for now, since it seems that she was blindsided by the news of Emory being in a relationship. But if I find out otherwise...

"One caramel latte', please?" I stopped at a coffee shop around the corner from the yoga studio.

The couple behind me laughed loudly, causing me to look behind me.

I froze.

Alan and I made eye contact.

I glanced at the woman beside him, confused.

Mimi.

Emory's Mimi?

Mimi looked at me, unbothered. It was clear that she didn't know who I was. That still doesn't mean she didn't know Emory had a woman. She knew. She had to have known. She just doesn't know what I look like.

"I'm going to go to the ladies room," she said to Alan.

"I'm confused," I said to him, as soon as she was out of sight.

He chuckled. "What can I say? We actually hit it off."

I grabbed my latte out of the cashier's hand.

"And check this out, she thinks that she gave the STD to me. She says she had to have gotten it from some guy named Emory that she was sleeping with."

"And you let her believe that?"

"Hell yeah. Emory, that's your man, right? She was fooling around with him. And in case you're wondering, yeah, she knew he had a woman."

I knew it!

"But she's cool. I like her vibe. Not being funny, but I can see why your man wanted to hang out with her. She's fun. Sexual. And very low maintenance. But whatever they had going on, is over and done with. She called and cursed him out because she thinks he burned her. I was right there. He was pissed off. He said he knew for a fact that whatever she had didn't come from him. She blocked his number and hasn't spoken to him since."

"And you and her…"

"We're kicking it. She's cool. We'll see."

I shrugged. "Shit, I should get a partial refund or something for playing cupid. I'm just saying," I said behind me as I walked out of the coffee shop.

Well, I wasn't expecting that.

But at least Emory and Mimi are over.

I took a sip of my drink just as I got into my car.

I checked my phone. I had three missed calls from Emory. His days on the medication are over, and he's trying to have sex with me again.

Nope!

"Is that…"

I glanced across the street at Yana and Josiah.

They were talking. Well, arguing. At least that's what it looked like.

I called Josiah's cell phone. I watched him pull his phone out of his pocket, but he didn't answer it.

So, I called Yana.

She didn't bother to look at her phone. She was too busy pushing Josiah. Finally, she slapped him and walked away. He ran after her.

Hmm…

What in the hell is going on?

A few hours later, Josiah came back to the house.

"Hey, where you been?"

"Oh, I was just out sight-seeing a little bit," he lied. "I didn't see your call."

Why is he lying?

"Are you ready for your flight?"

"Yep."

"Josiah, is there anything you need to tell me?"

"Nope. Why you ask that?"

"I'm just asking. I just want to make sure everything is okay."

"Everything is fine."

Whatever is going on between Yana and Josiah sure as hell didn't look fine to me. But for now, I'll let it be.

I'll just get Yana to tell me what's going on later.

About an hour later, I took Josiah to the airport. I hugged and kissed him at least a hundred times because I wasn't sure when I would see him again.

"I love you, Peanut Butter," Josiah grinned.

"I love you, always, Bread," I laughed at Josiah, to keep from getting emotional. I waved goodbye, and then walked away.

Using our little pet names brought back memories.

I was Peanut Butter. Jacob was Jelly. And Josiah was Bread. We ate peanut butter and jelly sandwiches so much as a child, that one day, Jacob decided to compare us to the sandwich. He said no matter what, we would always be as close as a peanut butter and jelly sandwich. And then, he gave us each our names. Over the years, it just sort of stuck. Although, we weren't as close as we used to be.

With Jacob all the way in California, with his own family, and Josiah always disappearing, we don't keep in touch these days like we used to.

Hopefully, with the two of them living together, and Josiah getting himself together, maybe things can go back to how they used to be.

Leaving the airport, I made my way to Emory's shop.

"Damn, y'all gotta' do better with communicating. He just pulled off about five minutes ago," Kojo said.

"Did he say where he was going?"

"Nah."

I gave Kojo eye contact. He towered over me, taunting me with the aroma of his skin.

"Well, I guess your dinner is on me today. It's fried chicken, mac and cheese, cabbage and cornbread. I got it from that place right up the street."

Kojo examined the plate. "Damn. It smells good too. Thank you. Good looking out," he smiled.

Time to make another move on him. Just a small one.

"You've been working out, I see."

"I do a little something."

"It's starting to pay off," I rubbed up and down his arm. I waited to see what kind of reaction he would have.

Kojo just smiled.

From what I know about him, he was a star running back in college. He hurt his knee his last game of his senior year. He spent months trying to get his knee back to where he needed it to be, but he failed. And just like that, his chances of being in the NFL were gone.

Kojo's life went downhill from there.

He felt as though he couldn't do anything other than play football. He started partying and drinking. One night, while driving drunk, he got into a car accident. The guy he hit, survived and he recognized him from his college days.

Instead of calling the police, he drove Kojo to his house and once Kojo sobered up, he told him he wouldn't report the accident if Kojo helped him fix his car.

That's where it all began.

Kojo fell in love with using his hands and decided to become a mechanic. He's good too. Almost as good as Emory. From listening to Emory, Kojo plans to open his own shop someday soon. Working for Emory is just a small stop along the way.

"Big arms. Big hands. I wonder…is everything else big too?"

There's the bait. If Kojo couldn't tell before, he would have to be as blind as a bat not to know that I'm coming on to him after my comment.

Kojo didn't say a word. He just kept a small, enticing smile on his face.

Ugh!

So, I guess Kojo wants to play hard to get.

I exhaled loudly.

"Well, let me get out of here. Enjoy the rest of your night. Don't work too hard."

I walked out of the shop disappointed.

I was sure that Kojo would jump at the thought of getting a piece of all this. It never crossed my mind that he just might be a little too loyal to Emory and their friendship.

I called Emory once I was back inside my car.

"I came by to bring you dinner, but you were already gone."

"Funny," Emory chuckled. "I just left the grocery store picking up things to make dinner for you. I just wanted to do something nice for you since things between us have been off lately."

Yeah, because you're a liar and a cheater!

"I just want us to get back on the right track. So, I wanted to make you dinner."

I exhaled loudly.

My love for Emory is different.

I've never loved any man as much as I love him.

Or should I say loved?

These days, most days, I hate Emory more than I love him. And then, there's some days that I remember why I loved him so much in the first place. I just know that no matter what I feel, the desire to hurt him is what I feel the most.

"Are you on your way home?"

"No. And I already ate," I lied.

I hung up the phone on Emory, completely in my feelings.

I hate him!

But I love him.

Ugh!

Feeling tempted to go home and confront him about everything, I had to do something to take my mind off the situation. I had to do something to make me feel better.

I…

I pressed the green phone icon and listened to the phone ring in my ear.

"Hey, Ox…can I come over?"

~***~

"Why are you lying?"

"I'm not. I don't know what you're talking about," Yana grabbed her mug and walked away.

It was days after Josiah left for California. I'd tried getting in touch with Yana the same day he left, but she wasn't answering her cell phone, and she was never home when I came by.

Until today.

"I saw the two of you arguing on the sidewalk. I saw it with my own two eyes. It looked intense. The way you pushed Josiah and the way he ran after you. Hell, you even slapped him! So, what was that about?"

Yana sipped her drink. "I don't kn—"

"If you say you don't know what I'm talking about one more time, I swear I'm going to punch you in the face!"

Yana giggled. "Just let it go, Nova."

"What do you mean, just let it go? He's my brother."

"And he's also a grown ass man."

I stared at her.

Yana pretended not to notice me looking at her as she continued to sip her tea.

"Oh, my god!"

"What?" Yana looked confused.

"You fucked my brother!"

"Sssh!" Yana hushed me being that her husband was in the back room.

"You did! Didn't you? When? And you didn't tell me?"

"It was a long time ago."

"He's just a baby!"

"Girl, he isn't a baby. And he doesn't have a baby sized dick either."

"Yana!" I folded my arms across my chest. "When? How?"

"It was years ago. He was legal. I promise. We ran into each other one night and it just happened. No big deal."

"No big deal? It sure as hell looked like a big deal."

"It's fine. Really. We just had a disagreement."

"About what?"

Yana didn't respond.

"Are the two of you still sleeping together?"

"No."

"Then why did the both of you seem upset?"

"I wasn't upset. He was."

"Why?"

"He just was."

"Why?"

"You'll have to ask him."

"I did and he lied," I mumbled. "Why did you slap him?"

"Because he deserved it."

"Why?"

"Damn, stop grilling me, okay? Josiah and I are both adults. We had sex. We had fun. We had an argument. Let it go, Nova. There's nothing there."

Oh, but I believe there is.

We were both quiet for a few seconds.

"So, what's going on with you and Emory?"

"Nothing."

"What do you mean nothing?"

"Like I said, nothing."

"Oh, so you're going to be an asshole now?" Yana chuckled. "Your nosey ass will be okay. You don't have to know everything. Some things, I would like to keep to myself, if that's okay with you," Yana kept a smile on her face. "Does Emory know that you know he cheated on you yet?"

I rolled my eyes at her. "No. And did I mention that he got an STD from one of them?"

Yana spit out her drink. "Oh, hell no!"

I didn't bother telling her that I was the cause of the whole STD situation.

"Dang, Emory. But that's what he gets for cheating."

"And he keeps trying to act like he's the perfect man. It's driving me crazy."

"What are you going to do?"

"You mean who am I going to do...next?"

"Next?"

"He started it and I'm going to finish it."

"Friend, just fuck his friend and leave his ass."

I smiled at her. "Great minds think alike. But what I have planned is just a little more than that. Well, a lot more than that. He'll never see it coming," I admitted to Yana.

"It just sucks. After all the frogs you've kissed... I really thought Emory was your Prince."

"Maybe a happily ever after just doesn't exist for me. I might have to go off to another country to find a man that will actually do right by me."

"Does such a man exist?"

"Just give me one that doesn't lie and cheat. That's all I want. That's all I've ever wanted," I stood up with my purse in my hand.

"Keep your ringer on just in case I need you to come bail me out of jail."

"Nova! What the hell are you going to do?"

"Something to make me feel better."

"Nova…"

"What?"

"You and your craziness. See, I told you. You need to go to therapy."

"Why? It didn't work for you."

"Bitch, shut up! Yes, it did! A little bit. And for the record, I think you should tell Emory that you know. If you plan on getting him back, it'll make the revenge even sweeter to have him think that you forgave him. He'll think that everything is going well between the two of you and then… BOOM! You fuck his friend. Take him all the way up and drop his ass right back down."

Hmmm…

I like that idea.

And by telling Emory that I know, I get to show my ass a little bit instead of trying to play it cool all the time.

Lord knows I'm tired of pretending.

I smiled at Yana. "See?"

"See what?"

"I told you your therapy didn't work."

"Baby!" Emory yelled a few hours later as soon as he walked into the house. "Baby, where you at?"

I heard his footsteps coming down the hall.

"Baby, what is that smell?" Emory entered our bedroom.

He spotted me, standing behind the ironing board with the iron pressed down on one of his shirts.

There were stacks of other shirts all over the bed.

"What are you doing? Ironing?" Emory picked up one of his shirts. "Nova, what the hell?"

Emory noticed the iron mark on the front of the shirt from me leaving the iron sitting on it too long.

He shuffled through the rest of the shirts.

I'd put iron marks on all of them.

"Nova? What the hell is this? Why are you messing up all my shirts?"

Quietly, I lifted the iron from the shirt and unplugged it.

"What is wrong with you? Do you know how much money some of these shirts costs? Why are you in here messing up my shit?"

"Who is Mimi and Christina?"

The look on Emory's face was priceless.

"What...what?"

Without warning, I threw the hot iron at Emory's head.

He ducked and then scrambled to pick the hot iron up off the floor.

"Are you fucking crazy!"

"You thought I didn't know about them, didn't you? I know! I've known for a while that you cheated on me! You fucking cheated on me, Emory!"

Emory sat the iron down on the nightstand. "Nova, baby, it's not what you think."

"Oh, and I guess the gonorrhea you had isn't what I think either, huh?"

Emory's mouth dropped open.

"Man, you ain't shit!"

"Nova, let me explain."

I brushed passed him, nearly knocking his shoulder off his body.

"Nova. It was nothing. Neither of them meant anything to me."

"Oh, classic fucking excuse!"

I grabbed a vase off the table in the hall.

"Mama gave us that vase," Emory said behind me.

"Oops." I dropped the vase, smiling as it shattered against the hardwood floor.

"Goddamn it!" Emory yelled. "Look, babe, I messed up. Let's just talk about it. Stop destroying shit!"

Telling Emory that I know about the cheating was definitely the right thing to do. Now, I feel so free.

Free to let out all the anger and hurt that I've been holding inside of me. Free to let out the scary side of me. And I don't give a damn what he thinks about me either!

"Please, just sit down on the couch. Please."

I stopped at the kitchen table.

"I would say go give one of them the ring you gave me, but…there isn't much left of it."

I played with the pieces of the ring with my index finger. I'd smashed the ring Emory gave me with a hammer.

"Are you kidding me, right now? Do you know how much that ring cost, Nova?"

"Oops," I shrugged, and headed into the living room.

I took a seat on the sofa. Emory sat right beside me as though I was no one to be afraid of.

"Wait. Is this my…"

Emory noticed the items on the coffee table.

I'd crossed his name out on his birth certificate and wrote "Emory Lying Cheating Ass Marcelis" in permanent marker at the top of it. I drew titties all over his associates degree and certifications and I'd played tic-tac-toe all over his high school diploma.

"Wow," Emory mumbled. "You've really been in here messing up my stuff."

I didn't respond.

That's nothing.

I put bleach in his body wash. Ketchup and mustard in about ten pair of his shoes. And I put crazy glue on all the lids of his expensive cologne bottles, so that he won't be able to take them off.

"I cheated. Not because I don't love you. Not because I'm not happy."

"Then why, Emory? Why?"

This is the first time I've ever asked why.

Usually, I do my damage and simply disappeared.

The why a man hurt me or cheated on me never really mattered. The fact that they did it was enough for me.

"Honestly, I don't know. The opportunities presented themselves, and I guess…I don't know. I just did it. Neither of those women mean anything to me. I don't love them. I love you."

"If you loved me, you wouldn't have cheated on me."

"I wasn't trying to hurt you. It wasn't about you. You're perfect. A little crazy, I see, now. But perfect. And all I want is you. I'll never cheat on you again. Just tell me what to do. I'll do anything to make this up to you."

"Kill both of them," I said with a straight face.

"What?"

"You said you'll do anything. Kill them."

Emory stared at me. "You're not serious right now…are you?"

No. I'm not.

I'm a lot of things. A killer isn't one of them. I think.

If I was, I would've killed Emory or one of my other exes a long time ago.

"There's nothing you can do, Emory."

"Don't say that," Emory touched me.

"Get your cheating ass hands off me!"

I stood up and attempted to walk away.

Emory grabbed me.

"I'm not losing you. I love you. I made a mistake. Two mistakes. They won't happen again."

"Get off me!"

"No."

Emory pushed me towards the living room wall.

"Get your hands off me!"

"No," he repeated. "I'll never hurt you again. I promise. I love you."

Emory tried to kiss me.

I turned my head.

"No! Go kiss Mimi, or Christina!"

"Nova?" Emory said, calmly. "I love you. I love you."

"Move, Emory!"

He kissed me mid-sentence.

"I love you," he mumbled through kisses. "I love you."

I squirmed trying to get free of him, but Emory continued to kiss me.

"Forgive me, please. Forgive me. I love you. I love you."

He kissed me over and over again, until finally, he picked me up.

"Put me down!"

Emory carried me down the hall and into our bedroom. He placed me on the bed on top of the shirts I ruined. And then he started to tug at the workout leggings I was wearing.

"No! Move! Get away from me!"

Emory didn't say a word as he pulled down my leggings. Next, he ripped off my panties.

"I said move!"

"And I said I love you. I love you. Let me show you how much I love you."

I squirmed as Emory pushed my knees apart. And just as I opened my mouth to curse at him, he placed his mouth on me.

"No! Get your damn mouth off me!" I punched at the back of his head.

My punches didn't stop him. Emory licked faster, harder, no matter how many times I hit him.

"Move, Emory! Mo---mo---move!"

Emory has always been blessed with a golden tongue.

"Get away from me, Emory! And get out! Just get out," I mumbled. "Just get out." I exhaled loudly. I could no longer ignore the satisfactory sensation his tongue was delivering to my thumping clitoris.

"I love you," Emory moaned in between his sucking and slurping. "I'm so sorry."

I cooed, unable to speak.

Needless to say, Emory sucked the anger out my coochie, temporarily.

I didn't even put up a fight when he turned me over and entered me from behind.

Though having sex with him is the last thing I planned to do, it means nothing.

Having sex with him changes nothing.

Emory's thrusts from behind demanded my attention, but no matter how good his dick felt going in and out of me, it didn't remove the malice from my heart.

Payback is a bitch.

And it's me…I'm that bitch!

~***~

"I thought you wanted a baby," Dr. Gemini asked.

"I do. Soon. Very soon. But today, I need that morning after pill. I know, I could've went to the pharmacy to pick up one, but since I'm already here…"

After having sex with Emory, I had to make sure I didn't accidentally get pregnant by my boyfriend, while trying to purposely get pregnant by his friend.

That's if I can even get Kojo to have sex with me.

Emory woke up this morning with a smile on his face. He thinks that everything is going to be okay between us.

I squirted two whole bottles of lotion all over his car this morning on my way out just to remind him of how pissed off I am. Although, I am going to pretend to forgive him over time. And then, hopefully, I'll start having sex with Kojo right under his nose.

"Well, I guess I could've gone to the pharmacy," I remember. "Because I need that liquid prescription that you gave me last time to help me go to the bathroom. I've been backed up again lately."

I popped the pill on my way out of the doctor's office, and then I headed to drop off my prescription.

I called my brother Josiah as I drove.

He didn't answer.

He hasn't answered his cell phone since the day I dropped him off at the airport, so, I called my brother Jacob. He hasn't been answering his phone either, but hopefully he will today.

"Hey, sis, what's going on?"

"Nothing. How are you? How is Reeva, and the kids?"

"Everything is everything my way. We're all good."

"That's good. I can't wait to see y'all. I was calling because I haven't heard from Josiah since I dropped him off at the airport to head there."

"Really? I thought he changed his mind. He never showed up and he hasn't been answering my calls either."

"What? I dropped him off at the airport myself."

"Well, he never made it here. And I've called him a few times. You know how he does. He just disappears at times. I figured he changed his mind about the job."

Hmmm...

Where in the hell is Josiah?

And what is he up to now?

I talked to Jacob for a little while longer, and then I called Josiah over and over again, while I waited for my prescription to be filled.

He never answered.

I sent him a few text messages, and then I headed into work.

"Good afternoon, beautiful," Ox smiled as he knocked on my office door.

"Hey, you."

He closed the door behind him.

"How are you?"

"I'm doing good. A lot going on at home, but good nonetheless."

"When can I see you again? Outside of work?"

I knew this conversation was coming, and I was prepared.

"Ox, what we did was fun. It was good. Damn good. But I still feel how I feel about mixing business with pleasure. Shit, you're my boss…and my friend. Us fooling around was exactly what I wanted and needed at the time, but it can't happen again."

Ox is a distraction and I can't allow him to get in the way of what I'm trying to do to hurt Emory.

"Cool. One day, you'll be ready," Ox smiled. "And I'll be waiting."

I chuckled. "You just don't give up, do you?"

"Nah. I don't. Not when it's something I want."

Genuinely, I smiled at him just as there was a knock on my door.

"It's open."

"I was told I could find…" the woman paused once she spotted Ox. "Ox."

"Shanice? What are you doing here?"

Ox tugged at his blazer.

"What? I can't come and see my *husband* at work?"

Did she say husband?

"Ex-husband."

"Funny, I only remember getting legally separated. I don't remember signing any divorce papers, though."

"Yeah, because you've been running all over the place for years to avoid being served. So, again, what in the fuck are you doing here, Shanice?"

She smirked at Ox, and then glanced at me, jealously.

I've known Ox for years, and never has he mentioned her or that he's married. I almost became pissed that I'd had sex with him, because I don't *do* married men, but from the looks of it, their marriage has been over for a very long time.

I checked out his wife.

She's definitely his type.

And to be honest, we look a lot alike; not so much as facial features, but our hair, the color of our skin, or body structure and size are all very similar. Almost exact.

"I need to talk to you."

"We don't have anything to talk about. I haven't talked to you in years, and I don't want to start talking now. But you know what, come on, while you talk, I'll get my lawyer up here to serve you these damn papers," Ox buttoned one of the buttons on his blazer. "I'll see you later, Nova."

Ox walked towards the door.

"Yes. He'll see you later, Nova," Ox's wife wiggled her fingers at me, as he nearly pushed her away from my office door.

Whew!

I'm glad I don't actually want to be with Ox.

His wife seems like a handful, and the two of us going head to head would've been a complete disaster!

For the rest of the day, I worked, and when I wasn't working, I was texting and calling Josiah.

He never answered.

I know there's nothing to worry about.

As Jacob said, this is Josiah's normal; to just disappear. But I am curious as to why he would let me drop him off at the airport and then not catch his flight.

Josiah, in my opinion, didn't catch as much hell as Jacob and I did growing up. By the time he was old enough to really understand our parents crazy, they were on the whole religion wave.

I do remember mama tying him to the swing set we had in our backyard, for hours, one day. It was hot as hell outside that day too, and I kept trying to take him water, but every single time, no matter how hard I tried, my mother would attack me and take the water from me. She said she was trying to teach him strength and patience. He was only eight or nine for God's sake!

Finally, I gave up and just went outside and laid in the grass beside him. I remember catching a glimpse of my father in the window. He just looked out at us, but he didn't do or say anything.

That day, Josiah and I were as hot as roasted pigs but I made him laugh and I kept telling him that everything was going to be okay. Josiah cried and told me that he didn't understand the things our mother did to us. I told him that our mother was sick but that she loved us as much as a sick person could.

I wonder if that's the day.

The day that she broke something inside of him.

The day she made Josiah the man that he eventually, inevitably, turned out to be.

And still, he didn't have it as bad as Jacob and I did, but maybe the things that she did to him were more than enough.

Before Emory, my brothers are the only men that I can say I loved with my whole heart. I always felt bad about not being able to protect them from my mother. And it took me a long time, and lectures from Jacob, to realize that the way Josiah turned out isn't my fault. I did as much as I could. Everything else, my mother has to answer for in heaven…or wherever she is.

By the time I got home that evening, Emory was already there and dinner was already done and on the table.

He had candles and roses all over the place.

"I know it's going to take time for you to forgive me, and I'm not expecting you to forgive me today, or tomorrow. But if it's the last thing I do, I'm going to show you how much I love you."

Emory pulled out my chair.

The food smelled and looked good, so, I decided to act civilized.

"I made your favorite."

"I can see that."

The smell of the meatloaf and potatoes made my mouth water.

Emory fixed both of our plates, and for a while, we ate in silence.

"Whose sex did you like better?"

"What?" Emory choked.

"Mimi's or Christina's? Whose sex did you like better?"

"Nova, really? You want to talk about this right now?"

I gave him a death stare.

"Fine. Neither."

I exhaled loudly and placed down my fork. "So, if I knock all this shit off this table…"

"Nova, I don't know! I didn't look at it like that, damn! It was just sex. Just something to do."

"Just something to do? Wow! So, you ruined our six-year relationship just because you wanted something to do?"

"I didn't mean it like that. I'm just saying…they didn't mean anything. You mean everything. That's all I'm trying to say. I know it's going to take time for you to trust me again. Sorry, I shouldn't have yelled. Can we just finish eating, please?"

"I'm sorry. Suddenly, I've lost my appetite."

I pushed away from the table.

Once inside the master bathroom, I locked the bathroom door and turned on the shower.

And then…

I cried.

I haven't cried since I was in my teens.

Over anything or anyone.

I smiled when both my parents died. When others hurt me, I smiled because I always got even.

And in that moment, as I cried my eyes out, as I cried from the deepest part of my soul, I realized that getting even with Emory still won't be enough.

But damn it, it'll have to do!

*****

CHAPTER FOUR

"Stop touching me," I mumbled through a fake smile as we waited for Cece or Rick to open the door.

It's Cece's birthday, and she's having a gathering at her house to celebrate.

"You're wearing the hell out of that red dress," Emory flirted. "I can't wait to take it off you tonight."

"In your dreams," I groaned just as Rick opened the front door.

"Hey! My favorite couple," Rick moved to the side so we could walk into the house. "Gifts go on that table. Drinks right over there. And the birthday girl is...oh, there she is!" Rick pointed at Cece, who was also wearing a red dress, and a black feather boa. "Let's get fucked up and have a good time, shall we? Games are on the way!"

Emory and I looked at each other.

What kind of games are we playing?

With Rick and Cece...you just never know!

After grabbing drinks, Emory and I went in opposite directions. I headed towards Cece.

"Happy birthday, doll," I kissed her cheek."

"Yay! You're here! I've been waiting to see your face all night!" Cece hugged me. "Come on, drink that so I can get you another one." Cece tapped her glass against mine, and together, we gulped down our drinks.

She smiled. And then, she noticed someone across the room.

"I'll be right back."

Cece ran across the room as I made my way over to the tables full of food.

Cece is one of the best cooks and bakers in town. Maybe even the world. I keep telling her to open her own restaurant, but she said she doesn't want to. She says she cooks to relieve stress. And that running her own restaurant has stress written all over it. So, she refuses.

Cece decided to cook everything for her party. So, I know it's going to be good.

"There's so much food," I mumbled to myself.

"There sure is," someone agreed.

I glanced up with a smile but immediately, it became a frown.

Christina.

Cece invited Christina to her party?

The same bitch that was sleeping with my man?

Of course, Christina has no idea who I am, because she smiled at me and continued to talk about the food.

"I want to try it all. That woman can cook her ass off!"

I didn't comment.

I wanted to stab her with the fork in my hand.

"How long have you known Cece?" she asked, making conversation.

Oh, you want to talk?

Okay…let's talk!

"Almost three years. I met her when my boyfriend, Emory, and I bought our house a few houses down."

Christina coughed. "Oh," was all she managed to get out.

"How do you know her?"

Just like that, Christina's vibe was different. It was clear that she no longer wanted to talk to me. She wanted to get as far away from me as possible.

"We, um, go to a class together."

"Yoga? She's been trying to get me to go with her to one of those classes for forever! I might give it a try. I could definitely use some stretching, well, not really. I get enough bending and stretching out in the bedroom, if you know what I mean. But yoga might be fun," I took a bite of the chicken leg in my hand. "Enjoy the party."

I walked away from her.

I found Cece sitting outside on the patio with a few of her other friends.

"How's the chicken?" She smiled at me.

"Fine." I took a seat next to her, and then I whispered in her ear. "Why would you invite Christina, knowing I would be here?"

Cece pulled her ear away to look at me.

"I invited the whole class. I didn't think about..." Cece smiled at the other women sitting close by. "I'm sorry," she said to me.

I sat quietly and ate my food while everyone around me talked and laughed. Finally, getting up to throw my empty plate into the trash can, I glanced inside the house to see Christina standing in front of Emory.

I couldn't be sure of what was being said, but she was trying to talk to him and he was shaking his head. Christina pulled Emory by the arm as he tried to walk away from her. Emory looked back at Christina, said something that caused her to fold her arms across her chest, and then he hurried away.

Christina stormed off in the opposite direction.

I headed into the house to follow her. I scanned the room for Emory, and then I made my way down the hallway.

Cece and Rick's house is huge.

It's only one level, but I won't even attempt to guess how many square feet it is. It's the biggest house on our street.

I knocked on the bathroom door to see if Christina would say something from the other side.

Nothing.

Suddenly, I heard a shout coming from the end of the bedroom at the end of the hallway.

I glanced behind me at the few people visible and then I inched towards the door. I pressed my ear up against it. I couldn't hear anything. So...

"Cece! Are you in..." I opened the door, yelling as though I was looking for Cece. "Oh, I'm sorry! I was looking for your wife."

Rick and Christina were standing in front each other in what looked to be an office. I've been in the main areas and in their bedroom before, but never in this particular room.

Both Rick and Christina stared at me as though I was a stranger.

"Excuse me," I proceeded to close the door.

"Last time I saw her she was outside!" Rick shouted behind me.

"Okay!"

I closed the door, discombobulated.

What in the hell could they possibly be discussing in private?

Hurriedly, I rushed back to the front of the house and searched for Emory.

Christina goes to yoga class with Cece.

Christina is, well, she was sleeping with Emory.

Christina is having a private conversation with Rick.

Something just doesn't feel right about this Christina chick.

I stopped in front of the mixed drink bowls on the table laced in gold fabric. I found the blue one that Cece has been drinking nonstop all night.

I unzipped my wristlet. I'd worn it to work that day and decided to wear it to the party to hold our house keys and my cellphone. Luckily, I still had my bottle of prescription laxative inside of it.

Looking around, I poured the rest of the bottle in the blue mixed drink, and then stirred it around.

I hope Cece drinks the whole bowl.

Maybe she'll shit on herself in front of everybody.

I'm her *real* friend.

She could've…no…she *should've* conveniently forgotten to invite little Miss. Christina to her party knowing I would be here. So, for that, she deserves to have a little accident on herself. Unfortunately, I won't be here to see it.

"I'm ready to go," I said to Emory as soon as I approached him. "Seeing the bitch you cheated on me with has suddenly taken me out of the partying mood."

"I didn't know she was going to be here. I didn't even know she knew Cece."

I didn't respond.

I turned around, and Emory followed me all the way out the door.

"What did she say to you to break things off?" I asked Emory as we walked to our house.

"She didn't break things off with me. I broke things off with her."

"What?"

"I broke things off with her. Officially, only a day or two before you told me you knew about her and Mimi. Though I wasn't having sex with her because of the whole STD thing, as you know. But for a week or two, Christina had been acting different. Out of nowhere, she started asking for more. She was complaining and wanted to talk more than usual. She knew from the very beginning that I was in a relationship."

"What? So, she knew about me?"

"Yes. She didn't know your name or anything, but she knew I had a woman."

Hmmm...

"And since I knew I wasn't leaving you, I told Christina I couldn't give her what she wanted and that we shouldn't see each other anymore. The whole gonorrhea thing was enough for me anyway. I was done cheating. I stopped answering her phone calls and all. She saw me tonight, had a few words for me, after randomly talking to you. And that was it. Nova, I promise. She and I are over."

I listened to him, but I was thinking about seeing Cece and Christina talking outside the yoga studio that day.

Cece told me that she told Christina about me. She told me that Christina was so upset to find out that Emory had a woman, and that she promised to break things off with

Emory that same day. But according to Emory, Christina already knew about me, and they continued to fool around until he broke things off with her.

Did Christina pretend not to know about me to Cece?

Or is there something that Cece isn't telling me?

What did she really say to Christina that day?

"I guess I won't get to see what's underneath that dress tonight, huh?" Emory asked as soon as we entered our bedroom.

Without answering Emory's question, I headed into the bathroom, slamming the bathroom door behind me, so that I could continue thinking about this whole Christina woman in peace.

~***~

I stood, listening to Kojo's phone conversation.

He was telling someone that he was going to catch a movie at seven by himself.

"Uh, uh," I cleared my throat.

Kojo turned around.

"I'll talk to you later, bro." Kojo hung up. "Boss man is in his office."

I smiled at him, flirtatiously, before walking away.

"Damn, I didn't expect to see you here," Emory stood up.

"Actually, I figured you were lying about coming to work on a Saturday," I answered honestly. "And since I was already over here, I figured I would just come in."

Emory walked around the desk and sat on the edge right in front of me. Emory pulled me closer to him.

"You're so beautiful," he complimented me. "And you smell good too. Let me take you out tonight."

"Nope. I already have plans."

"What plans?"

"I'm going out."

"With who?"

"Christina," I stepped back.

Surprisingly, he chuckled. "Whew, you're really gonna' make a brotha' put in work to get us back on good terms, aren't you? It's okay, though. I'll do whatever it takes. Enjoy your night out---with whoever. I'll be waiting for you when you get home. I need to stay here late tonight anyway."

"For what?"

"Paperwork. Some new contracts. Ordering parts online. I'm a little behind. It's time to hire an assistant at this location."

I used to help out with everything before taking on that big project at work. After that, I just didn't have the time. And as of right now, though I'm free again, I'm not helping him with shit.

"Go on, so I can watch you walk away," Emory smiled greedily.

I gave him the middle finger before backing out of his office and slamming his door behind me.

At first, I didn't really have any plans.

But I do now.

I'm going to show up at the same movie Kojo is going to see. Perfect time to make another move on him.

Every man in the shop watched me as I walked out the building.

"Are you busy? Want to go get our nails done?" I said once Yana picked up the phone, just as I got inside my car.

"I wish. Lord knows I need mine done, but I'm about to get on a plane."

"Lord, and go where? Dang, you can never just sit still, can you?"

Yana laughed. "This wasn't planned. Hubby has to check on his mom. She's in the hospital and he wants to see what's going on with her. We'll be back in a few days."

We chatted for a few more minutes, and then she was gone.

I definitely need more friends.

I've never really been the friendly type. Only with Yana, and Cece practically forced me into liking her.

Speaking of...

"Hello," she growled.

"Have you recovered from last night? You were pretty wasted, birthday girl," I tried to sound cheerful.

"Girl, I was so drunk that I don't hardly remember anything. All I know is by the end of the night, I had shit running down my legs."

I laughed. "What do you mean?"

I knew exactly what she meant because I was the cause of it.

"It's like diarrhea came out of nowhere! I couldn't hold it. I ended up with shit all over myself and woke up this morning on the floor beside the toilet."

I howled in laughter.

That's what she gets for inviting Christina.

"Where was Rick?"

"Girl, passed out in a chair outside by the pool."

"It was chilly last night. He must've been freezing."

"I don't know. I feel like crap. What time did you leave?"

"I can't remember. I was mad at you."

I decided to mention what Emory said to me.

"Mad at me? For what?"

"You invited Christina to your party, knowing she was sleeping with Emory."

"I swear it was nothing like that. I extended the invitation to the whole class. I didn't know if she would even come."

"That's not why I'm mad. I'm mad because you told me you told her about me and to leave Emory alone when I asked you. You also told me that she broke things off with him, immediately, but last night, I found out that wasn't true. Christina was still sleeping with Emory until he broke things off with her. And apparently, Christina knew about me from the very beginning. And you knew that she knew."

I wasn't sure if that part was true, but my gut told me I was right. If Cece denies it, I'll just tell her that she told me that while she was drunk.

Cece was quiet.

"Cece?"

"I gotta' go."

And with that, Cece hung up in my ear.

"What the----," I cut my sentence short as I pressed her name and number. She didn't answer the phone.

I knew it! I was right!

Cece didn't have to tell Christina about me, because Christina already knew. And Cece knew that from the very beginning. The question is, why the fuck wouldn't Cece tell me when it all first started? If she was my friend, why wouldn't she tell Christina to back off from the very beginning?

This is exactly why I've never had many friends.

You can't trust women.

The only woman I have ever been able to trust is Yana.

Later that evening, I got dressed in a tight pair of jeans, a canary yellow, off the shoulders shirt, big gold hoop earrings and headed to the movies.

I got there thirty minutes early, just to see if I could spot Kojo going in. About fifteen minutes before seven, he arrived by himself, and headed to buy a ticket.

I headed to do the same two minutes after he walked away.

"Nova?"

Kojo noticed me once I was inside, standing in line for popcorn. He had a bag of popcorn in his hand and a large drink.

"Kojo? What's up?"

"I just left Emory. He's still at the shop."

"I know, hence why I'm seeing a movie alone."

"Which movie are you seeing?"

I showed him my ticket.

"Shit, me too! I been waiting on this movie to come out."

"Where's your date?"

"No date. I'm solo."

"Oh. We could've sat together."

Kojo didn't respond.

He waited for me to order what I wanted, and he paid.

Then, we walked together to theater that was playing our movie.

We went our separate ways, but once the movie was about ten minutes in, and seeing that no one was yet sitting beside Kojo, I went to sit beside him.

The movie was a horror film. I would've never come to see this movie without Emory, but it was all in hopes of getting close to Kojo. I'm going to make him want to fuck me if it's the last thing that I do!

"Ahhh!"

I jumped. Instinctively, I grabbed onto Kojo.

He chuckled.

"Hold my hand," I said to him. He did as he was told.

For the remainder of the movie, I buried my face into his big left arm, or squeezed his hand every time I got scared.

"That movie was scary."

Kojo laughed. "I liked it."

"You're a psycho. You weren't scared at all."

Kojo didn't respond. He walked me towards my car in complete silence.

"You don't say much."

"I do when there's something that needs to be said."

"Why are you single?"

"I'm focused."

"Too focused for a woman?"

We reached my car.

"Pretty much. Women are trouble."

"Don't you get lonely?"

"I'm good," Kojo mumbled.

"Kojo?" I called out to him before he could walk away. "What if I'm not?"

"What do you mean?"

"What if I'm not "good" as you call it?"

I walked a little closer to him.

"Then, I guess you gotta' do what makes you happy."

"You sure about that?"

I was so close to him that I could smell the natural oils on his beard.

"What if doing something bad makes me happy?"

"Like what?"

"Like you?"

There it is.

I put it out there.

Now, let's see what he does with it.

Kojo stared down at me for a long time. It was as though I was a puzzle that he was trying to figure out.

Finally, he stepped back from me.

"Get home safely, Nova."

And with that, Kojo walked away.

Damn it!

He's one of the good ones!

I slammed my car door once I was inside. If he's going to be a good friend to Emory, this messes up everything! This blows up my entire plan!

I want to hurt Emory so bad that he never cheats on another good woman again. I want to hurt him so bad that he double checks his will just in case he decides to off himself. Hell, I want to hurt him so bad that every time he eats and swallows, he thinks of me swallowing another man's kids, the same way I used to swallow his. I want

Emory to hurt so bad that he refuses to eat, loses forty pounds, and ends up looking like a crackhead.

That's what I want!

And I need Kojo to do it!

I wonder if Kojo will tell Emory that I came onto him.

If he doesn't, there's still hope.

I called Yana because I was finally ready to tell her about my plan and Kojo, but she didn't answer her cell phone.

So, I headed home.

Emory was already there, so, I sat in my car for a while to do a little digging.

I'd gone through Cece's friends list on social media. Of course, Christina was one of her friends. From her profile, as much as I could see, she seemed pretty normal. And going through some of her photos and posts, I could see that both Cece and Rick commented on quite a few of them. They cracked jokes with her and made other quirky remarks to her.

Apparently, they *know* Christina.

A lot more than just from some damn yoga class!

A lot more than Cece led me to believe.

Hmm…

There's something weird going on with the Freaky Wilsons and Christina.

And I'm going to figure out what it is.

Emory stepped out onto the front porch.

Finally, getting out my car and approaching the steps, I could see that he was wearing a smile.

If he's smiling at me, that means Kojo didn't tell him.

So that means…

Kojo just might want my *goodies* after all.

~***~

"Your little wife isn't lurking around somewhere, is she?"

Ox chuckled. "She's not my wife."

"Oh, yes she is. She made that crystal clear."

Ox held open the door as I walked outside.

"I hadn't seen her in years, before that day she showed up here. She cheated on me, with my first cousin, years ago. We legally separated and when it was time to make the divorce final, she basically disappeared. One day, she was just gone," Ox shrugged. "She moved, changed her number, I didn't know where she was or what she was doing. Or if she was dead or alive. She was just gone. After a while, shit, I pretty much forgot that I was still married at all."

"Shit, all that money you make, she didn't stick around to get her cut of it?"

"Nah. She doesn't want or need my money. And she ain't getting shit from me, but a goodbye."

"Well, she's back in town. She must want something."

"She says she wants me. Some bull about missing me and making the worst mistake of her life. She says I'm the only man that she has ever truly loved."

"Aww. Can you forgive her?"

"Hell no. I just need her signature on the dotted line. That's it."

"See, that's why I've never been in a rush to get married. It seems as though marriage either leads to divorce or a lifetime of pain."

"Marriage is beautiful...when it's with the right person."

"That's what everyone says. But is there ever really a "right" person?"

Before Emory cheated on me, I truly thought he was "my" person. I felt as though all my other relationships failed because I was destined to be with him.

So much for that.

"Trouble in paradise?" Ox said with a smile.

"What paradise?"

Ox smiled. "There really is a God!"

I rolled my eyes.

"That's why you hooked up with me, isn't it?"

"Ox, it wasn't like that. I gave you the choice to take it there, remember?"

"Well, I choose to keep taking it there."

I kissed Ox on the cheek.

Without saying another word to him, I got into my car and I headed over to Yana's house.

Yana is still out of town, so, I used my spare key to let myself in.

I miss her.

I need her.

But right now, her new husband needs her more.

I grabbed one of the fluffy white pillows and stretched out on her white sectional.

The vibe of Yana's house is so calm and soothing. So, when I just need relax and clear my head, whether she's home or not, this is where I always end up.

I used to travel with her sometimes.

Yana would pay for everything and refused to let me pay her back. She even offered to help me start my own business, a few times, but I never wanted her to feel like I was using her or as though I needed her.

I love her rich.

And I would love her if she was broke just the same.

I really hope her new husband has good intentions.

He doesn't speak much English, which isn't an issue for Yana since she's fluent in five different languages. But from his body language, the few times I've been around, I can't really tell if he truly loves Yana or not.

For his sake, I sure hope he does.

Because if he does anything to her, Mr. Brazil will have to deal with me!

After lying there for a while, I got up and headed into Yana's bedroom. Her bedroom is all white. Literally! The entire room and everything in it is white.

It smelled like cinnamon and honey for some odd reason, but everything was in its proper place.

I turned on the light inside her enormous closet.

There were tons of clothes, shoes and purses that still had tags on them. Most of it, Yana would end up giving away or reselling anyway.

"Oooh, I like this bag!"

Yana always told me to help myself to whatever she had. If I wanted it or needed it. I could have it.

No questions asked.

I stared at the bag on my arm in the mirrored wall inside the closet.

"Cute!"

I sat the bag next to the chair by the door and continued to rummage through Yana's things. We aren't the same size in clothing, but she had tons of new jewelry that caught my attention.

For a second or two, I eyed the prettiest diamond bracelet that I've ever seen. I can't even imagine how much money she'd spent on it. I placed it on my wrist, just to see what it looked like.

"Diamonds are truly a girls best-friend," I mumbled taking it off. I placed it back where I found it just as something else caught my eye.

I picked up the gold chain.

It's Josiah's gold chain.

The same chain he was wearing the day I dropped him off at the airport.

This chain is the only thing Josiah kept from our father. It's a simple chain, with a cross dangling from it. I turned over the cross. It has the initials of my great, great, great grandfather on the back of it. It's been in our family for decades, which is the only reason Josiah decided to keep it.

Why is it in Yana's closet?

I closed my eyes as I thought back to the day I hugged Josiah goodbye at the airport. I'm ninety-nine percent sure that this chain was around his neck. He always wore it. He never took it off.

How did it get here?

To this day, Josiah hasn't called or texted me back.

This means that Yana saw Josiah after I did.

After I dropped him off at the airport.

I rushed to find my phone.

I called Yana. She didn't answer, so I left her a voicemail to call me when she could.

Maybe she knows why Josiah never made it to California. Yana never would elaborate on what they were talking about the day they appeared to be arguing on the sidewalk.

What's really going on between Yana and Josiah?

~***~

"Let's have a baby," Emory rolled over.

I pretended as though I was asleep.

"I know you're awake. Let's have a baby, Nova. Let's start our family. We've talked about it long enough. I'm ready to be a dad. I'll be a good man to you. And a good father to our child. I promise."

Emory was hellbent on becoming a better father than his father was to him. Emory's dad has always been in and out of his life, since his parent's divorced when he was twelve. He talks about how his father just disappeared during the stage of life where he needed him the most. He married another woman and basically created a whole new family leaving Emory and his brothers behind.

"Having a baby won't fix what's broken between us, Emory," I mumbled, though I smiled evilly with my back towards him. The one thing he wants from me, I'm going to give to someone else.

I can't wait!

"I know. But we've wanted a baby for so long. I think now is the time. I love you and I'm not going anywhere. You love me and we're going to work things out. So, let's make something that we both can love together."

"I don't know if I love you from one day to the next."

"Wow. Really?"

"Getting cheated on does that to a person. In case you didn't know."

I sat up. I checked my phone.

Still no call from Josiah or Yana.

"Okay, Nova. Just okay."

Emory rolled out of bed. "If you're not going to forgive me…"

"Uh, uh, you don't have the right to make any demands," I interrupted him.

"I'm just saying…"

"And I'm just saying, if I didn't want to be here…I wouldn't be."

The doorbell started to ring.

"It's early. Who is that?"

"Go and see."

Emory slipped on his shorts and hurried out of the bedroom. I checked my calendar on my phone. My ovulation days for this month have passed. Next month, I have to get pregnant.

Or I have to leave.

No matter how I tried to look at things, and no matter how much I feel like I love Emory, my want, my need to get him back overpowers it all.

I could tell him that I had sex with Ox. I cheated back. Yet, it just isn't satisfying enough for me.

"Nova!" Emory yelled my name.

I already knew what he wanted. I could hear her big mouth all the way down the hall.

Emory's mother, Ethel.

Ms. Ethel is one nosey, old lady, but for the most part, she's okay. She and I have always gotten along. She just asks a lot of questions and has an opinion about everything, all the time.

"Hi, how are you doing, darling?" she asked as I approached her.

"I'm doing good," I hugged her.

Emory tried to hug me afterwards but I moved away from him.

"Uh, oh, did I pop up at a bad time?"

"Nah, ma. You're fine. Let me take your bags."

Emory picked up her bags and carried them away.

"What happened to the vase I gave to you guys when you moved in?" Ms. Ethel noticed that it was no longer where it used to be.

"I threw it at Emory."

"What!" She grabbed her chest.

"You asked."

I walked towards the kitchen. I thought she was going to follow me to ask questions, but instead, she went to find Emory.

Good.

He can tell her his version of the story. And I don't care if it's the truth or not.

I made a cup of coffee, and with Emory and his mother talking in the guest room, I showered and got ready for work.

"You're not mad that she popped up, are you?" Emory asked entering our bedroom.

"No. She's fine."

I eyed myself in the full-length mirror. The tight black skirt hugged my hips, and the royal blue blouse looked good up against my skin.

"I told her I cheated on you."

"Oh."

The room was quiet.

"Look, if you don't want to try anymore, I get it. We can do whatever you want to do."

I picked up my purse. "I'm fine, Emory," I lied with a smile. The truth is, I know in my heart that there isn't a future for us. Whether I get to fully execute my plan or not. I would prefer to hurt him and move on, but I may have to just settle with moving on.

I didn't speak to his mother as I passed by her. I simply smiled in her direction and headed out the front door.

My phone started to vibrate just as I got into the car.

"Hey, girl. I've been so busy. I kept forgetting to call you," Yana said. "I just got back. My hubby stayed in Brazil. His mom isn't doing well. I may go back in a few days or next week. What's up?"

"Have you heard from Josiah?"

"No. Why?"

"When was the last time you spoke to him?"

"I don't know. The day before he left. Or maybe it was the day of. Why?"

"Did you see him on the day he left?"

"No. Nova, you're scaring me. Why are you asking me about Josiah?"

No?

Yana is lying.

Just like I thought, Josiah was wearing the chain at the airport that day. I went through my pictures to check the selfie that we took together that day at the airport and Josiah was wearing the chain in the picture.

Yet, I found the chain at Yana's house, and she's saying that she hasn't seen him.

Why is she lying about seeing Josiah?

That's the real question.

"I haven't heard from him. No one has. He's not returning calls or anything. I figured since I saw you guys arguing, maybe you guys talk a lot more than I know about."

"I can try calling him. But I haven't heard from him."

"Can you at least tell me what the two of you were arguing about that day? Maybe it will help me try to figure out where he is."

"We weren't arguing. We were talking. He didn't like what I said. I didn't like what he said. There wasn't an argument."

"Well, what were the two of you talking about?"

"It's personal. Something about him."

"And you can't tell me? Your best friend?"

"I could…"

"Yana, what aren't you telling me?"

"Nothing."

"Tell me."

Yana exhaled. "Josiah was mad that I got married. Okay!"

"Why? I thought y'all just fooled around once."

"It was a little more than once. It was for a while. Off and on."

I shook my head. "But why would he be upset about you getting married?"

"That's something you'll have to ask him."

"If I knew where he was…I would!" I yelled at her.

"Look, we may have fallen in love, briefly. Things happen. We lost touch. Next time he saw me, I was on social media with a new husband. I guess he was in his feelings and came to tell me about them."

"He came all the way here because he was in his feelings about you get married?"

"Basically."

"And you haven't seen or spoken to him since he left?"

"Nope. I'll try calling him and see if he picks up for me. But you know how he does. I'm sure he's fine. He's just in his feelings. That's all."

Something doesn't feel right.

I trust Yana with my life.

More than anyone in the world. More than Emory. More than my brothers. But she's lying to me about something. For the first time ever, she's lying to me and I don't understand why.

"Everything okay on your end?"

"Everything is peachy," I commented. And before she could carry on the conversation, I told her I had to go.

I called Josiah's phone. I left another voicemail.

"Hey. I'm just checking on you. Please, call me and let me know that you're okay."

Yana said they were sort of in love a while ago.
Wow!

She never told me about them. But if what they had was years ago, why would it matter to Josiah now?

Why would he care about her getting married to someone else?

And clearly she saw him in order to get the chain from him…why is she hiding that from me?

I'm sure when Yana notices that the chain is missing, she'll know, that I know, that she saw Josiah after I dropped him off at the airport.

I exhaled loudly.

Where in the world is Josiah?

And what the fuck does Yana have to do with it?

~***~

The hot coffee splashed all over me.

"Uggh!"

"Oh, no, I'm sorry!"

I looked up.

I recognized her.

Shanice.

Ox's ex…current…whatever wife!

"Did you do this on purpose?"

"Of course, not. Why would I?" Shanice asked, politely. "It was an accident. I didn't see you there."

Ox walked over just in time.

I was just about to slap that stupid smirk off her face!

"It was an accident, Ox. I swear. I was looking for you, and I guess she just got in my way."

Before I could say anything or react, hurriedly, Ox ushered me into my office.

"Despite whatever, you're my boss. And this is my job. But your wife is about to get an Equal Opportunity ass whooping all over this goddamn place!"

I unbuttoned the top buttons of my shirt, as Ox closed my office blinds.

"Do you need a shirt?"

"I keep a few here," I headed towards the coat closet behind my desk.

"I don't know why she's here. I'll get rid of her. I'm sorry, Nova."

I didn't respond to Ox. I waited until I heard him leave my office to turn around.

If I ever see her in the streets…

"Knock, Knock," my office door opened.

Emory.

He was carrying roses and wearing a smile.

"What happened? Why are you half naked?" Emory closed the door.

"I spilled coffee all over myself."

"Oh. I just wanted to bring these to you."

Over the past few days, I've eased up a little.

Emory has his mother to thank for that. Her being around causes enough tension in the house, with her country, old school ways, so, usually, Emory and I end up lying in bed laughing and talking about her at the end of the night.

"Thank you. They're pretty."

"Not as pretty as you."

"You're so corny," I shook my head.

"Only for you, baby," Emory smiled. "I hope you have a good day." Emory kissed my forehead and turned to leave.

"She sleeps with married men," Shanice appeared out of nowhere and blurted in Emory's face.

"Excuse me! No I don't!" I answered hurriedly, with Emory's eyes on me.

"Oh. Just checking." Shanice shrugged and moved out of Emory's way.

A confused Emory walked past her, glancing back at me until he was out of sight.

"I've had just about enough of you!"

"Girl, sit your ass down. You ain't gonna' do shit to me," Shanice walked into my office and closed the door behind her. "I need your help."

"Ha! Picture that!"

I smelled the roses one last time before taking a seat behind my desk.

"I need your help getting my husband back. I see the way he looks at you. I figured the two of you were screwing each other, but I guess not. Anyway, I want him to look at me like that again."

"Girl, I can't help you. And even if I could, I wouldn't. I don't know you. I don't like you. And I don't want to."

"You're feisty. Just like me. I can see why he likes you."

"Ox is my boss."

"Yeah, with a hard dick for you," she huffed. "Look, from what I could gather from him, and even seeing how he jumped to your aid after your little coffee accident, the two of you are close. And if you're not screwing each other, that means you're closer than him just being your boss. You're friends. And if I'm right, he'll probably listen to you, or at least consider your advice. So, I need your help getting him back."

"You cheated on him. You had sex with his cousin. There's no coming back from that."

"See…he does talk to you," she smiled. "You can help me. And in return, maybe I can help you too."

"Help me? How can you help me? I don't need anything from you."

"Wanna' bet?" Shanice stood up and fixed her dress.

She was wearing a tight, leopard print knee-length dress, and black, leather red bottom shoes.

"I'm a woman with a lot of resources. And a few necessary connections. You'll be surprised by what I may can help you with." Shanice grinned. "Think it over."

And with that, she walked out of my office with a sense of evil trailing behind her.

Hmm…I think I like her.

~***~

"Why didn't you tell Emory that I came on to you?" I asked Kojo.

"Was I supposed to?"

"No. I guess I just thought since you turned me down…"

"He's my boy. That's what I'm supposed to do," Kojo finished. "I know he cheated on you and all that. He told me. And if you were trying to fuck with me, to get back at him, that ain't my type of thing."

"Why does that make me want to sleep with you even more?"

"People always tend to want what they can't have. Trust me," Kojo eyed me up and down. "I know the feeling." He walked away, heading towards the work van, as I walked inside the shop.

Yes! He wants me! I just have to get him to give in to his desires, some way or another.

I dropped off the papers that Emory needed from the house, and by the time I came back outside, Kojo was gone.

Damn it!

"It smells good in here," I said to Ms. Ethel once I was back home.

"Those are my turkey necks that you smell."

I took another sniff before taking a seat on one of the wooden stools.

"You're going to leave my son, aren't you?" She asked me out of nowhere.

Kojo basically told me that he wasn't going to sleep with me. And if he doesn't, leaving Emory is the only thing for me to do. I thought about getting pregnant by one of Emory's other friends, but I just can't do it. All of them are so unattractive. And I'm scared I might end up with an ugly ass baby if I sleep with one of them.

Kojo was the only option.

Some might say I should just get over it already.

I cheated too, with Ox, and maybe Emory learned his lesson. Maybe he'll never cheat on me again.

He will.

He'll probably just never get caught again.

That's the way I see it. That's the way my mind is set up. And no matter how bad I wish it wasn't, it just is.

And I can't change it.

Not even for Emory.

"Probably," I shrugged, finally answering his mother's question. "I'm not a fan of being cheated on. And he'll do it again, if I stay with him. He'll just do a better job at hiding it this time."

"People change."

"Rarely."

"My son isn't like that. If he cheated…"

"Not *if*…he did."

"Well, he must've had a reason to."

"Excuse me?"

Mrs. Ethel started to wash a pot in the kitchen sink. "We both know Emory. He's a good man. He's not like his brothers. I'm just saying, he had to have a reason to cheat."

"And what reason would that be?"

"You tell me."

"The only thing I can tell you is that your son ain't shit just like all the other men in this world who cheat on good women for no apparent reason," I rolled my eyes at her.

"He told me about all the stuff you did out of anger. I've always told him there's a side to you that he hasn't seen. A dark side. A side that I'm pretty sure he wouldn't want to marry."

I exhaled loudly. "Yeah. There is. And that same side would love to give you a senior citizen discount on a beat down right now, but you know what, I'm just going to walk away," I turned my back to her. "You can thank my good side for that. And like I said, your son ain't shit and now I see where he gets it from."

Mrs. Ethel gasped and she started talking so fast that I thought she was speaking in tongues. The only thing I could make out was that she said she was telling Emory what I said.

I don't care.

I don't care about anything.

Almost.

My heart skipped a beat at the sight of Josiah's name popping up on my cell phone. I opened the text message in a hurry.

"I'm okay."

That's it.

That's all it said.

I called him.

He didn't answer.

I called him again, and again, and again, and still, he didn't pick up his phone.

Is he really okay?

Is he?

*****

CHAPTER FIVE

Shanice does have some pretty good connections.

I guess.

After she popped up at my office, uninvited, again, the other day, being that Josiah's phone is now going straight to voicemail, I asked if she knew how to find people who might not want to be found.

I briefly told her I was trying to get in contact with my brother. I agreed to talk to Ox for her if she could find out where Josiah is.

Unfortunately, her resources couldn't find Josiah, but she did have a connection at the airport who was able to find the footage from the day that I dropped Josiah off.

Josiah lingered around for just a few minutes after I walked away, and then he made his way right back out of the airport. No one came to pick him up. And he didn't call a cab or car. He simply walked away from the airport until finally, he's out of sight.

He never intended on getting on that plane.

And since he never left that means…

Josiah is still in town.

Why doesn't he want me to know that?

"How are you doing today…" Ox glanced around, "…Sexy?" He finished his question with a smile.

"I'm doing good."

I promised Shanice that I would talk to him, but I didn't promise to be able to change his mind about her.

"Your little wife loves herself some you," I giggled.

"Man, she's delusional. She won't tell me where she's staying, so I can't have her served."

"She obviously still loves you. You really can't forgive her?"

"Hell no. Could you?"

I was trying to get pregnant by one of Emory's friend for cheating on me with women I don't know. I can't even imagine what I would want to do to him if he cheated with my first cousin.

"She screwed my family. How would I look taking her to another family function?"

"Like a husband who forgave his wife."

Ox shook his head. "Nah. I just can't do it. I thought about it years ago. And I only thought about it because I'd never had a woman who loved me the way that she did. But no. That chapter closed a long time ago. I'm waiting on you to close your current chapter, so our story can begin."

"You just don't give up, do you?"

Ox beamed as he walked away.

Well, I did what I said I would do.

Shanice is going to hear the same thing from me that I'm sure he's told her a thousand times.

He doesn't want her.

And I don't feel sorry for her. She shouldn't have cheated.

"Damn, what were you doing? Hiding behind a tree?"

Shanice appeared out of nowhere. "Something like that. What did he say?"

"He said no. He said he could never take you around his family again. He's too embarrassed and that he doesn't think that he can forgive you. He also said the chapter of his life with you in it is closed. I think he's done. For real."

"Well, good thing I didn't ask you what you think. I asked you what he said."

"And I told you."

"Indeed you did. I guess it's time for Plan B."

I didn't bother to ask her what Plan B is, but I was jealous that I didn't have a Plan B myself.

Kojo is loyal to his friendship with Emory.

And since I'll never let any of Emory's other friends or his brothers so much as pull a pubic hair off my pussy, let alone get pregnant by them…it would've been nice to have a Plan B.

Shanice and I walked in separate directions.

My stomach cramped, letting me know that Aunt Flow was about to make her monthly entrance again.

I was hoping to be pregnant by now.

I drove home in complete silence.

I passed by Rick and Cece's house.

When she saw my car, she went inside the house.

We haven't spoken since the day she hung up with me when I gave her the third degree about Christina.

I don't even care anymore.

I don't need her.

I don't need anyone.

I smiled at my empty driveway.

Emory's mother's car wasn't there.

Finally, she's gone.

She told Emory that I threatened her.

We got into a huge argument. I ended up packing a bag and going over to Yana's house. When I arrived, though she told me she wasn't going anywhere, anytime soon, she was gone again. When I called her, she was already at the airport. And come to think of it, I haven't heard from her since that day. Yana isn't answering her phone much either these days, and I'm convinced that she and Josiah are somewhere together. They're still carrying on their secret relationship, and they don't want me to know about it.

It's the only thing that makes sense.

Emory pulled into the driveway beside me.

He's calling, texting, and sending his location all throughout the day, trying to prove to me that he isn't still cheating on me. Emory says that he's trying to earn my trust back, but his actions aren't working.

No matter what he does, I still don't trust him.

"Come on," he said just as I got out my car.

"What?"

"Get in the car."

"For what?"

"Come on, babe. Just get in the car."

I hit the alarm on my car and got into his. Immediately, I noticed the bags packed in the backseat.

"What's this?"

"I packed you a bag. We're taking a little ride."

"A ride? Where?"

"We'll you've always talked about going to one of those food trucks events in Savannah," Emory pulled out of the driveway. "Well, we're on our way."

Wow.

He actually listens to the things I say.

Yana and I have always talked about going to Savannah for one of their food truck festivals, but we never seem to make it.

"That's a long drive."

"I know. I already have a hotel booked a few hours away. And a suite booked for the weekend. Oh, and you're off on Monday, so I can treat you to some shopping and take my time driving back."

"I'm not off on Monday."

"Yes. You are. I worked it out with your boss. I told him it was a surprise."

"You talked to Ox?"

"No. The other one. I recognized him when he came into the shop. I gave him fifty percent off on his wife's brakes. He gave you Monday off. He said he'll email you to let you know over the weekend."

This is sweet. Very sweet.

And I don't like it!

I want to feel anger towards Emory. I don't want to let him off the hook.

"If you did this just so you can get some…"

"Your period should be coming on today or tomorrow. I packed your tampons," Emory smirked.

Wow! And to that, I was left with no words.

This is not supposed to be happening.

Emory turned up the radio, and we drove off in the sunset, literally, to make new memories together.

~***~

"He's in love with you."

"What?"

"Ox. He told me himself," Shanice barked.

I laughed. "Trust me, he's not."

"You think this is funny?"

I rolled my eyes at Shanice. "Yes. Ox is my friend. And I'm definitely not in love with him."

"Well, he's in love with you," Shanice growled. "So…now…I have to kill you."

And right there, in my office, Shanice pulled out a gun on me. I saw my life flash before my eyes.

Every good, bad and ugly thing that I have ever done played in my head as though I was watching a movie in 3-D.

I was frozen.

I didn't know what to say.

I didn't know what to do.

All I know is that I'm not ready to die!

"Nova, did you…" My office door opened.

Shanice jumped, turned her attention towards the door, and pulled the trigger.

Bang!

"Oh, no!" She screamed right after the gunshot. "Ox!"

Shanice rushed to his side. Ox melted towards the floor, howling in pain as he held his arm.

I just stood there.

Still stuck.

Still speechless.

"I'm sorry. I didn't mean to shoot you, Ox. I'm so sorry," Shanice looked towards me. "Don't just stand there. Call the goddamn ambulance!"

The building was suddenly full of noise with people in a panic, and still yet, I just stood there, in the midst of all the chaos.

I watched Shanice and Ox, but it was all a blur.

"Hey! Hey!" Shanice snapped her fingers at me. "Little Ms. Friend to Lover, get your ass over here and tend to my husband! I need to make my exit before the police arrive."

Her voice was cold.

Nonchalant as though she hadn't done a thing. As though she hadn't just pulled a gun out on me. As though she hadn't just shot her husband!

And I thought I had issues.

Shanice definitely has me beat!

"Shanice!" Ox yelled after her as she practically ran out of my office. "Shanice!" Ox came out of his blazer and pressed it up against the gunshot wound. "Nova? Nova? Are you alright? Nova?"

I couldn't respond.

"Everything is gonna' be alright. I don't know what was going on in here...but go!" Ox panted. "Get out of here. Go! I'll handle it."

Go?

There's nothing I wanted to do more.

In slow motion, I grabbed my purse and keys. As I stepped over Ox, he touched the side of my leg, causing me to jump. As I walked away, I heard him calling different employee names and giving them instructions.

I walked slowly.

Finally, I made it outside. Then and only then was I able to breath. Each breath was a struggle, but I inhaled and exhaled, loudly, over and over again.

That bitch was going to shoot me!

Over a man that I don't want and who doesn't want her!

Anger.

Fear.

Regret.

I was feeling so many different emotions, all at once, that I started to feel dizzy.

Finally, I made it to my car.

Now, I feel safe. But not safe enough.

In this moment, all I want is…Emory.

I sped across town to his shop.

When I arrived, it was pretty much a ghost town.

I've been nicer to Emory for the past two weeks after he surprised me with a road trip to Savannah.

No, I'm not over him cheating on me, but right now, all I want is to feel safe in his arms.

"Where is everybody?"

The sign on the door said closed, but when I used my key to get inside, Kojo was there, watching TV on the couch in the fancy lobby area that I'd decorated.

"The pipes burst this morning. Emory closed the shop down today. I'm waiting for the people to come out and fix it. I've been waiting all day. Emory drove to the store in Chestnut Park."

I stood there.

I started to breathe faster, and faster, and faster.

"Yo, Nova. Are you okay? What's wrong?"

Kojo stood up.

"I---I---I was almost shot at work today."

"What the fuck?" Kojo questioned, just as I started to tremble. I didn't have to ask him to hold me. Immediately,

Kojo pulled me close to him and wrapped his big arms around me.

I wanted to cry, but I couldn't.

Shanice could've killed me.

Right now, I could be dead.

"It's alright," Kojo rubbed my back.

I've accomplished a good bit, career wise, in my life.

But what about everything else?

The warmth of Kojo's chest caused me to close my eyes.

"I could've died today," I mumbled.

"Come on, don't talk like that."

Kojo pulled away from me and held my face in his hands. "What happened? Who almost shot you at work?"

I stared into Kojo's eyes.

"You're okay, Nova," Kojo kissed my forehead. "Come on, let's call Emory."

He attempted to pick up his cell phone from the red table, but I grabbed his arm.

I want to feel something in this moment.

I'd come to Emory---but Emory isn't here.

Kojo is.

Kojo eyed me, as though he was a weak little puppy eyeing a big, new bone.

I pulled at his arm, until he gave in and wrapped it around my waist.

"Nova…"

"Just kiss me."

Life is too short.

I could be dead right now.

But I'm not. I'm alive. I'm still here.

And I'm here with Kojo.

"Nova…"

I slid my hands underneath his shirt,.

"I know you want me," I rubbed Kojo's now bulging dick through his work pants. "And I want you."

I pushed at Kojo until finally, he sat down on the sofa.

"Emory is my boy…"

"Emory is your boss. And Emory isn't here."

I sat on his lap.

Yes, I just had a near death experience.

Yes. This is wrong.

No. I don't care.

I pulled my shirt over my head.

I could tell by the look in Kojo's eyes that he wanted to tear me apart.

"Nova…"

"Shut up and fuck me."

I kissed him. It took him all of two seconds before he started to kiss me back.

I made a mental reminder to check the camera surveillance footage before I left. I know that the cameras outside the building work, but last I checked, Emory rarely turned on the cameras inside the building. He said he trusts his team, and never felt the need to watch over them.

Kojo stood up with me still on his lap. He held me with just one of his massive arms, all while kissing me and walking towards the wall.

Up against the wall, still holding me, Kojo fondled with his belt buckle. I tapped his shoulder, signaling him to put me down so that I could take off my pants and panties.

We didn't speak. We both breathed heavily. And once my pants and panties were on the floor, Kojo scooped me up in his arms again, and without hesitating...

"Ohhhhh shit!"

Kojo filled my pussy with so much dick that it almost came out my mouth.

I've never been a fan of overly large penises.

A nice *normal* sized dick, six to eight inches was always good enough to me. I want to enjoy the sex. Not damn near die trying to have it.

One of my exes, Speedy, had a dick so big that he could fuck you from across the room. I don't think I ever came from penetration the entire time we were together. It was too much for me. He's one of the only guys that I actually broke up with, instead of him cheating on me. I told him he would have to go and find a prostitute, or alien or something. Someone who could actually enjoy what God blessed him with because that person just wasn't me.

I groaned as I tried to find a rhythm. I tried to find a way to enjoy it. The good thing is that Kojo wasn't just ramming his big dick in and out of me like a hammer pounding a nail. He pumped slowly, with a little swirling motion in between. At least he wasn't trying to cause me to need a hysterectomy.

The longer it lasted, the more it started to become enjoyable.

Nah. Not really.

Honestly, I couldn't wait for it to be over!

I hissed in pain with every, single pump, until finally, Kojo was done.

Shame was all over Kojo's face as he placed me down.

Silently, he got himself together and I did the same.

Suddenly, the doorbell rang, startling both of us.

Kojo rushed in the direction of the door and I rushed to check the cameras. The cameras inside the building were off. I could just tell Emory that I came by to see him and since he was here, I sat and talked to Kojo for a while. That's if an explanation was ever needed.

"Is he fixing the pipes?" I asked Kojo as I headed out.

"Yeah."

I opened the door to leave.

"Now I know why you're single."

"And why is that?" Kojo asked barely able to make eye contact with me.

"You got a Greek god dick. That's why," I frowned. "Nobody in their right mind would want you ramming that thing in and out of them every day. The Big Dick Myth. That's your new name."

Kojo chuckled.

I winked at him and walked away.

My phone stopped ringing just as I opened my car door. I'd left it in there on accident.

Damn! I had thirty missed calls from Emory.

"Hello?

"Oh, God! Thank God you're alive!" Emory yelled in my ear. "I saw it on the news! The shooting at your job. They aren't saying who got shot or what happened. And when you weren't answering, I thought it was you! I thought it was you!"

Emory started to cry.

I've never heard or seen him cry before and it caught me off guard.

"I thought...I thought..." he couldn't finish his sentence.

"I'm okay, Emory. I'm okay."

He cried for a few moments.

He thought he lost me. He thought I was dead.

"I love you so much. I don't know what I would do without you. I just thought...where are you?"

"I'm on my way home."

Emory sniffled. "I'll meet you there."

I beat Emory home. I hurried to take a shower, and just as I stepped out, I heard Emory come through the front door.

Emory ran into the bedroom, and though I was soak and wet, he hugged me.

"I'm glad you're okay."

He started to kiss all over my face.

In that moment, I could literally feel the love he had for me oozing out of his skin.

"What happened?"

"An angry wife shot her husband," I told the truth. I started to leave out anything concerning me, but I couldn't be sure of what Kojo would mention. "It was Ox. His wife shot him. I was right there. I could've been shot too."

"Is he alive?"

"Yes. She shot him in the arm."

Emory hugged me again. "That shit scared me half to death! Don't you ever leave me! Don't ever die on me! I swear, when we get old, I better die first because I can't live without you."

Aww.

Such a sweet thing to say after I just fucked his friend.

Emory started to kiss all over me again. Eventually, he made his way to my lips.

I tried to pull away from him, but he kissed me so passionately that my heart started to melt like butter.

"I love you, baby. I love you."

Emory's kisses turned me on and though I knew I'd just had sex with Kojo, I figured that men do what I'm about to do all the time. Emory was having sex with two other women and then he would come home and perform for me.

Those tables turn, and they turn so fast, I tell you!

I was horny because I couldn't get satisfied by Kojo, so, I didn't resist. I allowed Emory to have his way with me for the rest of the night.

Over and over again.

~***~

"Yana?"

The front door was cracked open.

I walked in to see that Yana's house was completely cleared out.

"Hello," a lady said coming out of the kitchen.

"This is my friend's house. Where is all her stuff?"

"Ms. Hampton put the house on the market. She moved abroad," the realtor answered. "If she's your friend, shouldn't you know this?"

"Yes. I should."

I took out my phone to call Yana.

Now, it's been about a month since I've spoken to her. It isn't uncommon for us to go without speaking while she's traveling, but normally, she would've told me something like this.

What in the hell is going on with her lately?

She answered the fourth time I called her.

"Yana? Hey. You're moving? To Brazil?"

"Hey," she said dryly. "Yes. I've already found a temporary house here until I can find a house to buy."

"Why wouldn't you tell me?"

"I was going to. Things have just been a little busy. My husband's mother died. It's just been a lot going on."

"Wow. I really thought you and Josiah had ran off together somewhere."

"Why would I be with Josiah? I'm married."

"I know. I just thought…"

"You know, me moving here for now doesn't matter. I can travel back and forth."

"I know. It's just a huge decision. It's something we would've talked about before, but here lately, I don't really know who you are anymore."

"I'm still your best-friend," Yana said. "It's just…" Yana paused. "Nova, I'll talk to you later."

She hung up.

And it felt as though I was saying goodbye to my best friend. She's not acting like herself. And no matter what she says, I know it has something to do with whatever is going on between her and Josiah.

I called him, but his phone went straight to the voicemail as always.

Hanging up, I ignored Ox's phone call for the third time today.

He told the police what happened was an accident.

He said his wife was toying around with her gun and it went off. No charges are going to be pressed.

Needless to say, I'm pissed!

I'm mad as hell that he covered for her!

Shanice could've killed me! And I wanted her crazy as locked up!

Ox tried to explain why he did what he did, but I didn't want to hear it. His wife pointed a gun in my face. And apparently she isn't scared to pull the trigger.

I've never been afraid of anyone, and I'm not afraid of Shanice. But I be damned if I die over Ox's little fantasy of us being more than what we are; which is nothing more than friends.

After the shooting, work was closed for three days, but I texted Ox and told him I wouldn't be coming in today. I need a few more days. That's probably why he's calling. The truth is, as much as I love the job, I don't think I'm ever going back.

I drove towards the auto shop.

I told Emory I would come help him get caught up on bookkeeping and place an ad online for an assistant.

This is his first day back at the shop.

Emory has spent the past few days, by my side, every second of the day. We had some real deep conversations. I even told him that I cheated on him to get back at him. I told him I wanted to hurt him just like he hurt me.

Emory got so upset that he punched a hole in the wall and broke a lamp. He was so angry that another man touched me. I just looked at him and told him now he knows how it feels.

I didn't tell him who I cheated on him with and I lied and said it was months ago when I first found out about Mimi.

After that conversation, things got real deep. He told me about some insecurities that I didn't even know he had, and somewhere along the way, I ended up opening up to him a little about my mother.

I told him enough for him to know that I've been getting hurt all my life. And I'm tired of people hurting me.

Emory promised to never hurt me again. And call me crazy, but I almost believe him.

"What's up, baby?"

"Hey."

Emory must've seen me pull up on the cameras and met me at the door. Secretly, I glanced around for Kojo.

I didn't see him.

"Thank you for coming to help me today."

"No problem."

"I really need the help. And on top of everything else, Kojo is gone."

"What do you mean gone?"

"He said it's time for him to move on. He's ready to open up his own spot. I'm proud of him and shit. He was one of my best guys, but I know what it's like to want to jump out there and make your own thing happen."

Kojo probably quit because of me.

Because we had sex.

He didn't have to leave though. He damn sure didn't have to worry about me ever coming onto him again. I wouldn't have sex with him again with my worst enemies pussy. My guts wouldn't be able to take it.

I'm sure he just doesn't want to look Emory in the face every day, since they are…or…were friends and all that.

Oh well.

I got what I wanted. I wanted to fuck one of Emory's friend's and...

Shit!

I forgot to go get a morning after pill!

I spent the past few days locked away with Emory in my face and in my space, that I hadn't had time to go and pick one up.

Originally, I wanted to get pregnant by Emory's friend to hurt him. But with something not feeling right with Yana and Josiah, having a gun pointed in my face, seeing how Emory reacted when he thought I was dead, and after the long deep conversations I had with Emory...I can't believe I'm saying this but...I've changed my mind.

Fucking Kojo was enough.

And if he ever finds out, so be it.

But the whole getting pregnant by Kojo thing...

I'm no longer interested.

"So, I need to hire an assistant and another guy."

"Emory, I need to run to the store right quick. Do you want something?"

"Nah. I'm good."

It's been three to four days.

The morning after pill is good for up to five days. Although by now, the percentage of it working has decreased tremendously, I'm still going to get one just in case.

I had sex with Emory and Kojo on the same day. If I end up pregnant, I really wouldn't know who the father of the baby is. And that wasn't a part of my plan!

A few minutes later, after purchasing the pill, I swallowed it before I even walked out of the pharmacy.

My phone vibrated in my back pocket, just as I unlocked my car door.

I smiled seeing that it was my brother Jacob.

"Hey, Jacob. How are…"

"Nova…Josiah is dead."

What?

I didn't hear anything else he said.

~***~

"It's been a long time since you've been home," one of my aunts on my mother's side said to me.

As far as I'm concerned, they aren't my family.

They never tried to help us. They had to have known my mother was sick. And they knew some of the things that she'd done to us because I told them.

But no one believed me. And no one ever tried helped us. No one saved us. Had it been up to me, I wouldn't have invited anyone to Josiah's funeral, but Jacob insisted.

Josiah was found dead, all the way back in Houston, Texas, inside the condo he'd purchased years ago with his half of our father's life insurance policy.

I remember talking him into purchasing it. I told him it was a smart move, because he was always getting into trouble. At least he would never have to worry about a place to lay his head. While he was at my house for those few days, Josiah told me that he was going to rent the condo out once he was settled in California. Josiah also told me that he never planned on going back to Texas, and if he did, it wouldn't be any time soon.

So, how did he end up here?

Dead?

Jacob found him.

He said he had to fly to Houston for a business trip and since Josiah hadn't been answering his phone, he decided to go by the condo. Josiah was inside, slumped over on the couch, with an open bottle of scotch and pills scattered all over the coffee table beside him.

Dead.

Josiah been dead for weeks, according to the coroner.

They're saying that Josiah killed himself.

There was no pill bottle. No way of knowing where the pills came from, since they weren't prescribed to him, but there was leftover residue on the sides of his mouth.

His phone was right beside him, turned off, which is why it was going to voicemail. Going from the date that I last saw him alive, once the phone was turned on, we saw tons of missed calls from me and Jacob, two missed calls from Yana, and the one text message that Josiah sent to me saying that he was okay.

No matter what I was being told, I don't believe for one second that Josiah killed himself. After all we went through as kids, after all he's been through as an adult, if he was going to kill himself, he would've done it a long time ago.

Why now?

Unless there's something that I don't know.

Something that I'm missing.

Something that someone isn't telling me.

Yana.

I'm willing to bet that Yana knows what pushed Josiah over the edge.

The bag that Josiah was carrying when I dropped him off at the airport wasn't there. And all of his other things were still packed and stored in the attic, so, it was clear he had no intentions of staying there.

What made him come back to Houston in the first place?

Yana approached me.

She cried when I called to tell her that Josiah was dead.

Her cry was hard, long, and heartbreaking.

There was more to the story about her and Josiah. If I had to guess, they were still in love. Deep love. But something went wrong.

"Are you okay?"

"I guess," I shrugged.

I noticed that she wasn't wearing her wedding ring. She flew into Houston last night to be here for the funeral.

"I'm just glad it's over. It's been a long week," I exhaled. "I just don't understand. Josiah wouldn't do something like this to himself."

"Maybe he was going through something none of us really knew about."

"No. He seemed better. He was on medication. He seemed happier. He was excited about starting his new life in California. No. Something happened. And it was something big."

Yana didn't say anything.

"How did you get his necklace? The gold chain that he kept from our father? I'm sure you know by now that I found it in your jewelry box. I know you've noticed that it's missing. How did you get it?"

I watched her body language. Yana dropped her head.

"Josiah gave it to me."

"What do you mean he gave it to you? He wouldn't give you that chain."

"I don't think he intended for me to keep it forever. Josiah left an envelope at my front door. Me and Hanz came home one day, the same day Josiah was supposed to leave for California, and there was an envelope with my name on it on the front porch. Inside, there was a letter from Josiah and the chain."

"What letter? What did it say? Where is it?"

"I don't have it anymore. I tore it up and flushed it down the toilet. I didn't want Hanz to find it and read it."

How convenient!

"What did the letter say, Yana?"

"What didn't it say? He talked about us and how we were so in love, at one point, and how he wanted to marry me. He wanted us to be together. Like I told you, he only made the stop in Mississippi because he saw on social media that I'd married someone else. I guess he came to try to change my mind about us. And to try and get back what we had. But it was gone. We were over."

"The two of you really had some big romance behind my back?"

"It wasn't behind your back. We were adults. We didn't know what it was and we wanted to keep things light and fun. Sure, we fell in love along the way. Josiah was there for me at times when I needed someone the most. And yes, I loved him. But love ends. Love changes. Love goes away. At least being in love with someone does. I moved on. I met someone else. He was having a hard time accepting that," Yana shook her head. "Because he was ready, he wanted me to drop everything and go running back to him. He was just too late."

Yana helped pay for the funeral.

I didn't ask her to. She wanted to, so, I know that she loved him. It seems to me that she felt just as strongly for Josiah, as he'd felt about her.

"Now, he's at peace," Yana concluded. She kissed my cheek although she was wearing bright red lipstick. "I have a flight to catch and a husband to get back to. I'll call to check on you later."

I hugged her.

My friend.

My sister.

My current bottle of confusion and mystery.

"Love you."

"I love you, too."

I watched Yana walk away from the burial site.

Emory approached me and placed his hand on the small of my back.

"Take me home, Emory. Take me home."

Jacob and the family headed to one of our aunt's houses to eat and fellowship.

Emory and I headed to the hotel to pack our bags.

"Did you tell Jacob we were leaving?"

"Yes."

"Are you okay?"

"No." I sat down on the edge of the bed. "I just can't believe that Josiah is dead. For years, I expected to get that phone call, you know? Because of the life he lived. We just never knew where he was or what he was doing from one day to the next. And then, I saw him. He seemed so much better. He seemed just fine."

"But maybe he wasn't. Maybe he wanted to be better and look better for you."

"Yes. That could be true too. He and Yana were in love."

"Really?"

"Yes. And apparently, he still wanted to be with her. He didn't like the fact that she'd gotten married. She could've been his last string of hope and once that was taken away…maybe he just gave up."

"I know this is a horrible way to look at this, but at least you don't have to worry about him anymore. You used to be so worried when you didn't hear from him or know where he was for months at a time. Now, he's resting."

"Now, he's at peace," I mimicked Yana's words. After taking a deep breath, I stood up and grabbed my bag. "The faster we get out of this city, the better. I never want to come back here again. Ever."

"Your wish is my command," Emory held open the room door.

And then there were two.

Now, it's just me and Jacob.

Our parents are gone, our brother is gone, and I don't want anything to do with my extended family.

It's time that I create a family of my own….

With Emory.

"Do you mind if we get a refund on our flights, and drive? We can stop along the way a few times. What do you say about that?"

Emory opened the door to the rental car for me. "Now, baby, you know I'm always down to ride. Let's fuck this highway up," he smiled.

I touched his hand just as he started to close the door.

"Emory, I love you," I said for the first time in a long time.

"Nova…I love you, too."

~***~

"I was starting to think you were quitting on me."

"Actually…I am," I said to Ox. "I figure you could use these past two weeks that I haven't been here as my two-week's notice," I started to pack my things in the bag I'd brought in from the car.

"Wait a minute, wait a minute, Nova. You don't have to quit. Come on, now."

"I do. I really do. It's time for me to go."

I didn't have a plan, or a new job, but I was okay with that. Emory was okay with me quitting and I could take time to figure out what I want to do next.

"Look, Shanice will never bother you again. You never have to worry about her again. She's gone. I'm going to be fine. Everything is going to be fine."

"I know it will be," I smiled at him. "I'm going to miss how things were with us, before all of this. Even before the…you know. I've enjoyed our friendship these past few years. And I made you a lot of money, boss," I grinned. "Take care of yourself, Ox. I'll see you around."

I kissed him on the cheek, and with him chasing behind me, I walked on until I was outside of the building.

I looked back at it.

It's been a nice run.

Now, it's time for something new.

Who knows, I may even give marriage another thought. Emory would want nothing more. As for what I want...I think I just want something different.

Stopping at my favorite coffee place, I closed my eyes as I took the first sip.

"Damn, that must be some good ass coffee," I turned around at the sound of his voice.

Kojo.

"Hey," I giggled, embarrassed. "How have you been?"

"I'm good. You?"

"I'm getting there."

"Yeah, Emory told me about your brother. I'm sorry to hear that."

"Thanks." There was an awkward pause. "So, Emory said you were opening your own auto shop."

"That's the plan."

"That's good."

"Yeah."

We both just stood there, unsure of what to say next.

"Well...it was nice to see you," I said finally.

"Yeah. It was."

I started to walk away.

"Nova, I can't stop thinking about you since that day," I heard Kojo say behind me, but I didn't turn around. I just kept walking.

Once inside my car, I drove away without so much as glancing back at the coffee shop.

Kojo is sexy and all, but there's nothing there.

It was just sex. Unfair sex, to be exact, because he got something out of it and I got nothing.

Goodbye, Kojo.

~***~

"I heard about your brother," Cece stood next to my car. She looked nervous and uncomfortable.

I haven't spoken to her since the day she hung up on me to avoid telling me whatever the truth is about Christina.

"I'm sorry."

"Yeah. But not sorry enough to call."

"I didn't think you wanted to talk to me."

"Why? Because you were hiding something from me about Emory's *ex* side chick?"

"Yes," Cece answered honestly.

We lived only three houses down, but I haven't seen Cece up close in what seems like forever.

She looks different. She looks stressed.

"I wanted to call you. I really did."

"Look, unless you're going to tell me whatever it is that you were hiding about Christina…"

"We had a threesome with her," Cece interrupted me.

Why am I not surprised?

"Quite a few times. We have to pay her though. But Rick really liked her so…a one-time thing became…" Cece exhaled. "One evening, she saw Emory as she was leaving our house. The next time she came over, she asked about him. Rick and I joked about the two of you. We told her that the both of you were stuck up and that we'd wanted to have some fun with you two a long time ago, but you always turned us down."

138

"So, Emory was telling the truth? Christina did know that Emory was in a relationship from the very beginning?"

"Yes," Cece admitted. "She didn't know what you looked like or anything, but she knew that Emory had a woman. Anyway, what was just light trash talking turned into some kind of dare and bet. Christina made a comment that everyone cheats. Rick bet her that she couldn't get Emory to cheat on you with her. She told him she could. Rick put a price on it. Honestly, neither of us thought Emory would cheat on you with Christina, but Rick said if he did, it would just show that the two of you aren't as perfect as you two wanted to be."

They did what?

They paid Christina to pursue Emory?

Oh, I'm about to whoop Cece's old ass!

I prepared to attack, placing my keys and my purse on the hood of my car.

"It didn't take long. Emory slept with her. And Christina proved it with pictures and text messages the next time we had her over. Rick paid her, and we thought that was it. A one-time thing. At least I did. Well, apparently, Rick enjoyed her getting in between the two of you a little too much. Rick likes what he likes, and always hated that you wouldn't give in. He hated that he would never get to touch you. And it made me slightly jealous. But you aren't the one I should've been worried about. Not only did Rick have Christina reporting back to him every time she slept with Emory, but he also started sleeping with her even when I didn't want to. I would always be there, but he would have a fit if I told him no. And now…"

I inched towards her. As soon as she finished her next sentence, I planned on punching her in the mouth.

"Now, she's pregnant, and she doesn't know if it's my man's…or yours."

"Hold up…what?"

"Christina is pregnant. Trust me, I made sure. And from the number of weeks pregnant that she is, compared to the text messages of the times she slept with Emory, and then came to sleep with us…sometimes it was on the same day. So, there's no way to know whose baby she's carrying, and I'm sick. I'm literally sick!"

I placed my hand over my heart.

I was stuck.

Maybe even in shock.

Christina is pregnant?

And it could be Emory's?

"I told you that night when you were drunk about Christina, because I was trying to make it right. In my own weird way, I was trying to confess. But from her ultrasound, the damage was already done. She's pregnant by Rick or Emory. If she's pregnant by Rick…my marriage is…"

Before she finished her sentence, I punched Cece in the mouth.

"If I were you, I would get the fuck away from me!" I threw another punch, but Cece caught my fist.

"I'll give you that first punch. I deserved that," she squeezed my hand. "But unless you want to get your ass whooped out here in your own front yard, keep your goddamn hands to yourself! I'm old school. And I whoop ass back in the day style too. Now, I messed up. Allowing that shit to go that far was wrong. That's why I'm here. That's why I'm telling you," Cece pushed my hand away from her. "Emory doesn't know. She didn't find out until after my birthday party. She doesn't plan on telling him until she has the baby and finds out for sure. I just thought you should know." Cece backed away from me. "I am sorry. It's up to you whether you tell Emory or not. One of us will have to share the man we love with this woman for the rest of our lives. And I hate to say this but…I hope it isn't me." Cece walked away, leaving me there with information I didn't know what to do with.

See, this is exactly why it's a waste of time to forgive!

Emory and I are just getting back in a good place, and now, one of the women he cheated on me with is pregnant!

And she doesn't know if the baby is Emory's or Rick's.

This can't be my life!

And to find out it's all Cece and Rick's fault!

What in the hell is wrong with them?

I was so angry that I started to scream.

I'm going to make Rick and Cece pay for purposely putting another bitch in my relationship!

And that's a fact!

I pulled out my phone to call Emory.

Suddenly, I paused.

If Christina is pregnant by Emory, she wins.

He wants a baby so bad that there's no way in hell he won't try to do everything he can to be a family with her. He'll leave me, when I should've left his cheating ass!

Christina will have the man.

She will have the baby…

Wait a minute.

What's today?

I checked my calendar.

"I know damn well…"

I didn't finish my sentence.

I rushed to the drug store. I grabbed four pregnancy tests. My period is two days late. And I'm never late. My period is always on time. I took the morning after pill almost four days after having sex with Emory and Kojo.

Did it work?

Or not?

Back home, I grabbed a small cup and I practically ran to the bathroom to pee.

I've never been so nervous in my life.

Thoughts about Christina popped in and out of my head. I wonder how far along she is. I wonder…

I fought to stay focus. I dipped all four pregnant tests inside the cup of urine, and I talked to myself in the mirror while I waited.

"This is my karma. It has to be. For all the fucked-up shit I've done to people. But they fucked with me first. I never went looking for trouble. Trouble always came looking for me."

I started to sweat, knowing that whether the tests are positive or negative, either result will be life changing.

If I am pregnant…well…

And if I'm not, there's no way in hell that I'll wait around to see if Christina's baby is Emory's.

Knowing who he is, and how he feels about being a father, I wouldn't set myself up to be broken by him again.

Despite how we seem to be mending our relationship, I'll just go and never look back.

But if I am pregnant…

I gasped at the sight of a plus sign on all four pregnancy tests.

I'm pregnant!

But by who?

Damn!

I don't know who the father of my child is either!

I am Christina.

Christina is me.

Were both having a baby.

And we both have the same question…

Whose baby will it be?

******

CHAPTER SIX

I'm going straight to hell for this.

I placed the pan of macaroni on the table.

Today, I'm telling Emory that I'm having his baby.

And I'll never tell him or anyone else otherwise.

I made up my mind that I wouldn't try to figure out who the father of my child is.

My child is Emory's.

Not Kojo's.

The end.

If Kojo ever sees me pregnant, I'll simply say I got pregnant after or before he and I fooled around. Emory will never know the truth about the baby and neither will I.

And to be honest, I don't really care who the father of my baby is. After thinking long and hard, I concluded that Christina isn't taking Emory away from me.

So, I have to do what I have to do.

I don't plan on telling Emory about Christina being pregnant. The only way he'll find out is if she contacts him and tells him herself while she's pregnant, or if she comes asking him to take a blood test once the baby is born.

Now, that I'm pregnant, I want my child to have the family I never had. The parents I never had. And no one is going to take that away from my baby!

No one!

In all honesty, if Christina wasn't pregnant, I would've gone to the abortion clinic the same day I found out.

Being that I don't know who the father is, I would've taken care of it, healed, continued trying to figure out my relationship with Emory, and then Emory and I would've gotten pregnant when we were ready.

But because Christina is possibly pregnant by Emory, I don't have time for that.

Now, I want Emory more than ever.

And I'll do what I have to do to keep him.

"Damn, it smells good in here. What did I do to deserve this?" Emory smiled at the spread on the table.

"I just felt like cooking today."

Emory chuckled. "You miss going to work, don't you?"

"A little," I admitted.

Emory washed his hands.

"I've been dying to get home to you all day."

"Really?"

"Really," he kissed my lips.

"Well…"

I sat two plates in front of him. I'd written in black marker on the back of them.

"Flip the plates over," I smiled.

"What?"

"Flip them over," I pointed for him to flip the one on his left over first.

"You're never going to believe this," Emory read aloud. Then, he flipped over the other plate. "We're pregnant! Wait. We're pregnant? Like me and you?" Emory jumped to his feet. "We're pregnant?" He questioned again.

All I could do was nod my head and smile.

"Hell yeah!" Emory punched the air. "Hell yeah!"

He was so happy he started to jump up and down. "For real? Are you serious right now? Are we really pregnant?"

"Yes. We're pregnant."

Emory picked me up and turned me around in circles. "Oh wait, I'm sorry. You're pregnant. Are you okay?"

"Yes. I'm okay."

Emory touched my stomach. "We're really having a baby?"

I placed my hand on top of his. "We're really having a baby."

Emory's kiss caught me off guard. "I love you. I love you so much!"

"I love you too."

"And I love you," Emory spoke to my flat stomach. "I'm going to be the best daddy in the world!"

I believe him.

"Baby, please, can I go call some people? I know you cooked but…"

"Go on, Emory!"

He kissed my forehead, touched my stomach again before zooming down the hallway.

And there it is.

Emory and I are having a baby.

And I'll never tell a soul anything different.

~***~

I listened for the fire trucks in the distance as I played with Josiah's chain in my hand.

I smiled at the few fun memories we had together as kids.

Once, our mother got very sick. She stayed in bed for days, away from us, and we had the time of our lives. We ate all the food we wanted and stayed up late to watch TV. One night, we decided to sleep outside in the backyard.

All three of us; Jacob, Josiah and myself, stared up at the stars, while lying on big fluffy blankets. Who knows where our father was, but just for that night, we didn't have a care in the world.

Josiah had the idea for us to tell made-up scary stories. Yet, his story ended up being the least scary of them all. His was more adventurous and heroic. I truly believe it's how he tried to see himself to help him get through the reality of each day. The smile he had on his face as he held the flashlight and told his story was priceless. I don't think I ever saw him smile like that again.

Shaking away my thoughts, I stepped onto the front porch.

I smiled at the smell of smoke.

I set Cece and Rick's backyard on fire.

I know, I know, my pregnant ass should be doing literally anything else, but I have a few more things up my sleeve to do to them, before I get too far along.

They deserve everything they have coming to them.

They had no right to try and ruin my relationship. And now, another woman could be carrying Emory's baby, all because they paid her to sleep with my man!

I don't pray much.

But I've been praying extra hard that the baby is Rick's. Hopefully that'll teach them that marriage is supposed to be between two people. Not fifty.

Cece is going to have a fit when she sees that her precious garden is destroyed. I'm sure she'll suspect that I had something to do with it, but where's the proof?

She's been begging Rick's cheap ass for who knows how long to put cameras around their house. All he would say is that the neighborhood is safe and that no one else had them, so they didn't need cameras either.

So, I walked from my backyard, through the two backyards in between ours, to get to Cece and Rick's backyard to set the fire.

I poured gasoline on everything and set that shit ablaze! And I made sure to do it on a school day, and when I knew Rick would be at work, and Cece would be at one of her many classes that she takes to waste her husband's money.

I'm not sure which neighbor saw the flames and called the fire department, but not caring, I went to grab my keys, and decided to go for a drive.

I've been calling to tell Yana my pregnancy news for almost a week, but of course, she isn't answering her phone.

Emory and I had our first doctor's appointment, just to confirm the pregnancy. What will become *my* baby, is just a little bubble on the screen. Emory is on cloud nine. He's so happy that some days, I feel guilty. But I can live with the guilt. I have to because after seeing that it's actually a little something there, attached, waiting to grow inside me, there's no way in hell I'm getting rid of it.

What if I never get pregnant again?

And I don't know Kojo. I don't know anything about him, other than what Emory has told me. But I do know Emory. And I know that he's going to be the best father my child could ever ask for.

So, it's all pretty simple to me.

Emory and I are having a baby.

I passed by my old job.

I miss it. Oh, how I miss it.

Speaking of…

Ox still calls me at least twice a day, since I quit.

I would be lying if I said I didn't miss his presence. He set a goal to make me laugh or smile every chance that he could. Some days, I really need a good laugh.

Screw it! I decided to text Ox.

"Take a lunch. Meet me at Sheema's Café."

Twenty minutes later, Ox walked through the door, grinning from ear to ear.

"I miss you." He sat across from me.

"Honestly, I miss you, too." I looked around. "Your crazy wife didn't follow you here, did she?"

I'd heard what she said that day.

She said Ox is in love with me.

"She's gone. I told you she was leaving. She won't ever bother you again."

"Whatever you say," I sipped my water. "In a way, her pulling that gun out on me, helped me get some things in my life together."

"You and ole' boy?" Ox asked.

"I'm pregnant."

Ox froze.

"Don't worry. It's not yours. And yes. I'm pregnant by ole' boy as you call him." I smiled. "He's done some things. I've done some things. And now, we've done something together. I'm about to be someone's mother. I can't believe it. It just opens my eyes about a lot of things. You know?"

"Not really. I've always wanted kids. Shanice couldn't have kids. She didn't tell me that she had a hysterectomy until after we were married. I should've known right then that she couldn't be trusted. I've always wanted kids though. Doesn't look like it's in the cards for me."

"It is. You'll make a damn good dad. Had I never gotten involved with Emory...I would've been all over you, a long time ago. Well....never mind. Your wife is crazy as hell. Oh no!"

Ox chuckled. "You know, if he doesn't treat you right..."

I interrupted him with a smile. "I know, Ox. I already know. And I know where to find you."

~***~

"Aw, don't tell me you're still salty about the little incident in your office," Shanice smirked.

Damn! I knew I shouldn't have met up with Ox last week! Ox thought Shanice was gone, but nope! Her crazy ass is still around, watching, and lurking close by.

"Little incident? You pointed a gun at me! You were going to shoot me!"

I was in the mall, and Shanice was following me around the shoe store.

"Girl, I wasn't going to shoot you."

"Shit! You could've fooled me! And you shot your husband."

"Yeah. But I didn't mean to. He startled me," she shrugged.

I walked away from her.

"He loves you, you know that, right?"

"I don't know why. I don't love him. Ox and I are just friends. I'm in a relationship. I don't want him."

"That doesn't change the fact that he wants you. The question is why? What is it about you that he finds so intriguing? Other than that cute ass of yours, there's nothing particularly special about you. Yet, he seems to want you more than his next breath. Why?"

"That's something that you'll have to ask your husband."

"Ex-husband, unfortunately. In order to smooth things over with the police to save me from getting in trouble, Ox made me agree to sign the divorce papers. I just signed them last week. He's a free man."

"Good for him. And good for you. Now, maybe you can move on and find someone who actually wants to be with you."

"Hmmm, maybe. Any suggestions?"

"Never in a million..." I paused. "Wait. How do you feel about middle aged, rich men?"

"Just my type."

Cece and Rick put Christina in my relationship.

What in the hell would they do if I put a bitch like Shanice in theirs?

"Did I mention that he's married?"

"And your point is?"

I shook my head.

Shanice and I have quite a few physical similarities, so there's no doubt in my mind that Rick wouldn't want her as bad as he obviously wants to have a go with me.

I want to get them back for what they did to me but sending the woman their way who was clearly going to shoot me over a man who had been trying to divorce her for years…am I ready for that type of karma?

"Never mind. For now."

Shanice eyed me from top to bottom. "You're glowing."

"Because I'm happy."

"Why are you so happy?"

"I just am."

"Is it A or B that has you all lit up like a Christmas tree?"

"A or B?"

Shanice smiled. "A…your man. Emory. That's his name, right? Or B…that stallion of a man who fucked your brains out that day at the auto shop?"

"Excuse me?"

"Girl, play dumb with your mama. Not me," Shanice rolled her eyes. "I followed you there. I was just curious to see where you would go after I dangled my pretty gun in your face. It looked as though the building was closed, but you went inside. I'm a little nosey, so they say, so I got out of my car. Instead of using the door that you clearly left unlocked, I walked around to the open area. You know, the garage part where the three cars being worked on were pulled in. And boy, did I get a show! I never would've been able to see it from the street, but from there, I got a glimpse of some real, hot, steamy action! I like when they're strong like that! Yes! Hold me, and fuck me up against the wall, daddy," Shanice shivered.

Oh no!

Of all people, Shanice saw me having sex with Kojo!

"I made my way back to my car just as a work truck pulled up. So, again I asked, which one of your little options is causing this glow?" She questioned. "It looks good on you by the way."

I had to say something. She knows the one thing I never wanted anyone to find out.

"Look, Emory and I went through something. He cheated on me with two women. I cheated on him. Now, we're even. And we're moving forward. He's the one making me happy. There's no other option. Just him."

"Good. I wish Ox would've been as forgiving with me for sleeping with his cousin as your man is with you for sleeping with his employee."

I cringed, knowing I had to come back with something witty. "Oh, he cheated and got an STD. Believe me, I'm the one doing the majority of the forgiving."

"Ouch!" Shanice shook her hand as though it was on fire. "And so, the stallion man, he's fair game then?"

"Yep. He's free game. Knock yourself out. But just as a warning…he has one of those multiply by three, carry the one, times the seven, type of dicks! I'm telling you…his dick will give you acid reflux. But please, shoot your shot! And he's single, too."

"Humph. I just might do that," Shanice said, placing on sunglasses inside the mall, and then walking away.

As soon as she was out of sight, I let out a deep breath. Damn! Damn! Damn!

Why did she have to be the one to see me having sex with Kojo? Why, God? Why?

Shanice has no reason to tell Emory what she saw, but who's to say that she won't tell him just for the hell of it?

She's one of those misery loves company type of people. I can tell. And I can tell that she'll be sticking around a lot longer than Ox thought she would be.

And I don't like it.

I don't like it one bit.

I sat down to try on the shoes that were in my hand.

Emory pointed out that I only have two pair of flat, comfortable shoes. So, I decided to come and get a few pairs, since I'll need them during pregnancy.

I stood up to look at myself in the mirror. I smiled at the sight of the shoes on my feet. But my smiled turned into a frown seeing her in the mirror standing in front of the row of shoes behind me.

Christina.

Immediately, I glanced down at her stomach.

If she is pregnant, she isn't really showing. I mean there's a tiny pudge there, but nothing extravagant.

Cece never mentioned how far along Christina is supposed to be, but she had to be at the least two or three months.

Hmm…I'm about to find out.

I walked up to her. When Christina realized who I was, she jumped and stepped back from me.

"Please, you got what you wanted. Please, leave me alone."

"Girl, what in the hell are you talking about?" I asked her confused.

Christina stared at me. "I lost the baby, okay? So, just let me be."

"First of all, I don't know what the hell you're talking about."

"Yeah. I bet. I know it was you who attacked me. I talked to Cece and she said…"

"What? I didn't attack you. I don't have time to be out here trying to attack and fight nobody these days. I'm pregnant and wouldn't want to hurt my baby."

"You're pregnant?"

"Yes. I'm pregnant. And I sure as hell didn't attack you!"

Christina looked confused. "Cece told me that she told you that the baby I *was* carrying might've been Emory's. A few days after she told me that, I was attacked one night as soon as I got out of my car at home."

"She told me. And for your sake, I was hoping that it was her husband's baby. You don't want these problems. Trust me. But I didn't attack you. You better check with your girl, Cece. She has a hell of a lot more to lose than I do."

"She was sure it was you. She even said she thinks you set her backyard on fire."

"Who me?" I chuckled. I refused to deny it.

Fuck them people!

"Like I said, I didn't attack you. Emory will have a fit if something happens to our baby. I wouldn't dare put it in harm's way. If you know what's good for you, you would leave them folks alone. Those people are crazy. Haven't you figured it out yet? After they paid you to sleep with my man?" I rolled my eyes. "Oh, and only if the baby wasn't Emory's…sorry for your loss. If it was, then God sure does answer prayers."

I turned my back to Christina.

As I paid for my shoes, different thoughts flooded my head.

Christina isn't pregnant anymore.

That changes everything!

I don't know who the father of my baby is.

And Shanice knows I had sex with Kojo.

Now that Christina is definitely not having Emory's baby, I don't have to have this baby. I don't have to be unsure. I could just get rid of it, pretend I lost it, and get pregnant again.

What do I really want to do?

I walked out of the store with a head and heart full of questions that I don't really have the answers to.

Decisions. Decisions. Decisions.

~***~

"If something ever happens to me. Ask Yana."

Who left this on my porch?

I came home to see an envelope with my name on the front of it.

I opened it, and on a sheet of paper, that's what it said.

"If something ever happens to me. Ask Yana."

Who wrote this?

Josiah?

Josiah is dead.

Who left this here?

Is this some kind of sick joke?

Immediately, I called Yana.

No answer as always.

I practically ran to our bedroom with the note in my hand. I had letters from Josiah, somewhere. While he was in and out of jail over the years, he would write me letters. And I kept them all.

"I know I saved them," I spoke aloud to myself. I wanted to compare the handwriting. "Where are they?"

I tore my closet apart looking for the letters, but they weren't there.

"Wait a minute…"

I rushed back to the living room.

I glanced over the fireplace.

Josiah sent me a card last year for my birthday.

I stared at the birthday card, and then at the sheet of paper.

Yep.

Same handwriting.

Josiah wrote this.

When?

And what did he mean by ask Yana if something happens to him?

Something did happen to him.

He died.

So, who put this note, in his handwriting, on my front porch?

Confused, I called Yana over and over again like a crazy person, before finally giving up.

I called Jacob to tell him about the note.

"Babe, guess who came to the shop today?" Emory said as he walked into the house from work.

I'd been sitting in the same spot for hours, holding the note; lost, confused, and trying to figure out what it means.

"Ox's wife came by the shop. Didn't you say she shot him?"

"Shanice?"

"Yes. That's her name. Did he press charges on her? Or did he let her off the hook? If he did, he must really love her. Although, she's convinced that he's in love with you."

"She said that to you?"

Emory nodded. "Yeah. But she didn't say nothing I didn't already know. I could tell by the way he looked at you that the fool had a thing for you. But you're mine."

Emory kissed me. "What's wrong?"

I reached him the note.

I have too much on my mind to think about Shanice's messy ass right now.

"What is this? What does it mean?"

"I don't know. I don't know what it means. But it's Josiah's handwriting. Someone left that note in an envelope addressed to me on the porch today."

Emory read the piece of paper again. "Ask Yana….ask her what?"

"I don't know."

"So, this means he knew something was going to happen to him? Or he knew he was going to die? Or maybe he knew he was going to kill himself and Yana knows why. Did you call her?"

"Probably a hundred times. She's not answering. She never answers the phone for me anymore."

"Yeah. I noticed that the two of you don't talk as much as you used to. I'm willing to bet it has something to do with whatever this is," Emory reached me the note.

I exhaled.

"Yeah. I was just thinking the same exact thing."

~***~

"He came back," Emory said as I stared at Kojo. "The building he was thinking about leasing ended up getting sold to someone else. I told him to come back and help me out until I can find someone to fill his shoes. I told him sixty days, tops. But I'm hoping he ends up wanting to stay a little longer."

I could tell that Kojo was trying not to make eye contact with me.

"Your first interview should be here any minute."

Emory asked me to interview three candidates for the office assistant position.

Emory left me alone in his office and as soon as he was out of sight, Kojo finally looked in my direction. I closed the office door.

I was hoping to never see him again. Or at least not any time soon. And especially not here.

Luckily, once an assistant is hired, Emory won't ask me to stop by as often.

I'm choosing the oldest and the most unattractive of the candidates for the assistant position.

Point. Blank. Period!

I'm the only cute piece of ass sashaying around here on a regular basis.

There was a knock on the door, and I waited to see who would walk through it.

"Hello, I'm Nova," I stood up to greet her.

Nope. Hell no. Hell to the double no!

"I'm Genesis," she smiled.

I pretended to be interested in what she was saying the whole interview, knowing that she was definitely not getting the job. She was a cute as an eight-week old puppy; very charming and she had a nice smile.

I wouldn't dare trust Emory around her.

Hell, I'm straight and a few times, I caught myself wanting to lick the side of her face. She is just that adorable.

Nevertheless, I have enough going on and I don't have the time to worry about Emory's tempted flesh.

After receiving the note, that was clearly written by Josiah before he died, I've been driving myself crazy trying to get in touch with Yana and trying to figure out who left the note on my porch. I planned to go back to Houston for a few days. Jacob was handling selling Josiah's condo, but I wanted to go by there to look through his things, just to see if I could get an idea of who he was hanging around weeks before his death.

I've gone through every number in Josiah's cell phone.

Most of them were of his friends.

He had some old therapy text messages reminders.

A few old text messages and voicemails from women that he must've fooled around with here and there.

Nothing that stood out.

I was hoping to find something, anything in the condo.

There has to be something I'm missing.

I finished the interview with Genesis.

The second woman I interviewed was average looking. She has been married to her high school sweetheart for the past fifteen years. And here resumé was really good. She just might be the one for the job.

I exhaled as I waited on my last interview to come in.

"I'm here," she smiled as soon as she opened the office door.

"Shanice? What in the hell are you doing here?"

She chuckled. "I'm here for my interview."

"What? No. I'm waiting on a Regency Scott."

"Yep. That's my stripper name. It's cute, ain't it?" Shanice laughed as she took a seat. "Relax. I don't really want the job. Your little man mentioned that he was hiring when I came by to get my transmission serviced. He told me you would be doing the interviews. I thought it would be nice to drop by, again. I wrote the hell out of that resumé, didn't I?"

This lady is the textbook definition of a lunatic!

She's like that one little annoying gnat that just won't go away!

"What do you want, Shanice?"

"I see Mr. Stallion is out there. They're out there laughing it up. Your man doesn't know that you slept with him, does he?"

"He doesn't need to know the who. He's knows the what and the why I cheated. That's all he needs to know."

Shanice glared at me. "A little birdie told me that you're pregnant."

"And what little birdie would that be? Ox?"

"You've spoken to Ox? When?"

"I'm surprised you don't know. I assumed you were following me or somewhere watching us eat lunch the whole time."

"I must've been busy. How is he?"

"Who? Ox? Fine, I suppose. I told him I was pregnant. If he didn't tell you, who did?"

"Christina."

"Christina? How do you know Christina?"

"I don't know her. When I passed back by the shoe store that day in the mall, I saw you talking to her. I continued on the candle store next door. A few minutes later, she came into the store. She looked as though she'd been crying. I asked her if my "friend" was still in the shoe store. I told her your name. She said no. And then, she said to tell my friend she hopes she loses her baby too."

I rolled my eyes.

"What do you want, Shanice?"

"For now…an introduction. You said I need to get over Ox. Best way to do that is to get on top of someone new. I want to give Daddy Big Dick a spin! Unless you're giving out the name of that married rich guy you mentioned."

"You're not going to go away, are you?"

"I'm just here to take your advice."

"Has anyone ever told you…"

"If I were you…I wouldn't call me crazy," Shanice interrupted me.

I stood up from the chair behind the desk. Quickly, Shanice glanced at my stomach before standing to her feet.

"If you hadn't tried to shoot me, maybe we could've been friends," I mumbled.

"I didn't try to do anything. If I really wanted to shoot you, I would have. I wouldn't have hesitated. My jealousy got the best of me. It does that sometimes."

"Now, that is something I can relate to."

I'm not sure about introducing Shanice to Kojo.

She clearly has a problem with obsession, but remembering that I could be carrying his baby, and the comment he made to me, about not being able to get me off his mind, a woman like Shanice would be perfect to keep him occupied.

I've still been wrestling with the idea of terminating the pregnancy. It really is the better decision for everyone involved. There's no doubt about it. Emory will be completely heartbroken after I lie and tell him I had a miscarriage. The upside to me taking this baby from him is that finally, in my mind, we'll officially be even.

I approached Emory who was laughing with Kojo.

Briefly I glanced at Kojo, before smiling at Emory.

"Hey, baby. What's wrong?" He asked, recognizing Shanice. "You again. Is something wrong with your car?"

"No. Actually, I came by to see your girl."

Emory looked at me confused, remembering the things I'd said to him about her.

"Unfortunately, she can't seem to stay away from me," I grunted. "Shanice, this is Emory's friend, Kojo."

"Oooh, hey, Kojo. I'm your future wife," Shanice teased. And then she started to purr like a cat.

Both Emory and Kojo chuckled. I looked at her like the crazy person that she is.

"What's up? Nice to meet you," Kojo shook her hand.

"Uh, Emory, I think you should hire the woman I interviewed second. I'll leave all the information on your desk."

"Y'all look like y'all could be sisters," Emory pointed out. "I mean, y'all don't look alike in the face, but…"

"I get it. Anyway, I'm going to get out of here. I'll see you when you get home," I kissed him.

Both Kojo and Shanice looked on.

"Bye, daddy's little man," Emory rubbed my stomach. "I hope it's a boy."

I could tell by the look on Kojo's face that Emory's comments caught him off guard. Emory hadn't told him that I was pregnant.

Shanice followed me back to the office to get my things, and then out the door.

"I'll pass on the stallion. I can see it all over his face. He's already in love with you too," Shanice frowned. "Damn! What is it about you?" Shanice walked ahead of me. "Set that married guy situation up. Shoot, I feel like destroying a marriage this week anyway," she chuckled. "Should we exchange numbers at this point?"

I walked towards my car. "Nope. I'm sure when you want me…you'll find me," I spat at my new unwanted best-friend.

~***~

I opened another box.

I've been going through Josiah's things all day.

I'm not sure what I'm looking for, I just want to make sure that nothing was overlooked.

My eyes lit up as Yana's name and face appeared on the front of my cell phone.

"Hello? Hello?"

"Hi, friend."

"Where in the hell have you been?"

"Busy," she complained.

"Well, I've been calling you. There's so much that we need to talk about."

"Well, talk."

"For starters, I'm pregnant," I finally told her my big news.

"Oh, my God! Seriously? Congratulations. Wait...is it..."

"Yes. It's Emory's." I never got around to telling Yana that I had sex with Kojo. And there's no point in telling her now.

"Good. I'm so happy for you! I'm glad everything is working out for you. I really am."

"Yeah. I just thought I would always go through something like this with my best friend by my side."

Yana didn't respond.

"In other news, I received a note from Josiah."

"What?"

"Someone left a note on my porch. The envelope had my name on it. The note is in Josiah's handwriting. It said: *If anything ever happens to me, ask Yana.* What does that mean?"

"I don't know."

"What do you mean, you don't know?"

"I mean...I don't know. I don't know why he would have said that."

"What would he want me to ask you?"

"Maybe about our relationship that we hid from you, but you know all about that now."

"But he said if something happens to him…that means he knew there was a possibility that something might happen. Obviously, he was making it clear that you would know the *why*."

"Like I said, our relationship was deep. We were in love for a while. Josiah wanted us to work a lot more than I did. I moved on. He didn't. I got married. He got mad. That's as much as I know. That's it."

"Why didn't the two of you come to me about whatever was going on between y'all? Obviously, he was hurting. He was sad. He was miserable. I could've done something. I could've helped him."

"You couldn't help Josiah."

"What does that mean?"

"Josiah had issues. Issues that no one could fix or change. He struggled with decisions that he'd made. I tried to help Josiah. I tried to save Josiah. He didn't want to be saved."

"What aren't you telling me, Yana?"

"I'm telling you all you need to know. He was your brother, but I knew him better than you. In a different way than you. He's at peace now. Maybe he left the note hoping I would tell you some of the things I know about him, but I won't. His past and his pain died with him."

Neither of us said a word for at least a minute.

"I miss you," Yana said, finally.

I forced myself to say it back to her. "I miss you, too."

The secrecy from her rubs me the wrong way.

I don't like it.

We've always told each other everything.

When did that change?

"I don't know when I'll be back. Hopefully soon. Until then, send me plenty of pictures of your stomach as it grows. I love you, with all my heart, all the way from Rome."

"Rome? I thought you were in Brazil."

"To live…yes. But I'm in Rome for a few days. I needed a little vacation."

Yana said another sentence or two, and then, she was gone.

Despite what Yana said, I checked a few more boxes, and once I started to feel lightheaded, I concluded that it was time for me to go. Whatever the truth is between Yana and Josiah, she's only going to tell me what she wants me to know. And no matter what she tells me, it won't bring Josiah back anyway.

I left the condo in a hurry to get some food in my belly. For a while, I didn't feel pregnant at all. I didn't have any symptoms. But here lately, my body feels like it belongs to someone else.

The clock is ticking, and I still don't know if I should go through with having the baby or not.

As I took a bite out of my sandwich, I rolled my eyes as I deleted the fourth friend request from Shanice off my social media account.

With her on the prowl, and knowing what she knows, it's only a matter of time before the truth comes out.

And I need to be one step ahead.

I finished my food, and then I drove by the house I was raised in. I stared at it.

So much went on inside that house.

So many things I'll never speak of.

My brothers and I never had a chance.

Not really. Not coming from this.

Somehow, we tried. Not really knowing what love was, we tried to love. We tried to live. We tried to be better than the monsters who created us.

We tried.

I tried.

The house is abandoned.

It looks as though no one has lived in it in years. Probably since my father died. After living there for about thirty years, I have no idea why my parents weren't buying the house in the first place.

I got out of my car and slowly walked towards it.

I felt so many different emotions.

All I could do was thank God that they're dead.

I can count on one hand the number of times I spoke to or saw my parents once I moved out of Texas.

There wasn't anything to say.

Appearance wise, I'm a younger version of my mother. There's no doubt that her beauty is what drew my father to her. And from what I could gather as a child from my aunts, she used to be pretty normal. It wasn't until her twenties that things about her started to change. They called her fun and loving. They said that she was always the life of the party and always made everyone smile.

I wish I'd gotten to know and experience that version of her. I can't remember her ever being fun or loving. I don't think she ever made me smile.

Not once.

My mother never called me beautiful or told me how special I was. She never really taught me much either.

She only taught me how to cook because she said I would need to know how in order to get and keep a good man; but it was never fun cooking with her. She would stand over me, yell and hit me if I didn't do something right.

She also always told me not to trust people who tell you they love you. She said they're the ones who will hurt you the most.

Well, she was right about that.

In the backyard, the old swing set was still there.

I remember the Christmas our father brought it home. And then, I remember my mother refusing to let us play on it for months.

Once we were finally allowed to play on it, we played on it for hours that day. There were three swings, one for each of us. And it came with a slide. I spent hours out there, swinging back and forth, wishing that I was someone else. Wishing that someone would come and save us.

But no one ever came.

I took Josiah's chain out of my pocket and placed it on the seat of the middle swing---his swing.

I had no plans of passing it on to my child; whether it's this one, or one that I may have in the future.

"Goodbye, Josiah," I smiled. "And if for some strange reason mama actually made it to Heaven…push her down for me, one time."

~***~

Kojo wanted to say something, but I could tell that he didn't know what to say.

"The baby isn't yours," I spoke up.

"Are you sure?"

"Yes. Apparently, the pregnancy was already in process before we…well, you know," I glanced around for Emory.

He was in his office talking to his new assistant.

"I was wondering. If it was, I would help you take care of it. No questions asked."

"I'm sure you would. But it's not. It's Emory's."

"Okay," Kojo said.

"Okay."

We both pretended to do other things for a few minutes, before I decided to say something else.

"Why did you come back here? Did someone else really buy the building you were trying to lease?"

"No," he answered honestly. "As long as I'm here, I can see you."

"You know, what we did, was a one-time thing, right?"

"You sure?"

"Oh, hell yeah! Even if I wasn't pregnant, and even if Emory and I didn't work things out, I don't ever want that… whatever you call it, anywhere near me, again!"

Kojo laughed. "Damn, so, you really can't take the dick, huh?"

"Sir, that is NOT a dick! I don't know what that is. But a dick is the one thing it is not!"

Kojo grinned. "And nah, I didn't come back just to see you. Emory begged me to. He said he needed my help. And honestly, I don't know if I'm ready to be on my own or not."

"You're ready. You know just as much as Emory, if not more. You're good at what you do. If you weren't, he wouldn't have come begging you to come back."

Kojo didn't say anything.

"You didn't tell him what we did."

"Neither did you."

"Because I don't regret it."

"Neither do I," Kojo proclaimed.

I turned to walk away.

"And you're sure the baby isn't mine?" I heard Kojo ask behind me.

"I'm sure," I lied.

The baby isn't going to be anyone's.

I made up my mind the night I got home from Texas and saw that Emory had gone out and bought tons of neutral color baby items, diapers and wipes.

Emory said he went into the store for batteries and somehow, came out with all kinds of baby stuff.

I realized then, that I actually do have a heart.

And Emory has a big piece of it.

The hurt that he's going to feel from my fake miscarriage, will save him from the hurt that he would feel if the truth ever came out.

The visit to Texas made me realize that there has been enough hurt.

I don't want to hurt anymore.

And I don't want to hurt anyone else, anymore either.

Well, except maybe Rick.

I saw Rick in the store the other day, and he spoke to me as though he hadn't done anything. As though he hadn't dared some random woman to mess up my relationship. I told him to go fuck himself, and he respond with he'd rather fuck me instead.

Cece probably didn't tell him that she told me what they did, but I got a little something, or should I say, a little *someone* up my sleeve for him.

My appointment at the abortion clinic was only an hour away. I snuck out of the shop without interrupting Emory. I texted him and told him I would see him at home.

"You really should pick a better password for your e-mail. I figured it out in two guesses. Your password is: *NovalovesEmory*. Why would you make it that easy?"

Shanice.

"What in the hell are you talking about?"

"Why are you getting an abortion? I came all the way down here just to ask you that," Shanice sat on the hood of my car.

"You went through my e-mails?"

"Isn't that what I just said?"

"Why the fuck would you go through my e-mails?"

Shanice shrugged. "I was bored. I wondered what you were up to. You have your email address on your social media pages, so, I wanted to see if I could guess the password. I did. Why are you getting an abortion? Does Emory know about this?"

"Why are you here!" I screamed at her. "Why are you bothering me? Why won't you leave me the fuck alone? I don't understand why you're even here right now! I don't want Ox! The two of you are divorced...like, why are you still here!"

I yelled in her face.

"Calm down. You're going to upset the baby," Shanice giggled. "And I'm still around because you need a friend."

"What? I don't need a friend! And I sure as hell don't need a friend like you!"

"Oh, yes you do."

I rolled my eyes are her. "Lady, you really are crazy!"

Shanice cleared her throat. "Well, I've been told that a time or two. But I own that shit. Own your shit, Nova." Shanice and I stared at each other for a while.

"I don't think you should have an abortion."

"Guess what, I don't give a damn what you think!"

"You could end up regretting it. Trust me...I know." And with that, finally, Shanice walked away.

Fuck her!

She doesn't know what the hell she's talking about!

I glanced at my cell phone. I only have twenty minutes to make it there. I drove like a bat out of hell towards the clinic. I arrived three minutes before my scheduled appointment. An e-mail popped up on my phone just as I opened the door to the clinic.

Emory will never forgive you for this. I couldn't stop you. Maybe he can.

I glanced at the sender.

Shanice!

Why is she in my business?

She already tried to shoot me, why won't she just let me be?

I stood there for a minute and re-read her e-mail.

Would she really tell Emory?

I let go of the door handle of the clinic.

Hell yeah! She would!

Damn!

I can't even get an abortion in peace!

Once I was back inside my car, the first thing I did was block Shanice's e-mail, and then I changed my e-mail password.

Shanice.please.go.to.hell!

I bet she won't guess this one!

I drove out of the parking lot.

"That's okay. There's other ways to get rid of a baby," I mumbled to myself.

No one is going to make me have a baby if I don't want to!

Not Emory.

Not Kojo.

And not Shanice!

*****

CHAPTER SEVEN

"When will you start to show?" Emory smiled.

"I don't know. I still have a long way to go."

Morning sickness is officially whooping my butt, and I don't like it at all. For a while, I just felt bad, but now, I can't seem to stop throwing up, and most days, all I want to do is stay in bed.

"I can't wait! I hope he or she looks just like me."

Every day, I tell myself to fall, or punch myself in the stomach. And every day…I don't seem to have the strength to do either.

I'm just going to have to go back to the clinic.

And I want to go before it's time for my next doctor's appointment, which Emory keeps reminding me about.

"I think that woman has a thing for Kojo," Emory mentioned.

"What woman?"

"Shanice. She came by the shop today, again. It's like she's doing stuff to her car on purpose, just to come and have it fixed."

"She has some issues, so I wouldn't doubt it."

"As long as her money spends, I don't give a damn. But she talked to and flirted with Kojo the whole time. She had him sweating and shit. The shit was hilarious!"

"She's basically stalking me," I rolled my eyes. "I'm sure she only came by hoping I was there."

"Maybe she just wants to be your friend."

"Friendships are overrated."

"Speaking of friends, I saw Yana earlier when I was leaving the post office. She didn't see me, but I saw her getting into a brand-new Jag."

"She's here?"

"Oh, I'm guessing she didn't tell you she was back in town?"

"No. She didn't."

"What's going on with you two?"

"Your guess is as good as mine."

Emory offered to go pick up dinner, and I called Yana as soon as he was out the door.

I was surprised that she answered this time.

"How's everything with you and the baby?" She answered without saying hello.

"Not so good. I don't like being pregnant. I'm always sick."

"But you'll have the cutest gift ever when it's all said and done," Yana said. "I'll be in town in a few weeks. You're my first stop."

Hmmm…

"You're in Brazil?" I questioned Yana.

"Yes. That is where I live now, you know," Yana seemed to move her mouth away from the phone. I heard some whispering, and then finally she spoke to me. "Well, I have to run. Sorry I can't talk longer. I'll call you soon. Love you."

She's lying about being in town.

She's lying about everything these days!

I can't trust her anymore.

I can't believe anything she says.

The doorbell rang and I forced myself out of bed.

"I don't have anything to say to you," I said seeing that it was Cece. I attempted to close the front door, but she stopped it with her hand.

"Emory told Rick you're pregnant."

"So? And I'm sure you already knew that from Christina."

"I haven't talked to Christina," Cece confirmed. "She lost the baby."

"Oh, I know. I wonder who attacked her, because it sure as hell wasn't me like you told her!"

Cece looked surprised that I knew that information.

"I did one of us a favor. You should be thanking me."

"Bitch, please! It's you and your nasty ass husband's fault for daring her to sleep with my man in the first place!"

"Emory is a grown ass man. He could've said no," Cece growled. "Why didn't you tell him what we did?"

"Oh, it's on my to-do list; especially now, since he's still speaking to Rick. I'll be sure to tell him what the two of you did when he gets back home."

Cece exhaled. "Look, Nova, I came by because I miss you. Over the years, you have become one of my best friends. I know what Rick and I did was wrong. We never thought Emory would cheat on you, at least I didn't. So, I thought it was all talk. That's it. I didn't expect Christina to actually sleep with Emory. That's why I told you about her. I felt bad."

"How would you like it if I did something like that to you? If I intentionally, sent a woman in Rick's direction, hoping that he would cheat on you with her? Oh, wait, never mind. You would allow your husband to screw her anyway, and most likely join in. So, I guess it really wouldn't matter. Now, would it?"

"No. I'm done…we're done with all that. After Christina, we agreed that it's time for us to get back to what our marriage was in the beginning. Just the two of us."

Umph. I'll see about that.

"Did you burn up my backyard?"

"Did your mama burn up your backyard?" I shot back.

"I worked for years on that garden."

"That has nothing to do with me. Maybe it was Christina, or who knows who else lives you and your husband have toyed with and tried to ruin."

"Yours isn't ruined. You're having a baby. You still have Emory. Everything worked out fine. Let's be friends again. Like the good ole' days. Let's just let the past be the past."

"Okay. I'll take your advice. Goodbye, past," and with that, I slammed the door in Cece's face.

I don't need any friends like her in my life.

Hell, these days, I don't really have any friends at all; except for Emory. But I don't care.

Once Emory got back, I told him everything.

I told him about Rick and Cece, and how they dared Christina to get him to cheat on me. And told him that they paid her and I told him that Christina *was* pregnant.

"I'm so sorry, Nova. I never meant to hurt you."

"Yeah, yeah, yeah. Come eat my pussy and shut up."

Emory didn't hesitate to get me comfortable so that he could put his mouth on me. I just wanted him to stop talking, so I gave him something to do.

But for the first time, ever, while Emory was licking and sucking, my mind was somewhere else.

Or should I say on someone else.

Shanice.

~***~

"I knew you would show up sooner or later," I rolled my eyes as Shanice took a seat in front of me.

"Actually, I was here first. I saw you when you walked in."

Her hair was different. She'd cut it into a short style and added a few highlights. With her full face exposed, now, you can really see how beautiful she is.

"Are you still pregnant?"

"Are you still interested in a married man with money?"

"Always," she laughed. "People didn't care about my marriage, so…"

"Wait, Ox cheated on you?"

"Plenty of times. And I kept forgiving him. And then the one time that I cheat back…BOOM! He wants a goddamn divorce!"

Okay, despite the little hiccup with her putting a gun in my face in all, I knew there was a reason I somewhat liked her in the beginning.

"I mean, yeah, yeah, I cheated with his cousin, but does it really matter who the dick was attached to? I just did it to get even with him. To get him back for all the whores he'd brought into our marriage."

"He never told me that."

"Of course, he didn't. He only told you what he wanted you to know. After all, don't we all do that at some time or another? Only tell what's necessary?"

"I guess. Why did you come back? He said you were missing for years."

"We separated and I spent months trying to get him to understand why I did what I did. He treated me like shit. It was best that I leave; especially for him. I'd killed him 432 times in about 50 different ways in my head, and it was taking everything in me not to try out one of my ideas on him. It was best that I just go away. I'd spent years loving a man who damn near drove me crazy trying to figure out why I wasn't good enough. So, I went. I lived. I had some fun. I got my mind together…"

"That last part…whatever you did, to get your mind together…it didn't work," I interrupted her.

Surprisingly, Shanice laughed.

"And then, you came back because you thought he would've forgiven you over time?"

"I loved him. I still love him. No matter what or who I fooled around with over the years, Ox and the life I thought we would have crossed my mind every now and then. After talking to a friend about love, I decided to come back and see if with time, came forgiveness. I'd forgiven him for the hell he put me through. It would've been nice if he'd been able to do the same."

"That block of ice that you call a heart has a soft spot for Ox."

"It has one for all the people I love. And for the ones that I don't…"

"Fuck them."

"Exactly," Shanice ran her fingers through her short curls. "So, this married man…how much money does he make? Does he like to share it? Where does he live? And what in the hell did he do to you?"

~***~

"Who did you cheat on me with?"

"What?"

Unfortunately, I'm still pregnant.

And Emory and I are at the doctor's office, waiting to be called back for my appointment.

"You told me you cheated on me, once, after finding out about Mimi and Christina. But you never told me who. Who did you cheat on me with?"

I looked at him with a blank stare.

"Tell me. I won't be mad. I'm sure it's not someone I know. So, tell me."

"Why do you even want to know?"

"I don't know. I just do."

I thought about telling him it was Ox. But Emory confessed to having his suspicions of Ox being in love with me for years, so, I didn't want to start any trouble. I wouldn't want Emory to run into Ox one day and throw a punch or end up exchanging words with him.

"You don't know him. Just leave it at that."

"What's his name?"

"Why?"

"Why don't you want to tell me?"

"Because I don't."

The nurse finally called my name. Quietly, we headed to the back. Emory didn't say anything the entire time that I spoke to the nurse. He didn't speak again until we were alone in the examination room.

"Is the baby mine?"

"What? I know you didn't just ask me that."

"Why not? Obviously, you're keeping secrets. So, again, Nova, is this baby mine?"

"Of course, it's yours. I cheated months before I got pregnant. How could you ask me that?"

Emory didn't respond.

"Do you really want to know who I slept with?"

Emory waited for my next words.

Fuck it.

"Ox."

Emory jumped to his feet.

"I knew it! I fucking knew it!"

I could see the anger all over his face.

"Like I said, it wasn't until after I found out you were cheating on me. And it was only once," I lied.

"That motherfucka' wanted you from the very beginning! And he got you! Of all people, you slept with him, Nova?"

"Look, you slept with who you wanted to sleep with. I slept with who was available. It's all in the past. Now, do you want to keep talking about it? Or are we going to get excited about what we're going to see or hear from our baby today?"

"Did you like it?"

"Emory…"

"Did you fucking like it?"

"Did you like fucking Mimi or Christina?"

Emory glared at me.

"It was what it was. And it happened at the least two months before I got pregnant. I don't work with him anymore. I don't have to see him. There's nothing to worry about."

If he ever found out about Kojo, Emory might try to kill him.

Luckily, the doctor came in before either of us had a chance to say anything else.

The weeks are rolling by and before long, and from the looks of it, I'm definitely having this baby. After hearing the heartbeat and seeing how the tiny bean has started to form, no matter who the father is, this baby is mine.

And I'm keeping it.

"I'll give you a blood test, if you want one," I threw it out there hoping to ease Emory's mind. Of course, I wouldn't want to have to do that just in case the baby is Kojo's.

"No. I believe the baby is mine. I just can't believe you slept with Ox. But it's my fault. You never would've did it if I hadn't cheated on you. I'll be al'right."

Emory and I drove in silence for the rest of the drive home.

"Does Shanice know you slept with Ox?"

"Nope."

"Are you going to tell her?"

"Nope. They weren't together when it happened. I don't owe her anything."

"But the two of you are…"

"We're not friends."

"Does she know that?" Emory nodded as we got out of the car.

Shanice was pulling up in front of our house. Emory shook his head and walked towards the house as I approached Shanice's car.

"I'm not even going to ask how you know where I live."

Shanice chuckled. "Why didn't you tell me that the married man was your neighbor?"

"I told you what you needed to know. I hate him. I hate his wife. I hope you milk that cow for as long and for as much as you can."

A few days ago, I sent Shanice in Rick's direction.

She supposedly wanted to talk to him about stocks, but I told her that he had a whole lot of money that he didn't mind giving to her as long as she gives him something in return.

"He's a pervert. It took all of five minutes into our conversation before he came onto me. I liked it though."

"You're one weird woman," I exhaled. "His wife is going to have a fit. She told me that they were giving up adding people into their marriage. Obviously, Rick lied to her."

"Hell, does he have a wife? I swear, he could've fooled me if I didn't already know. He reminds me of Ox, back in the day, which makes me want to use him even more. Maybe his wife will catch on, leave him, and take half of everything he has. He deserves it."

"Did you get half? From Ox? He does make millions a year." I already knew she didn't try to get any money from divorcing Ox. I wanted to know why.

"Want to know a secret?" Shanice didn't give me time to answer. "I have more money than Ox has. Who do you think gave him his half of the money to start the company?"

"Really?" I questioned her.

"Really," she shrugged. "How was your doctor's appointment?"

"Stop following me, Shanice!"

She laughed loudly. "You're right. I need to get a life. For now, I like watching yours. Maybe Rick will keep me busy for a while."

I started to walk away.

"Oh, by the way. Kojo thinks your baby might be his."

"What?"

I looked towards the house to make sure Emory wasn't standing in the door or on the porch.

"I went by the shop, flirted with him enough for him to want to hook up. He loves you, just like I knew he did. I told him I knew about the two of you. He asked me if I knew how far along you were. He thinks the baby could be his. And I have a feeling that he's going to be pretty adamant about finding out the truth once the baby gets here."

Shit!

"Could the baby be his?"

"No. According to my dates, I was already pregnant before…"

Shanice grinned, "Before he ripped your insides apart! You were right. I couldn't walk for two hours once I finally got him to shut up about you and give me a little taste of it."

"Told you. Having sex with him should be considered attempted murder or at least assault with a deadly weapon. The size of his dick just don't make no damn sense!"

"Right. I stopped breathing like three times."

I laughed.

Damn!

She's wearing me down.

Well, this will surely get rid of her.

"I had sex with Ox."

Since she's practically trying to force me to be her friend, I might as well put it out there.

"I know. Why do you think I thought about shooting you?" Shanice shrugged. "He wouldn't admit it, but he wouldn't deny it either. I already knew. But that day in your office, I could tell that you didn't give a damn about Ox. You didn't want him. And he wanted you so badly. Oh, what satisfaction that gave me. Finally, there was something...someone...that he couldn't have. At least not entirely. That, my dear, is an answer to one of my prayers."

Shanice rolled up her window and drove away without saying another word.

That's gonna' be me in ten years if I don't change my way of thinking.

Alone. Petty. Desperate for connections. Stalking people for my amusement.

I thought about what Shanice said about Kojo.

Does he actually want my baby to be his?

Is he going to say something to Emory?

All hell is going to break loose if he does.

Emory already has his doubts, and I don't need Kojo giving him anymore.

My baby deserves a father.

A better father than I ever had.

A father who will love them, teach them, and show them more love and attention than they know what to do with.

And that father is Emory.

~***~

"Nova?"

Kojo glanced behind me. "How do you know where I live?"

"Shanice told me."

Kojo chuckled. "That woman...something is wrong with her."

"Everything is wrong with her."

Wow.

I didn't know that Kojo was living large and in charge.

His house is bigger than mine! It's so modern and neat. Nothing like I imagined his house would be.

"You can afford this house working for Emory?"

"I work for Emory because I want to. Not because I have to," Kojo mentioned. "My mentor left me a pretty penny, unexpectedly, when he passed away. Working for Emory gives me practice, and experience. But that's coming to an end...again. I've found another building, and I'm buying it."

"Good for you."

Kojo offered me a seat.

"Does Emory know you're here?"

"Of course not."

"So...."

"Kojo, the baby isn't yours. Shanice told me you have suspicions and I wanted to come and tell you face to face that I'm sorry, especially if you want a child, but my child is Emory's."

"The timeline just seems close. Too close. And if the baby is mine, I wouldn't want to miss out on any of the baby's life. I've already lost one child…"

"You too?"

Kojo looked confused.

Emory lost a child. And now Kojo is saying he did as well.

"You lost a child?"

Kojo nodded. "He was three. His mother wasn't watching him. He wandered into the swimming pool at her parent's house."

"Wow. I'm sorry to hear that."

"It was a long time ago."

"I'm sorry. I can't imagine. But I don't want any problems. I don't want anyone to be unsure. That's why I'm here. If there was any possibility, I would tell you, but it's not. I just wanted to make that clear."

"Why does Shanice think there's a possibility it could be mine?"

"Excuse me?"

"She's the one who brought up the conversation, and once I started to think about it, I started to wonder. She believes there's a possibility."

That bitch!

"You can't believe anything she says. She's the reason we had sex in the first place."

Kojo looked confused.

188

"She's the person who tried to shoot me at work that day. She shot her husband instead, but she came there to shoot me. And now she's trying to force me to be her friend."

"Are you serious?"

"Yes. Something is wrong with that woman. All she says is that she wasn't really going to shoot me. And now everywhere I go, she shows up."

"Sounds like she's obsessed with you."

"If something ever happens to me…Shanice did it."

Saying those words instantly made me think about Josiah. It made me think about his note. And it made me think about Yana.

"Apparently, her ex-husband was in love with me. I guess she has some kind of vendetta against me, although she's trying to make me believe she wants to be my friend or something."

"Nova, be careful."

I stood up.

"I can handle Shanice. I just don't need any extra drama in my life right now; which apparently she's trying to cause by giving you some kind of false hope."

"Understood," Kojo walked me towards the door. "I'll see you around, Nova. And if I don't, congratulations.'"

"Goodbye, Kojo."

He opened the door.

Both of us froze at the sight of Emory standing there. Emory looked back and forth between the both of us and then through clinched teeth he said:

"What the fuck are you doing here, Nova?"

~***~

"Hey girl," Yana yelled as soon as I opened the door.

She was ten drinks past drunk.

"How did you get here?"

"I drove, duh," she wobbled inside my house.

I spotted the new Jaguar that Emory was talking about parked beside my car in the driveway.

"How long have you been in town."

"Uh uh," Yana shrugged.

She flopped down on the couch.

"I thought you were pregnant?"

"I am."

And I don't want to be.

The other night, Emory said he was just stopping by Kojo's to talk. He said seeing my car there had him thinking all sorts of things.

We lied to him.

Kojo let me do most of the talking.

I told Emory that I came to talk to him about Shanice. Emory already knew that they had sex, but I told him that Shanice asked me to talk to Kojo for her.

I told Emory that Kojo ghosted her and she wanted to know why. Kojo agreed with everything I said.

Needless to say, Emory believed us.

I left Emory there that night with his friend, and once I got inside my car, I nearly had a panic attack.

I knew right then and there that I have to choose.

It's either Emory.

Or the baby.

And despite these crazy few months…I choose Emory.

With everything going on, he's the only one in my life I can truly depend on. In the past, I always had Yana.

These days, all I have is Emory.

And I can't lose him.

"I wonder if it'll be a boy or girl. Which do you want?" Yana slurred.

"It doesn't matter."

It doesn't matter because I'm not having it. I have a new appointment Monday at the clinic, and nothing…no one is going to stop me from going through with this abortion this time. I'm tired of going back and forth about it. I've made my decision. I'm doing it and putting this behind me.

Yana started to sing a lullaby.

"Twinkle…twinkle…little…"

"Where is your husband?"

"Who knows. He doesn't care about me."

"What? Why doesn't he care about you?"

"He wanted what he wanted from me…money. They always want my money. Everyone wants some of my money. Except for Josiah."

Suddenly, Yana's eyes became as wide as a four-lane highway. I could tell that she hadn't meant to reveal her martial problems to me. And she sure as hell hadn't meant to mention Josiah.

"Why didn't you just marry Josiah?"

Yana refused to speak.

"You didn't love him the way he loved you."

"I did!" She yelled. "I did love him. It's just…"

"It's just what?"

"He just wouldn't let it go. I just wanted him to let it be."

"What are you talking about?"

Yana closed her eyes. "I just want to go to sleep. I just need to sleep."

Within a minute or two, Yana was snoring.

I sat there for what seemed like hours, just staring at her. Staring at a woman I barely seem to know these days. A woman who I thought I knew like the back of my hand.

Yana had her ways about her, just like I did.

Her parents weren't abusive, physically, but emotionally and mentally, they were never available to her. They never wanted a child, and they made that crystal clear. She was their mistake, literally; and they thought money could fix everything.

I can remember Yana watching her phone all day on her birthdays, hoping her parents didn't forget. Sometimes, they didn't. But most times, they did. And then, they would call her a week later once they remembered, letting her know that they'd transferred a few thousands into her account to say sorry.

Money isn't what she wanted.

All she ever wanted was love.

And that's what I don't understand.

If what she and Josiah had was love, real love, the love she's always been looking for, then what went wrong?

Maybe it was Josiah.

He had problems. He had a temper.

Maybe that's why he got help. Maybe he wanted to be better for Yana and by the time he got himself together, it was too late. She'd married someone else.

I love her.

Still.

Though I don't know what's going on with her. Though I don't understand her. Though I don't trust her anymore...

I love her.

I got a blanket from the closet and placed it over her.

Her phone was on the floor. It chimed just as I picked it up.

New Message.

I put in her passcode.

Incorrect.

Yana has had the same passcode, on every phone, for many, many years. I tried it again. It still didn't work.

She changed it.

She's changed.

I placed her phone on the table and walked away.

"Is that Yana on the couch?" Emory asked once he got home.

"Yep. She showed up in the middle of the day, drunk."

Emory started to undress.

"You don't really seem happy that she's here."

"Something is off with her. I can't explain it. She did admit that she's having marital problems."

"Already?"

Emory walked into the bathroom and turned on the shower. He came back into the bedroom completely naked.

"Now, you know my hormones are crazy right now. Why would you come out here looking like that?"

Emory smiled. "You can come join me in the shower, if you want to."

"Don't mind if I do."

Emory and I were all of five minutes into hot steamy shower sex…

"Nova!" Yana burst into the bathroom. "Oooh…y'all nasty!" She didn't even bother to cover her eyes at the sight of me bent over.

Emory rushed to cover himself with the shower curtain.

"Yana! Get out! Get out!"

She smiled. "Okay, okay. You don't have to yell."

Still smiling, she exited the bathroom slowly.

All I could do was laugh.

I got myself together and found Yana pouring herself a glass of wine in the kitchen.

"Is pregnancy sex as good as they say it is?"

"You should try knocking next time."

"I didn't know he was here. But umph, now I know why you love him so much," Yana smiled childishly.

"Don't make me stab you, bitch."

Yana laughed.

I snatched the wine glass out of her hand.

"You just slept off some alcohol, you don't need any more today."

"My mother is dead, in case you forgot. You don't tell me what I need," Yana reached for the glass. I moved it. So, she grabbed the bottle and took a big gulp from it.

"What's been going on with you lately?"

"Nothing. I'm fine."

"I'm sorry that your marriage is having trouble, Yana. Are you going to get a divorce?"

"Yep. If I'm even really married. I found out that he was using a fake name. So, I guess legally, I was never really married at all." Yana drunk more of the wine. "It was all about my money. He said I looked like a woman with money at the resort that day. He approached me in a fancy suit that he stole out of one of the rooms. He was actually just one of the housekeepers. He played me from beginning to end. He made me trust him. He made me marry him. And then…he made me pay him."

"You don't have to give him a damn thing! Hell, you don't even know his real name. You're not legally married, so he's not entitled to half of anything."

"I didn't give him half. Just two million dollars."

"Two million dollars! To a man whose name you don't even know?"

"It's nothing. I have more money than I'll ever be able to spend. I just want to forget him, forget Brazil, forget everything."

Yana stood up with the bottle in her hand.

She then grabbed her keys that I'd placed on the table by the door.

"Where are you going? You're drunk, Yana! You don't need to drive!"

Yana shrugged just before walking out the door and slamming it behind her.

I couldn't help but wonder if I would ever see her again.

~***~

"I have nothing to say to you. You are the one who put the thought of my baby being Kojo's in his head."

Shanice grinned. "I just thought I would put it out there. He's a grown man. He can think for himself. I just mentioned the obvious."

"Well, obviously, you should mind your own damn business! You come around like you want to be my friend, but really, you're just trying to mess up my life. You want my life. You want what I have."

"And what do you have exactly? There's nothing that you have that I can't have, don't already have, can't buy or don't have more of. So, don't flatter yourself. Now, if you're out of your feelings, let me tell you about my night with Rick."

"I don't want to hear it. And I don't want to talk to you."

"Anyway, Cece showed up," Shanice sat down in front of me with a smirk on her face, knowing that I wanted to hear what she had to say next. "Rick had me meet him at a nice hotel, and a few minutes into fourplay, his wife comes through the door after getting the front desk to give her a key."

"And?" Shanice waited for me to ask.

"He asked her to join in. Needless to say, she had a damn fit! I actually had to punch her in the face when she tried to take her frustrations out on me. I broke my damn nail," Shanice frowned. "They're getting a divorce. At least that's what she yelled at him before storming out of the room."

"What did Rick say?"

"Nothing. We had sex. While he was asleep, I took his credit card and went to buy me a few things, then tossed the card in the trash. But they're getting a divorce. Whatever they did to you, you got your payback, thanks to me. You're welcome."

"Well, I guess I didn't expect the whole divorce thing."

"You can't tell Karma how to play her cards. You should be happy."

"I'm not happy. I'm satisfied. There's a difference."

"Nova?"

Both Shanice and I looked up at Yana.

Yana stared at Shanice as though she recognized her.

"Yana, this is Shanice."

"Do I know you?"

Shanice stood up. "I doubt it." She placed her purse on her arm. "See you around, Nova."

She walked away just as Yana took a seat.

"Who is she? Your new best friend?"

"Ha! More like my new pain in my ass! And why does it matter to you? You haven't been much of a friend lately."

"I know. I just have my own shit going on." Yana looked behind her at the door. "I've seen her. I don't know where, but I've seen her before."

"Maybe around town."

Yana didn't comment.

"How long are you in town?"

Finally, Yana turned to face me. "Until the wind blows me on a plane far away from here. I'm trying to figure out where I want to go next."

"What about the house in Brazil?"

"I never purchased a house in Brazil."

"Rome?"

"Nope."

"Hmmm…"

"I don't know if I want to find another house here, or somewhere abroad. I don't know what I want to do. These days, I just feel so lost."

"That's because you're trying to face whatever you're going through all by yourself. I've always been here, but you're shutting me out."

"It's because…" Yana paused. "You just wouldn't understand."

"Try me."

"Trust me…you wouldn't understand. And honestly, I don't expect you or anyone else to. This is something I have to work through and get through all on my own. And I will. I will."

"I'm here if you need me."

"I know," Yana picked up a menu. "Okay, lunch is on me, belly. Let's eat."

Yana and I talked for a while, and just as they brought our food to the table, I looked up towards the door.

Standing there, watching us from the window was Shanice.

She never left.

When she noticed that I was looking in that direction, she smiled, but she didn't move. She just stood there.

I took my eyes off her for one minute to taste my food, and when I looked back up…

She was gone.

~***~

"I'm surprised you're not with your little friend."

"She isn't my little friend. She's my best friend," I corrected Shanice.

"Well, excuse me."

Shanice just stared at me.

I was at the grocery store.

I had a cart full of groceries.

My new abortion appointment is tomorrow, and I have a feeling that I'm going to need plenty of comfort food.

With Yana around these past few days, I almost changed my mind. But she's unpredictable, and so is this crazy woman standing in front of me. I can't be sure of what the next month, or even the next day looks like with her lurking around, putting ideas in people's heads, so, making sure I maintain my only *sure* relationship is at the top of my list.

And with life's crazy twists and turns lately, I can't afford to lose Emory too.

"Are you cooking a feast?"

"No. Don't you have somewhere else to be?"

"No."

I stopped walking to face Shanice.

"My friend thinks she's seen you before? Why? Have you ever seen her?"

Shanice shrugged.

"Well, have you?"

"I've seen a lot of people. I've seen a lot of things."

I rolled my eyes at her. "You've probably been watching her the way you watch me."

"I don't watch you. I observe you. Sometimes."

"Why? Why won't you just go away."

"For a minute there, I thought we were bonding. Maybe even becoming friends."

"Do you even know what it means to be a friend?"

"More than you know."

"Because to me, it seems like you chase entertainment and self-satisfaction. You feed off chaos and meddling in other folks business."

"Or maybe I'm just trying to help."

"Help who?"

"You," Shanice said firmly.

"I don't need your help. You are the one who needs help."

"We all need a little help sometimes."

"Well, I don't. Especially not from you."

"You?" Cece interrupted our conversation. She walked closer to us. She was staring at Shanice, and then she looked at me. "And you?" She waited on me to say something, but I didn't.

She looked horrible.

She looked as though she hadn't slept in weeks.

"You put her up to sleeping with my husband, didn't you? To get back at me? You ruined my family!"

"Your family was ruined the minute you and your husband started bringing other people into your bed," I snapped at her. "And I didn't ruin anything! Your husband ruined your family. Your husband did what he wanted to do. Your husband is a grown as man...remember those words?"

Cece shook her head. "We agreed. We were going to focus on us and our marriage. And you sent this bitch in his direction!"

"I got your bitch in this purse. You wanna' see it?" Shanice swayed her Gucci bag back and forward.

"Emory isn't your husband. The two of you don't have kids...yet. You broke up a family."

"Girl, forgive the man and shut the fuck up," Shanice rolled her eyes. "To be honest, he sleeps around and likes threesomes or whatever because his sex is horrible. The added attention is his way of making himself feel better because he knows that he has sex like a ninth grader. Take him back. Be rich. And have boring ass sex for the rest of your lives. You're making a big fuss about nothing. If you want him, stop trying to teach him a lesson behind something that you've allowed him to do for years! And because you said it was time to stop, you thought he was going to," Shanice barked. "You look like shit. Your ass in those pants looks like it smells like shit. Put those goddamn grapes down and go get your husband back! You better hurry up while there's still a chance. Because if these new-aged whores get ahold of him, and his wallet, he's gone for good! Go on, now! And maybe fix your hair and put on some clothes before you go begging him to come back. I'm sure he doesn't want to come back home to someone looking like that."

Cece looked back and forth between Shanice and I. Finally, she did just as Shanice said. She threw down the grapes and rushed out of the grocery store.

"She better hope there's still time," Shanice mumbled. "I spent $10,000 on this man's credit card and disappeared. And he still left me a voicemail this morning asking if he could see me again."

"We're both going to hell," I mumbled.

"Speak for yourself," Shanice proclaimed. "I'll be turning over a new leaf sooner than later. I've had enough hell on earth. I damn sure don't want to deal with it for eternity."

A new leaf.

Once I get rid of my baby, I'm turning over a new leaf too. I might marry Emory, like he's been begging me to for years, and I'll get pregnant again as soon as I can to give him the one thing he wants most.

A new leaf sounds nice.

"The thing about me is…I am who you see," Shanice interrupted my thoughts. "Can you say the same thing about everyone else in your circle?"

"What is that supposed to mean?"

"Most people wear masks. But you can only wear a mask for so long before you need to take it off to breathe."

~***~

"Yana, can we have a minute alone, please?"

I could tell by the sound of his voice that something was wrong.

Yana scurried out of our bedroom.

Emory closed the door.

"So, tell me why I got an appointment reminder voicemail today…from the abortion clinic."

"Wh---what?"

Emory took out his phone and played the message.

"Nova Parks, this is Chelsey from Woman to Womb Abortion Clinic. I was calling to confirm your appointment tomorrow, October 27th, at 1 p.m."

I was stuck.

I didn't speak. I didn't move.

So, Emory played the voicemail again.

Why in the hell would they call Emory's phone?

How in the hell did they get his number?

This has Shanice's messy ass written all over it!

"Why are you trying to get an abortion, Nova?"

I tried to think of something to say.

A lie, of course.

"Why in the fuck are you trying to kill my baby behind my back?" Emory realized what he said. "It's because the baby isn't mine. Right? All along, you've known that the baby isn't mine. That's why you want to get an abortion. Right!" He yelled.

I knew I had to say something.

"Wrong," I mumbled.

"Wrong? You said wrong? What am I wrong about, huh? How am I wrong!" Emory yelled.

"The baby is yours…" I forced myself to say. "Getting the abortion has nothing to do with you."

"Nothing to do with me? You're pregnant with my child, so you say, and it has nothing to do with me?"

I finally figured out a direction to go with the conversation.

"I'm scared, okay. I thought I wanted this baby, but the more I think about it, I don't know the first thing about being someone's mother," I forced myself the whine. "I had a horrible mother, the worst mother a child could ever ask for. What if I'm just like her? What if I don't know how to love my child enough? I have all these thoughts, and I just wanted them to go away. I started to feel like getting rid of the baby is the only way. I'm not ready, Emory. I'm not ready to be a mother."

I was in full blown tears, because though I was trying to hide the truth from Emory, a lot of what I said is actually the truth.

"You act like you're doing this alone," Emory growled.

"I'm not. I just don't know if I can do it. I'm scared. And I knew you would never agree to getting rid of it."

"So, you were going to do it behind my back? What the fuck were you going to tell me, Nova?"

"I would've told you the truth. I would've. I wouldn't have had a choice but to."

Emory paced back and forth.

"I didn't want you to be upset."

"You didn't want me to be upset?" Emory mocked me. "But you want to kill my baby?"

"Don't say it like that!"

"How else do you want me to say it, Nova?"

"It's not like a real baby yet."

Emory howled sarcastically.

"I tell you what," Emory threw up his hands. "I'll leave it up to you. It's your choice. You don't want to have the baby, fine. It's your body. Do what you feel. But if you get rid of my child, I'll never forgive you. And you and I are done! Kill my baby, and we're over, Nova! But I'll let you choose."

Emory opened the bedroom door, stormed out of it, slamming it so hard behind him that the pictures fell from the wall.

Only a minute later, Yana came into the room.

"Why do you want an abortion?" She asked immediately. "He was so loud, I heard everything."

"Because…I'm just not ready."

Yana sat on the edge of the bed. "Okay, now that we got that bullshit lie out of the way…why do you really want an abortion?"

"Because…it might not be his."

Yana exhaled. "Who else could it be?"

"Some random guy I slept with just because Emory did it to me," I lied to Yana, though I'm not sure why. I'm sure it has something to do with me not being able to trust her these days.

"Some random guy?"

"Yes. I think it's Emory's, but I can't be sure."

"Do you want it to be Emory's baby?" Yana started to play with her fingers.

"What do you mean?"

"Just what I said. Do you want it to be Emory's?"

"Yes, of course."

"Then we'll just make sure it's his. On paper anyway. You have your baby, offer to give him a DNA test…I'll take care of the rest. Trust me, there's nothing, and I do mean nothing that people won't do for money. A truth I've had to learn the hard way," Yana gazed off into the distance. "I'll find the place, if the baby comes back not Emory's, I'll make sure the DNA test shows that Emory is the father. Problem solved. It's nothing a little money can't fix. You should've told me sooner," Yana smiled.

"What would I do without you?" I mumbled. "I'll never be able to repay you for something like this."

Yana giggled. "In your words…consider us even."

It was something about the way she said it.

"Even for what?"

Yana shook her head. "Nah, seriously, that's what friends are for. And who knows, maybe the baby actually is Emory's and I won't have to do nothing at all. What do we have about six months or so to find out? Girl, if I were you'll I'll be damn near a saint until then. You need to be on God's phone line, all day and night, praying," Yana laughed. "And if he doesn't answer…me and my checkbook will answer the call."

I exhaled.

To be able to keep both the baby and Emory is what I really want anyway.

I thought about the voicemail.

Shanice had to have found out about the appointment somehow and switched out my phone number for Emory's.

That's the only explanation because I didn't tell a soul about my appointment.

It's all pretty strange.

Shanice wants me to have this baby just as much as Emory does, but why?

What does my pregnancy have to do with her?

And why is she always in my goddamn business?

******

CHAPTER EIGHT

I spotted Rick moving back into his house.

Cece stood on the porch as he carried overnight bags from the car.

She took Shanice's advice.

Speaking of Shanice, she hasn't popped up in almost two weeks, which is like a breath of fresh air. Maybe she found something better to do with her time.

Finally!

I pulled into my driveway, and just as I got out of the car, his black on black Lincoln town car pulled up on the side of the road.

Ox.

I haven't seen him in a while, and the smile on his face told me that he missed me just as much as I've missed him.

"You can't be here."

"Well, hello to you too," he grinned.

"I kind of told Emory that we had sex, so…"

Ox nodded. "Oh, I see. Well, I was just in the neighborhood and thought I would stop by."

"In the neighborhood?"

"Yes. The woman that I'm seeing lives two streets over."

"You're dating someone?"

"Something like that." Ox glanced down at my stomach. "You're growing."

"Finally, it took forever for me to get this little pudge."

Ox studied my face as though he was looking for something in my eyes that wasn't there. "You look happy. And I'm happy that you're happy."

"I am," I paused. "Have you seen Shanice?"

"No. Why?" Ox questioned. "Once we signed the divorce papers, she disappeared again. I haven't seen or heard from her. She didn't want anything from me. She didn't even want the money back that she let me borrow to help start the company. All she said was: *There's nothing like being free. Enjoy it.* That's the last thing she said to me."

Sounds like something she would say.

"Why? Has she been bothering you?"

"She was...but then she just went away."

"Sounds like Shanice. Even when we were married. Some days, she was there...other days, she would just check out on me."

"Is that why you cheated on her?"

Yeah. I bet he didn't know Shanice told me that.

"Honestly, yes. That was part of it. I was young. You live and you learn. I cheated. Shanice cheated back. She got me. And she got me good. I learned my damn lesson. I'm not a cheater, anymore. And I don't plan on cheating on another woman. Ever. But now, if you tell me you want us, I'll drop..."

"Bye, Ox," I smiled.

"Damn. You just won't let me love you, huh? That's all I've been trying to do," Ox pouted, just before flashing his million-dollar smile. "Bye, Nova."

Ox drove away, and it wasn't until then that I noticed Cece staring at me from the sidewalk.

I stuck up my middle finger at her.

Cece just stood there with her arms folded across her chest until I walked away.

I answered the phone for Yana just as I walked inside the house.

"Hello?"

I haven't seen her in a few days, and she hasn't been returning my calls. I was starting to think that she was back on her bullshit, again. After I already told Emory that I was giving him a DNA test.

Emory is still somewhat mad at me, but I told him that I was keeping the baby. Also, I told him that I was giving him a DNA test as soon as the baby is born. Emory insisted that I didn't have to, but I told him I didn't want him to regret not getting one in the future.

Now, all I can pray is that the baby is his.

And if it isn't, I pray that the child at least looks just like me because if the baby comes out looking just like Kojo, no matter what strings Yana thinks she can pull, Emory isn't stupid, dumb or blind!

"Where have you been?"

"I'm still in town. I met a man at a bar, and I've just been enjoying him for the past few days, if you know what I mean."

"I know exactly what you mean. I thought you were gone, again. I figured you were somewhere on the other side of the world."

"Oh, it's coming. I'm just sticking around for a little while. I feel like you need me."

"I do."

Yana talked about the guy that she's been sleeping with for the past few days. I listened attentively since I didn't have anything better to do.

She said the man's name is Ray.

I dated a Ray once.

And just like almost every other man, he cheated on me too. Ray had me all in my feelings.

He was an artist. A musician.

He could sing, dance, draw, create. He was just this big ball of energy. I put my college education on hold for him. I wanted to be around him all the time.

Ray had me completely consumed…until I caught him screwing his so-called assistant in his art studio. That same night, I screwed the drummer in his band and destroyed every art project that he'd been working on for months.

"Nova? Are you listening?"

"Um huh."

"How are things with you and Emory?"

"He's still a little upset, but he's going easy on me because I'm pregnant."

"The two of you will be okay."

"Hopefully. Months ago, I was done with his ass! I planned on hurting him and going on with my life. Now, I feel like I need him in my life. I feel like I can't do this without him. Emory is one of the only people in my life that truly loves me."

"I love you," Yana said. "And hopefully, one day, I'll find a man that loves me the way Emory loves you. Minus the cheating," Yana laughed.

"Girl," I chuckled. "I pray Emory's cheating days are over! For real! I hope he got it all out of his system because if he ever cheats on me again…I can't be sure what I would do to him! But I'm sure it'll probably be something that sends my ass straight to jail!" I laughed.

"Oh, I'm sure it would be."

Yana talked a little while longer, and then she told me she would call me soon. She promised not to leave town again without letting me know first.

"Hey, baby," Emory walked in a few hours later with food.

"Hey. You're in a better mood today."

Emory shrugged. "Your weird friend helped me realize something today."

"Shanice?"

"Yep."

Damn!

She's back!

I should've known she wouldn't stay away too long.

"She came by the shop, again?"

"Actually, she approached me while I was picking up these wings."

"What did she say?"

"At first, she just asked if I was excited about the baby. And then, she started to talk about you. She reminded me of how hard pregnancy can be on a woman, her body and her mind. She said some women get scared of being responsible for a little human that they'll have to teach and mold. She also said the fear will go away once the mother looks into the eyes of her baby for the first time. She really helped me to understand what you were saying to me that day, and why you considered getting an abortion. If you ask me, she was clearly speaking from experience."

Ox said Shanice couldn't have kids. Maybe at one point in time she could and something went wrong.

Did Shanice have an abortion or lose a child?

"She's oddly concerned about you."

"And for the life of me I can't figure out why. She just popped up one day and now she won't go away! She wants something. I can feel it. I just don't know what it is."

"She doesn't like Yana."

"She said that?"

"She didn't have to. She called her a bitch. Her exact words were: *Nova has been hanging out with that bitch lately*." Emory chuckled. "I was like, dang lady, what did Yana do to you?"

"Nothing. She didn't do anything to her. Well, not that I know of. Shanice is crazy."

"I can agree with that." Emory kissed my forehead. "I'm sorry if I overreacted. I'm sorry I gave you an ultimatum. I didn't fully understand where you were coming from. Now, I do."

I nodded my head.

"I got your favorite wings. I got fifty of them cause lately…"

"Shut up! I'm pregnant. Don't talk about me!"

Emory laughed. "It's okay. Feed my baby. You can get as big as a house and I'll still love you."

"Yeah, and probably cheat on my big ass too!"

"No. I will never cheat on you again. You don't ever have to worry about that. Ever," Emory walked towards the kitchen. "Besides, you don't just take that shit. You cheat back. And ain't nobody got time for that!"

~***~

"Ma'am where were you between 10:00 p.m. and 11:00 p.m. last night?"

"Here. Asleep. Why?" I asked the officer.

"Your neighbor believes that you could be responsible for stabbing her husband, Mr. Rick Wilson."

"What? What do you mean stab?"

"He was stabbed last night in his driveway. He's still pretty out of it, but one of the children say a figure running away from the house last night. They said it looked like a woman, dressed in all black."

Rick was stabbed.

And Cece sent the police to my house.

Emory appeared in the living room.

"He's expected to survive, for now, but his wife believes that you may have had something to do with it. She says you've been out to get them because of something that happened between the two of you."

"Officer, I didn't stab anyone! And as you can see, I'm pregnant, so I'm not running anywhere."

"Carter?" The female officer called out to her partner. He took a look at what she was pointing at.

"Ma'am are these drops of blood on your porch?" He paused and stared at the doorknob. "And is that blood on your doorknob?"

Both Emory and I took a look.

"I don't know what that is, or where it came from. I was asleep last night. I didn't do anything to anyone."

The officer got on his radio. He made it clear that he was about to get a search warrant.

"Ma'am, I'm going to need you to come down to the station with me."

My heart skipped a beat.

"For what? I didn't do anything!"

"She was asleep like she said she was," Emory stepped in front of me. "I can prove it."

"Bring your proof down to the station. "Ma'am, please," the officer said. "Things will go a lot easier if you voluntarily go with me. I won't even put the handcuffs on you."

"Emory…"

"Don't worry, baby. Everything is going to be fine. I'll meet you down there."

The officer led me down my porch steps.

I glanced down the sidewalk to see Cece standing there.

"I didn't do shit to your stupid ass husband!" I yelled in her direction.

"Ma'am….you have the right to remain…."

The officer started to read me my rights.

"This is some bullshit! I didn't do anything! Hell, she probably stabbed her own husband because he cheats on her! She should be getting in this car! Not me!"

I got into the police car, completely embarrassed.

Mad doesn't even begin to describe what I'm feeling; especially since I'm innocent! I've done a lot of shit to people but attempting to kill someone isn't one of them.

Just as we pulled out of the driveway, I saw Emory, fully dressed, and coming out of the house. Cece ran towards him. Who knows what she's going to say to him.

All I know is that I didn't stab Rick.

But who did?

And why?

~***~

I spotted Kojo and Shanice as soon as I walked in.

After the longest two days of my life, I was meeting Yana for dinner. She was running late, as usual!

I followed the waiter.

"You're really showing now," Shanice said as I walked past their table. "And look at that booty! Pregnancy is going to be good to you."

I turned around to face her.

Kojo stared at my stomach. I could see something that looked like sadness in his eyes once he finally looked up at me.

"Hey, Kojo."

"What's up?"

Shanice stood up as I turned to walk away.

"Please, go back to your date."

"We're not on a date. We're talking business. Kojo is opening his shop soon. And with his ideas, he's going to be big. Even bigger than your little man. I'm going to be a silent investor."

I sat down at the table and asked the waiter for a glass of water.

Shanice sat down in front of me.

"How was it being in jail for your first time?"

I rolled my eyes. "You know what, I'm not even surprised that your stalking ass knows about that."

Surprisingly, the blood on my porch and doorknob did belong to Rick. And I don't have a clue as to how it got there.

After hours of questioning, and tearing our house a part, finally, the police allowed Emory to tell them what he'd been trying to tell them from the very beginning.

Apparently, every night while I'm asleep, since finding out about the pregnancy, Emory takes pictures and videos of me. He said he planned on making me a video and photobook to show me how much I grew, from day to day, throughout the whole pregnancy.

Isn't that such a sweet idea?

Well, the police ruined it!

Emory said he'd planned on giving the photobook and video to me the day I came home from the hospital, but he had to give them to the police to prove my innocence instead.

Emory's pictures and videos proved that I was fast asleep the night Rick was stabbed; at least between 10:23 p.m. and 10:45 p.m. And unless my pregnant ass stabbed Rick, ran home, and fell asleep without a care in the world, all in a matter of minutes, the photos and video was enough proof that whoever Rick and Cece's daughter saw that night…wasn't me.

The police let me go, but they made it clear that more questions would most likely be coming my way.

"They should've known you didn't do it. You don't have it in you," Shanice shrugged.

I stared at her. I waited for her to look at me.

"What?" She shrugged.

"You. It was you. Wasn't it? You stabbed Rick…didn't you?"

"What? I don't know what you're talking about," Shanice seemed amused.

"You stabbed Rick! Why? What did he do?"

Shanice shrugged. "He wouldn't stop calling me names."

Shanice's response surprised me. Accidentally, I chuckled. "What? Did you just say he called you names?"

"Yes. And I don't like to be called names," Shanice said seriously. "I told Rick to leave me alone, and that the fun was over. I told him to go back home to his wife. Rick kept calling me, and when he wasn't getting the responses that he wanted out of me, he started calling me names and all of that nonsense," Shanice exhaled. "I prayed about it. And once I opened my eyes, I realized that stabbing him was the answer. And so, I did."

This bitch needs to be in a straitjacket!

"I stabbed Rick in a "safe" place. I knew it wouldn't kill him. He should've just left me alone. But now, he will. Little do they know; I just saved their marriage. Me, stabbing Rick, is the best thing that could've ever happened to them. They'll be all in love and shit after this. Just watch." Shanice grinned.

"Shanice, I could've gone to jail, for a long time, all because of you! If Emory hadn't had some kind of proof…"

"Why are you yelling? The police only thought you stabbed Rick because I dripped a little blood from the knife on your porch. I touched your doorknob too. I knew they wouldn't be able to put it on you. So, relax. You're going to be fine."

I opened my mouth to say something else, but before I could…

"Nova? Is everything okay?" Yana asked appearing out of nowhere. Yana looked at Shanice. Shanice looked at Yana. Suddenly, Shanice stood up with a smile on her face.

"Well, I'll leave you and your friend to it," Shanice walked away.

"What's her problem?" Yana asked taking a seat.

"She stabbed Rick."

"What?" Yana looked behind her. "She told you that?"

"Yep. But I don't think she'll ever admit it again," I glanced over Yana's shoulder. Shanice was now seated at the table in front of Kojo again.

"Are you going to tell the police?"

"For what? She'll deny it. That's if she doesn't disappear first," I exhaled. "As long as they don't keep trying to accuse me of it, then, it is what it is. Rick deserved a little reality check. Maybe being stabbed will help him get his shit together, once and for all."

"Yeah, right. He'll be back at it again, just as soon as he's able," Yana smirked.

"I hope not."

Yana shrugged. "Well…I'm catching a flight tomorrow morning. But I won't be gone long. I'll be back in a week or two. I just need a little fun in the sun, on a beach, drinking fruity drinks and stuff."

We talked about Yana's trip for a while.

I noticed Shanice and Kojo get up to leave.

Kojo placed his hand on the small of Shanice's back and she allowed it to stay there.

Humph.

Business dinner my ass!

~***~

"It's a girl!"

Thank God!

Hopefully, she'll look just like me---just in case.

Emory smiled from ear to ear.

"Hey, daddy's baby girl. I can't wait to meet you! Can we name her Emerald?" Emory turned to me with the sweetest smile and the brightest glow on his face.

"I actually really like that. Emerald Sade. I like it."

Sade is Yana's middle name.

We made a pact a long time ago that if or when either of us had a little girl, we would give them something from each other's name.

"Your baby girl is growing just fine," the doctor smiled.

I'm having a little girl.

I promise to teach her all the things I wished my mother would've taught me. All the things I ever wanted to do as a little girl, I'm going to be sure to do them with her.

After the appointment, Emory and I talked with excitement the entire drive to the restaurant.

"Ox."

"Nova."

Ox and his lunch date were coming out of the restaurant that Emory and I were headed into.

The woman holding Ox's hand was stunning!

Her skin was only a shade and a half lighter than charcoal, but it was smooth and shiny. She had the brightest, whitest smile, and these big, bold brown eyes.

I could tell that Ox was proud to have her on his arm.

"Wow. You're growing."

I grabbed Emory's hand. I could literally feel the anger seeping out of his skin. I didn't know if I should say something back to Ox or not. I didn't want Emory to feel disrespected, but I also didn't want to be rude.

No matter what, I look at Ox as a friend.

"Thank you. It's a girl," I smiled.

"Congratulations," both Ox and his date chimed.

Emory remained quiet.

"Well, nice seeing you," Ox said.

I smiled as I led Emory inside.

"Emory?"

"I should've punched the fuck out of him! All I could think about was him putting his hands on you!"

"That's the past, Emory. Let it go. Or do you want to spend our lunch talking about the women you cheated on me with? I got time today if you do!"

Emory exhaled. "You're right."

"Thank you. Now, come on. Let's eat. I'm starving."

We managed to have a pretty good lunch.

I ate until I was literally about to explode. Emory kept trying to feed me more and more, saying that he wants a big, chunky baby.

"I'm going to run to the bathroom," Emory stood up.

"Okay. I'm going to hold mine until we get home. If I can."

Emory made his way across the restaurant.

His phone started vibrating on the table.

I picked it up.

It was a new message from D.M.

Who in the hell is D.M.?

Hurriedly, I typed in his passcode and read the text message. The message asked him when they could meet up again.

That was the only message from that contact in his phone; which means he'd deleted everything else.

No calls from the contact were in his call log either.

I started to breathe heavily.

I swear if he's cheating on me again...

"Are you cheating on me, Emory?" I asked him as soon as he approached the table.

"What?"

"Who is D.M. in your phone?"

Emory took his phone out of my hand.

"Come on, we'll talk about it in the car."

I slammed my right hand down on the table.

People started to look at us.

"No! We will talk about it now!" I screamed at Emory.

Emory smiled, embarrassed, as he looked around at everyone looking at him.

"You're making a fool of yourself," he said through tight lips. "And to answer your question, no, I'm not cheating on you. I told you, I'll never cheat on you again. But clearly, you still think I would," Emory shook his head. "I'll be outside in the car when you're ready. I have to go text D.M. back."

Emory walked away.

This fool is going to make me kill him!

I sat there for another minute or two until finally, I got up from the table full of rage. By the time I made it outside, Emory was parked in front of the restaurant, waiting for me.

"Who is D.M.?" I asked him as soon as I was inside the car.

"No one you have to be concerned about," Emory said calmly.

"Then tell me."

"No."

"Why?"

"Because I don't have to. And like I said, I'm not cheating on you, so that's all you need to be worried about."

"Emory, I swear to God, if you don't tell me who it is…"

"What? You're going to leave me?" Emory interrupted me. "Then, that will be on you. You'll be leaving me for nothing. Because I'm not cheating on you. Now, if that's what you want to believe, then that's on you. But I'm not cheating."

"Actually, I was going to say if you don't tell me…I'm going to kill you," I growled.

Emory chuckled. He looked at my face and immediately stopped laughing.

"Shit, you look like you're serious."

"You wanna' find out?"

Emory looked concerned.

"I'll get Shanice to give me a few lessons on stabbing your ass! Now, tell me who D.M. is!"

"What?" Emory asked.

I exhaled, loudly.

"Shanice stabbed Rick. Now, who in the hell is D.M.?"

"Shanice stabbed Rick? Why? How do you know that?"

"Because she told me," I rolled my eyes. "Stop trying to change the subject."

"So, you knew this, and didn't tell the police?"

"She didn't tell me until days later. And I don't have any proof. All she would have to do is say she didn't say it. And she could've been lying about it. I don't know. All I know is I didn't do it, and that she said she did. I would never hurt anyone…but you. If you don't tell me the truth!"

"And I did. I'm not cheating. That's all you have to worry about. Okay?"

And with that, Emory turned up the radio.

I stared at him the whole ride home.

If he's not cheating, then why won't he tell me who the person is?

What's the big secret if it's not another woman that he's sleeping with?

"So, you're really not going to tell me who it is?" I asked Emory, annoyed, as we pulled up at home.

"Nope."

"Emory?"

"Nova?" Emory opened his car door. "Don't be all angry and stuff. It's bad for my daughter. Now, come on so I can rub your ugly ass feet."

I pouted, but he couldn't care less.

Finally, I opened the car door.

I spotted Cece strolling up the sidewalk.

"I don't have a damn thing to say to you!" I barked at her. "You tried to send me to jail!"

"How do you know that woman?"

"What?"

"The woman that was sleeping with Rick. Shanice. How do you know her?"

"Why?" I walked up the driveway. Emory waited for me on the front porch.

"She sat out here for hours, today, across the street from your house. Just watching it. Or maybe she was waiting for you. Either way, something is strange about her. I found her on social media, and then searched her on the internet. She's been married three times, from what I could see. No kids. Not much family. I think I found a sister for her, but that's about it. On her social media, it seems like for a while, periodically, she just disappears. For months, once over a year, between posting. There's nothing but pain behind her smile on her pictures. And on top of everything else, I think she may have been the one who stabbed Rick."

"But you told the police I did it," I teased her.

"Sorry," Cece shrugged. "I thought you did, at first. Look, Nova, I know we're not friends or whatever like we used to be, but something is off with that lady. Something is wrong with her. Very wrong with her. And if you don't get away from her..."

"I'm a grown ass woman! I can handle myself. And I can handle her. And who I deal with isn't any of your damn business! Besides, you proved that you're not a very good person, and a horrible friend. She can't be any worse than you."

Emory helped me up the porch steps.

"She wants something from you!" Cece screamed behind me. "If I were you, I would figure out what it is. Before it's too late!"

Slamming the front door, though I hate to admit it...

I can't help but to wonder if Cece is right.

~***~

"Kojo, Emory is at the shop."

I forced myself to smile, although I was upset just a little that he'd woken me up from my nap.

"I know."

I waited to see what he was going to say next.

Kojo stared at my stomach. I closed my robe.

"What's wrong? What are you doing here?"

"I told you about losing my son."

"Yes."

"And since I've been fooling around with Shanice…"

"Fooling around? You like her crazy ass, don't you?"

"She's different. She challenges me to think bigger. I can't figure her out, at all, but it's something about her," Kojo admitted.

"Um, if you say so."

"She told me about her not being able to have kids."

"What does that have to do with me?"

Kojo hesitated. "I want a blood test with the baby."

"Kojo, I told you…"

"I know what you told me. I also know that you don't have a clue as to who the father of your baby is."

"And what makes you say that?"

"Trust me, I know."

"Bye, Kojo."

"Cool. I'll just go talk to Emory about it."

"You wouldn't."

"I would. Ain't no other man raising my child. I deserve to know."

I shook my head. "Kojo, where is all of this coming from? Again? I told you this baby is Emory's."

"Just agree to give me a blood test, and I'm out of your way until the baby gets here. As a matter of fact, I read somewhere that you can get it done while pregnant these days. I'll pay for it. You set up the time, and the place and I'll be there. But if that baby is mine, I'm not going anywhere, Nova. How this all plays out is up to you. The man in me won't let another man raise my daughter. It's a girl, right? That's what Emory said."

Kojo walked away.

As he got into his car and drove away, I spotted Shanice's car across the street. She just sat there, with her window rolled all the way down, wearing sunglasses.

Did she put Kojo up to this?

But why?

What the fuck is Shanice up to now?

*****

CHAPTER NINE

Oh, my God!

She lied!

I started to pant as I stared at Christina's big, round belly.

"You lied!" I shouted at her as soon as approached her.

Immediately, she place her arms around her stomach, as she glanced down at mine.

"Security!" She yelled.

"Seriously? What in the hell can my pregnant ass do to your pregnant ass?"

Christina had a stupid look on her face.

"Look, it's my baby. I lied about losing it because I don't care who the father is. I'm moving away. I don't plan on bothering anyone. I'll never tell Rick or Emory…"

"Tell me what?"

Emory had been parking the car.

We were at a new baby boutique downtown.

Christina turned to face him. Emory's eyes nearly popped out of his head once he saw her stomach.

"I thought…I thought…"

"She lied," I frowned. "She lied about losing the baby!"

"And it's mine?"

Christina glanced at me before answering him.

"I don't know."

"And you were going to keep it from me?" Emory looked at me as he spoke to Christina.

"I was just going to go away," Christina replied. "I don't want any problems and I don't want to ruin anyone's relationship."

"Too late!" I yelled at her.

I felt hot. I started to fan myself to keep from passing out.

"I get all of that," Emory spoke. "But if the child is mine, I need to know."

Ugh! Emory sounds just like Kojo!

"I pray that it isn't. But if it is, there's no way in hell I'm not being there for my child." Emory came to my side. "So, what's the plan?"

My heart felt so heavy.

We're right back to square one!

This can't be happening!

And listening to Emory, he said exactly what I always knew he would.

"Emory, I've forgiven everything over these past few months, but if her baby is yours…"

"Nova, this is a conversation that we need to have when we get home. But I said what I said. And I meant it," he looked at me. And then, he looked at Christina. "Is your number still the same?"

She nodded, keeping her eyes on me the whole time.

"I'll be in touch," Emory said. "Do you want to get out of here?" He asked me.

All I could do was nod.

The cold outside air helped me to breathe.

"Are you okay?"

"Hell no, I'm not okay! I thought this was over! I thought this was something I didn't have to worry about anymore! And now…what if her baby is yours?"

"What if it isn't? It might be Rick's."

"And it might be yours!"

Emory just looked at me.

Kojo is threatening to tell Emory that my baby might be his. Christina is still pregnant and it might be Emory's.

I just want to scream!

And so I did.

"Ahhhhhh!!"

"Calm down, baby. Calm down."

"Don't tell me to calm down! Imagine if this was happening to you!"

"Well, for a minute there, I thought it was a possibility that our baby wasn't mine, remember? But she is. And we're going to be just fine. Let's just hope that Christina's baby is Rick's."

"And if it isn't?"

"If it isn't---I meant what I said. If the baby is mine, I'm going to take care of my responsibility. I won't turn my back on my child, Nova. And you shouldn't want to be with a man who would do something like that to his kid."

I shook my head. "Just take me home, Emory. Just take me home."

Once we were inside the car, Emory continued to blabber about Christina, her baby, my baby, and everything else in between.

I didn't tune in until he said…

"I was working with Demi to plan your surprise birthday party…how about we turn it into a wedding reception? I just want you to know and be sure that I'm not going anywhere. If Christina is having my baby, it won't change shit. I love you. I want our family."

"Who the hell is Demi?"

"Oh, you heard that part, huh," Emory chuckled. "D.M. in my phone. Her name is Demi. She's been helping me plan a surprise party for your birthday. Yana referred me to her. I've already sent out the invitations. Everyone is going to be there...so, we can turn it into a wedding reception instead."

"So, you weren't cheating on me?"

"I told you I wasn't."

My birthday is a week away.

I figured we wouldn't go all out this year since I'm pregnant, but apparently, Emory has other plans.

"Marry me, Nova. We can go today, tomorrow, just marry me. I'm not going anywhere. No matter what. I can't change the past and what I did, but I can guarantee you a future where I'm the best father and husband that you could ever hope for."

I have to give Kojo a DNA test.

I don't have a choice.

I need Yana. I need her help.

I need her to pay whoever, to make sure the DNA test I take for Kojo comes back negative.

That will take care of Kojo.

I have to call Yana.

"Okay," I mumbled.

"What?"

"I said, okay. Let's get married on my birthday."

"Are you for real?"

I smiled. "Yes. Yes, let's get married!"

"I thought you would never say those words!" Emory smiled. "Wait…I gotta' get you a new ring since you smashed your other one with a hammer."

"Oh, yeah. I forgot about that," I chuckled.

"We're getting married," Emory smiled.

"We're getting married," I exhaled.

I can't control much of anything else.

But I can lock Emory down, before Christina possibly gets a chance to.

And that's exactly what I'm going to do.

~***~

"Say what?"

"You and Kojo. What is your plan, huh? You want my baby to be his so you can play step mama, or something?"

Shanice chuckled. "What in the hell are you talking about?"

"Kojo wants a blood test with my baby, or he's going to tell Emory about us."

I placed the red dress back on the rack.

I've gained over twenty pounds since being pregnant, and I look and feel like a pig in everything I wear.

"First of all, I don't know what you're talking about. Kojo and I are soon to be business partners. That's it."

"Yeah, right. He likes you."

"Oh, I'm not denying that. But there ain't a damn thing he can do for me, other than run a good business and send my thirty-percent every month. That's it," Shanice picked up the same dress that I'd just placed down. "He likes me, but I don't want him. This coochie and charisma does that to these men sometimes," she laughed. "Yet, it only does it to the men that I actually don't want. Ain't that something?"

"Whatever, I don't know what the two of you have going on, but you're not about to play "house" with my baby!"

"I have nothing to do with whatever you're talking about," Shanice rolled her eyes. "I would tell you, if I did. That day, the day Kojo came by your house, I was already outside. I was surprised when he pulled up. I thought maybe the two of you were fooling around, again," Shanice shrugged. "But if the man wants to be there for his baby…"

"It isn't his baby! That's the thing! My baby is Emory's!"

"Apparently, he thinks otherwise," Shanice said. "And I damn sure don't plan on playing *house*, as you called it, with him. I doubt I'll be around here much longer. It's almost time for me to move on."

"Where? To go stalk someone else? To go meddle in someone else's business?" I said, sarcastically. "If you stay out of everyone else's business, maybe you can find husband #4."

Shanice didn't look surprised by my comment.

"Maybe. Yes, I've been married three times, but Ox is the only one I'll ever claim," she laughed. "The other two marriages I call those Trial & Error. Those two don't count. Literally, one of them didn't last longer than a week." Shanice shrugged. "I guess you've been checking up on me, huh? What else did you find?"

"I didn't find anything. I was told that piece of information. Along with you having a sister."

Shanice cringed.

"I don't have a sister. She's no sister of mine," Shanice's facial expression was hard to read.

"Hmmm, whatever you say. Just stay the hell out of my business! And stop trying to convince Kojo that my baby is his!"

Kojo is serious about getting a DNA test.

He has sent tons of text messages with information on getting the testing done, now, before the baby is born.

I've been calling Yana like a crazy person all week, but she isn't answering her phone.

I need her help. And I need it now!

"I was seventeen, when my sister's college boyfriend raped me," Shanice said out of nowhere, getting my attention. "He was entitled. He came from parents with an ass load of money. My "sister" came home for the weekend and brought him with her. Our parents went out for the night, and my sister fell asleep downstairs. Somehow, her boyfriend found his way upstairs to my bedroom."

Tired of walking on swollen feet, I took a seat on one of the benches in the store.

Shanice continued.

"He came in and shut my bedroom door behind him. I was a virgin. A good girl. I was always reading. I read everything. Novels. Medical books. Anything I could get my hands on. That night, I was reading a suspense novel. It was just getting to the good part. He tried to act interested, but quickly, he showed his true colors. He said he saw how I looked at him during dinner that night. He thought I wanted him. And then, he tried to kiss me. I pushed him away, and…" Shanice paused. "Long story short, he held me down and raped me." She cleared her throat.

I'm not sure why she's telling me this. But maybe this will explain why she's so weird and crazy.

"The worst part wasn't the rape. It's that no one believed me. It took me days to get up enough courage to tell what happened to me. My parents didn't believe me. My sister didn't believe me. He denied it all, of course. He said I came onto him, and he turned me down. Everyone believed him...until I missed my period. He knew then that the truth was going to come out, so, he admitted the rape to his parents. They offered to pay me for my silence, if I got an abortion. They offered us a lot of money. Their son had big dreams and they didn't need something like rape ruining his plans. My parents were onboard because they didn't want to have a teenage pregnant daughter. No one asked me how I felt. My sister was too ashamed to even look at me. No one cared if I wanted the baby or not. No one even asked me what I wanted. All they talked about was getting rid of the baby, getting the money, and my silence."

"But you didn't want the baby...did you?"

"Hell no! But no one even asked," Shanice took a seat beside me. "I went to see his parents the day before the appointment. I told them that I was going to carry the baby for another month. I would then be eighteen and they could give me the money, instead of my parents. I wanted the check in my name. My parents weren't getting a dime of it. His parents didn't want to wait, but they didn't have a choice. My parents cursed me out and treated me like shit every day that I stayed pregnant. They didn't know I was holding out until I was eighteen. They just wanted it done, so they could collect. The day after my eighteenth birthday

I went to the abortion clinic. I went all alone, after I met my rapist's mother at the bank. With the money in my bank account, I had the abortion. I'd felt so dirty and disgusted with it growing inside of me, but once it was gone, I felt clean. I felt free. But that didn't last long. Apparently, something went wrong during the procedure. Two days later, I was in the hospital. I thought I was going to die. I had to have a hysterectomy."

I didn't know what to say.

"Just like that, the option of having a kid by a man who actually loves me, was gone. And check this out. Not even a week after I got out of the hospital, my sister found out she was pregnant."

"Did she have an abortion too?"

"No. She kept the baby. And she married the rapist too."

"You have got to be kidding me!"

"I'm not. They had a baby. Graduated college and got married, as though nothing ever happened. I wasn't around to see any of it though. Once I found out she was keeping the baby, despite what he did to me, I left, and I never looked back. I haven't spoken to her in twenty years. My parents, I barely talk to them. Every now and then I may call just to hear their voice. I took that money, at eighteen years old, and started my own life. A new life. A life where none of them existed."

"Sounds a little like me. Minus the rape. I just had horrible parents. I left and never looked back, until it was time to bury them."

"Mine are still holding on. And still holding out hope that I'll come back to them. I won't. I met my first husband when I was nineteen. He taught me a lot; business wise. He showed me how to make my money make more money. We divorced because he said I was too moody. We argued all the time. I was fighting within myself. Internally, mentally, I was in a bad place. So, he divorced me. I spent two years being wild and living life like there was no tomorrow. Eventually, I met my second husband. We annulled in a week. We both realized that what we felt for each other wasn't love. It was just lust. I was all alone for a while. No friends. No family. Tons of money. And tons of pain. And then, I met Ox." Shanice exhaled. "He made me feel safe. And though I didn't tell him everything about my past, Ox tried to help me get through it. He tried to help me get better. But...Ox was a *hoe*, chile," Shanice growled.

"Wow. Now, I understand why you're a little crazy."

"I don't like to be called crazy," Shanice stood up. "Even if it is true." Shanice paused. "If you ever tell anybody what I just told you...I'll kill you," she threatened with a smile. A chill slithered down my spine because in my heart, I knew she meant just what she said.

Shanice touched the clothes on rack nearby, and started to look through them, as I sat there, watching her.

I felt sorry for her, in a way.

But I don't have the time to worry about anything or anyone else.

I have my own shit that I have to deal with.

Still watching Shanice, I called Yana, again.

"Come on, Yana, answer the phone. Please, answer the damn phone!"

But as always...she didn't.

~***~

"You said this week."

"I meant next week. I'll make the appointment for next week," I told Kojo before hanging up.

The baby kicked, causing me to smile through my frustration.

Kojo is demanding a DNA test be done, now, so that he can plan accordingly if the baby is his. He makes it clear that he would rather lose his friendship with Emory than to miss out on a second of his child's life.

Yana is still M.I.A.

And I'm not going to be able to hold him off much longer.

In that moment, I tried calling her a few times.

I swear, I'm going to curse her ass out whenever she does finally call me! And not to mention, I'm getting married in two days! And my best friend has to be there!

Emory keeps telling me not to worry about it, because Yana knew about the surprise birthday party and planned on being there, so, he's sure she'll be in town.

I'm not so sure.

Maybe she forgot.

She's never forgotten my birthday, but she hasn't been herself lately. And I can't imagine getting married without her. Though we'll be going to the courthouse to get married, I still want her by my side as a witness.

And the wedding reception just wouldn't feel right without her sitting at one of the overly decorated tables smiling at me.

Luckily, Emory's rose gold, gold and cream theme worked well for both a birthday party and a wedding reception. We didn't have to change much. Our biggest change was swapping out five-hundred balloons, for two thousand dollars' worth of lilies. But the planner, Demi, got it done and everything was set and ready to go. A hundred guests are expected to be there; including my brother, sister-in-law and nieces. Emory had literally invited everyone who he thought was important to me, as well as his family and friends.

Rick and Cece weren't invited.

They're one of the reasons I agreed to marry Emory in the first place. It's because of their stupid dare that Christina may still be carrying Emory's baby.

Emory asked Christina if she was willing to get the testing done before the baby arrived. I'd mentioned the procedure to him as a suggestion. Christina said that she would rather wait until she had the baby. Emory is okay with that. He just wants to be sure that the baby isn't his.

According to him, he used condoms with her every single time, except once. I told him that it only takes one time to get pregnant, but he's almost eighty-percent sure that the baby isn't his. The twenty-percent of him that isn't sure is the part I want to strangle.

Still, being in the exact same situation, I figured by marrying him, if I had to accept a child from him…he would have to accept mine if Yana doesn't show up to make sure the results are negative for Kojo.

Outside of all the baby drama, a part of me actually wants to be Emory's wife these days.

A lot of things have changed inside of me since I've been pregnant. My thoughts, my wants, my needs…all of it is changing, daily. So, if everything does play out just right;

Christina's baby ends up being Rick's and my baby actually is Emory's...

I'll be the happiest woman in the world.

I'm no fool. These past few months, I've seen how much Emory loves me. I can only imagine that he will love me even more once I have his last name.

Consumed with my thoughts, I sat inside my car and rubbed my stomach for a little while. Since finding out that I'm pregnant with a girl, and deciding on her name, Emory has gone completely insane with having things customized for the baby. He has her name on everything!

Christina is also having a girl.

A car slowed down in front of my house.

I glanced out my rearview mirror at it until it sped away. It was black with dark tinted windows, so I couldn't see inside of it.

I haven't seen Shanice since that day in the store.

Call me crazy, or maybe I'm just desperate, but I'm tempted to find her and inquire about the many resources she claims to have. I know that she does have a few connections. Maybe she knows someone who would able to switch the DNA test results for Kojo, if need be.

But then, Shanice would know the truth.

She would know that I'm unsure of who the father of my child is.

What would she do with that kind of leverage?"

The same car from before, slowed down again in front of my house.

What are they doing?

After lingering for about three seconds, the car sped away again.

Feeling unsafe, I backed out of the driveway.

I'm not going to wait around and see what bad luck plans on coming my way today. I'm going to the shop with Emory.

I made it to the stop sign, and looking in my rearview mirror, the strange car stopped in front of my house again.

This time, the passenger side door opened.

Yana?

Yana got out of the car.

She had bags in her hands and ran towards my house. She placed the bags on the porch, and then, she ran back to the car.

I made a U-turn.

"Yana! Yana!" I beeped my horn as the car passed by me going in the opposite direction.

The car drove by and turned out into oncoming traffic.

What the fuck is going on?

Now, back in my driveway, I stared at the bags on the front porch steps.

"Pick up the phone!" I yelled as I called Yana over and over again.

What is going on with her?

She's in town. Yet, she's ignoring my calls.

Angry, I got out of the car to take a look at the bags.

There were five bags and each were labeled:

Something Borrowed. Something Blue. Something Old. Something New. Something for My Sister.

In the Something Blue bag, there was a set of blue and diamond earrings. They were probably worth more than my house and car put together.

In the Something Borrowed bag, there was a check for $50,000. And the name, number, and lab to have the DNA testing done. Yana left a handwritten note in the bag that said the money would cover the results being switched for both Kojo and Emory. She said her contact was expecting my call.

Yes! This is exactly what I needed!

In the Something Old bag, there was a photo book full of old pictures of us. Some pictures I hadn't seen in years. Some of them, I don't even remember taking. I smiled at the pictures through the tears that had started to fall from my eyes. Yana has always been there for me, until recently, and I truly miss the girl smiling in the photos next to me.

I sniffled as I looked inside the Something New bag.

It was a chain, almost identical to the one that my brother Josiah had from my father, who had gotten it from his father and so on. It was obvious that she was giving this chain to me to pass down to my daughter, who could pass it down to her child after her.

"Aww!"

The chain was gold, with an Emerald pendant in the center of it, surrounded by smaller diamonds. It was one of the most beautiful things I've ever seen.

I would've appreciated each gift a lot more if Yana had given them to me herself.

Angrily, I opened the bag labeled "Something for My Sister."

Inside that bag, was a copy of Yana's will.

And in her will…she left me everything.

Millions of dollars.

Why would she leave me this?

Is something going to happen to her?

Is she dying or something?

Is that why she's been acting so strange?

I called her phone again.

She didn't pick up so I left her a message.

"Yana, I don't know what's going on with you, but if you aren't at the courthouse on my wedding day, or at my wedding reception...this friendship is over!"

~***~

"I'll fill in as your maid of honor, or whatever, if you need one. I know what it's like not to have any friends."

Shanice always shows up at the strangest times, in the strangest places.

Here I am, the day before I get married, trying to get a manicure and pedicure, and she shows up and sits in the chair beside me.

"I do have friends."

Actually, I don't.

Yana isn't here and despite my threat, she never called me back. And I'm no longer friends with Cece.

"I was coming to your wedding reception tomorrow anyway as Kojo's plus one. I can stand in at the courthouse if you need someone on your side."

"I didn't invite you to my wedding reception."

"Hint, the plus-one comment I made," Shanice giggled. "Kojo insists that I come with him. And since I wasn't invited, I thought I would come just to have a look."

I was going to tell her to stay as far away from my wedding reception as possible, but what the hell.

She'll probably find her way inside anyway.

"If you don't like Kojo, but knows he likes you..."

"Him liking me is his problem. Not mine."

Shanice closed her eyes as the man started to scrub her feet.

"My offer stands. Yana won't be there."

"What? How do you know she won't be there?"

Shanice didn't comment.

"What do you know? What did you do?"

"I didn't do anything," Shanice finally opened her eyes.

"Then why would you say that?"

Shanice looked me in the eyes. "Nova, your best-friend is gone."

"What do you mean gone?"

"I mean---just gone. You'll be lucky if you ever see her again."

"Why do you say shit like that?"

I was getting so frustrated that I was starting to yell.

"Your best friend has a secret."

"I know all her secrets."

"No. You don't."

"And you do?"

"I know this one," Shanice assured me. "And the last thing she wants is for it to ever come out. And to avoid that, she has to stay away from you."

"Why? Why does she have to stay away?"

Shanice shook her head. "Because she loves you. And because she loves you, eventually, she'll get tired of lying to you. And if she tells you…she knows she'll lose you."

"What are you talking about? You're not making any sense!"

"They're not my secrets to tell. I have enough of my own. Stop calling her. If you insist on keeping that door open, be ready for what's going to be revealed on the other side of it."

Shanice closed her eyes again.

What in the hell is she talking about?

And as much as I hate to admit it, what she's saying somehow makes sense.

There has to be something going on with Yana.

There has to be a reason she's acting this way.

Maybe she does have some kind of secret.

Shanice always seems to know something that she shouldn't, so, there's no doubt in my mind that somehow she knows what Yana is keeping from me.

Maybe she's right.

Maybe my best-friend is...

Gone.

"Shanice?" I mumbled.

Jacob's flight won't be in until an hour after we're scheduled to be at the courthouse to get married. And the reception doesn't start until a few hours after that.

"What?"

I exhaled. "Could you be there for me, at the courthouse tomorrow?"

Shanice opened her eyes. "I was gonna' be there whether you asked me to be anyway."

~***~

"Do you, Nova Revae Parks, take Emory Luis Marcelis to be your lawfully, wedded husband? To have and to hold, for richer and for poorer, through sickness and in heath, until death do you part?"

I took a deep breath.

Am I really about to get married?

I never thought this day would come, so, I never tried to imagine what it would look like. Even as a young girl, I never dreamt of the big fairytale wedding.

My dreams were more like nightmares.

And there's no room for fairytale weddings in nightmares.

But here I am, as pretty as can be, wearing an elegant white dress, that hugged a stomach that now sticks out past my feet.

I'm standing in front of a man that I have loved more than life itself. But also a man who betrayed me, hurt me and let me down. Before him, before this, I've never forgiven anyone who hurt me. I've never even wanted to. But Emory changed that. He changed me. He has changed everything.

"Nova?" Emory smiled, eagerly awaiting my response.

By saying yes, I'm saying yes to forever.

Yes, to whatever the results are with Christina's baby.

Yes, if I have to lie to him for the rest of my life about "our" child. And yes, if I never see my best-friend again.

I looked beside me.

Shanice stood there, in a tight rose gold colored dress and matching heels.

Yana was nowhere in sight.

No matter how many messages I sent her, and threats I made, she never texted or called me back. She isn't here for me on one of the most important days of my life.

I'll never forgive her for this.

I'll never look at her the same again.

"I do," I smiled. "I do."

Emory beamed.

As I said, Emory is one of the only people in my life who actually loves me. I know that. I feel that. And I'll do anything to make sure things stay that way.

All of two minutes later, Emory and I were pronounced husband and wife.

He kissed me, slowly, passionately, and told me he loved me in a whisper.

"I love you, too."

Shanice stood there, quietly, with a smile on her face. Emory's brother, Drew, hugged him as soon as he let go of me.

"Hopefully, you'll only have to do this once," Shanice laughed.

"Hopefully. I don't want to be like you."

"Touché."

After the signing of the paperwork, I faced Shanice.

I hesitated. "Thank you, Shanice. For being here. I don't really know who you are or why you won't go away but thank you."

She nodded. "If I say I'm going to do something…I do it. I always keep my word. Always."

What "word"?

Is she talking about to me?

Or keeping her word to someone else?

Shanice sashayed away from me, and Emory's brother Drew, with eyes full of lust, ran behind her.

"We're married," Emory grinned.

"We're married."

Emory made a few nasty comments, and we rushed home to have sex.

A few hours later, we made our way to the reception space.

"It's beautiful," I said in awe.

"And it's all for you, baby. It's all for you."

I frowned. "I wish Yana…"

"Uh, uh. Don't do that. She's not here, but she did help a lot with all of this. Her advice and suggestions are all over this place," Emory assured me. "This is your day. No one else has to be here but you and me."

"Okay, baby."

"Okay."

And with that, the announcer introduced us as husband and wife, and the place went wild.

There were people at the reception who I haven't seen in years. College professors who helped me along the way that I told Emory about. It's like he remembered every little detail about me, and if it involved someone else, in a positive way, he made sure they were there.

I spent the night talking to people, and letting people rub my belly. I laughed, I danced, and I ate all my favorite foods.

Later that evening, Shanice found me hiding in one of the back rooms of the building, absolutely exhausted.

"I just thought I would bring you your wedding gift," she reached me a card. There was an address on it.

"That's where Yana is staying. You're one of those people who needs closure. When you're ready for it, go get it. But I promise you, some things are better left alone. This…she…is one of those things."

I stared at the address. It was in the next city over.

"If you think it should be left alone, why did you give this to me?"

Shanice shrugged. "It's your gift. It was either this or kill Kojo for you. This option is less messy and requires less work."

"Kill Kojo for me? What? Why?"

"The baby you're carrying is Kojo's. And he will want to be a part of the child's life. This little fairytale that you have going on will soon be over because Emory won't forgive you. You may think he will. But he won't. Trust me. And Kojo will want to be a father to his child. And there's nothing you can do about it. Well, other than kill him, but you know what I'm saying."

I touched my stomach. "Kojo isn't the father of my baby. Why would you say that?"

"A friend, of a friend, of a friend, owed me a little favor. I got some of Kojo's DNA and what I needed from your doctor and cashed in on that favor. Your baby is Kojo's baby."

I started to breathe harder and harder.

"Like I said…this gift is the only one I can give you. I don't like Kojo in the way he likes me, but I do like that we're going to make a lot of money together. Our auto shop will have a bar in it. Isn't that neat? Anyway, you have a head's up…"

"I already have it handled," I breathed. "Kojo will never know this baby is his," I said disappointed.

Damn it!

I was really hoping she was Emory's daughter.

"Good. Well, unless she comes out looking just like him. Then, girlfriend, just have your shit together, and prepare for a divorce. I know a good lawyer if you need one."

Shanice turned to leave the room.

"Whatever the secret is that Yana is keeping from me…will I ever be able to forgive her?"

Shanice froze. "No. You won't." And with that, she was gone.

~***~

"Thank you. I wasn't trying to give you a hard time, I just need to know," Kojo opened the door to the clinic.

The referral from Yana was paid and full, and no matter what the real results are, Kojo's results from the DNA test will state that he isn't the father of my baby.

"I just want this to be over. I know you aren't the father, and you're about to find that out too."

I opened my car door.

"If I am…I'll be here."

Kojo wants this baby.

Bad. It's all over his face.

But too bad. I'll do anything to save my marriage. I'll do anything to have a family with Emory.

Sorry.

I drove away feeling like a pile of horse shit, which is a common feeling that I've been experiencing these days.

Somebody take me back to almost a year ago, when I was still a G. Please!

All of this emotional shit is for the birds!

It's too much for me to handle!

I needed a drink so bad, but I headed to the closest restaurant instead.

"Is this seat taken?"

Ox sat down.

He seemed different. He didn't have his usual glow. He just didn't seem like himself at all.

"How are you?"

Of course, Emory hadn't invited Ox to the wedding reception.

I'm not even sure if he's aware that I got married.

"I've had better days," Ox said. "The funeral for Valerie was yesterday, and you know how that goes."

"Valerie?"

"Yes. The woman I was dating. She's dead."

"Oh. Wow. I'm sorry to hear that."

"She had some kind of allergic reaction and couldn't breathe. It's crazy because she always read everything to make it was nut-free. She was very careful. And she always kept her EpiPen with her just in case. Yet, somehow, in her home, she died from an allergic reaction to a piece of pie that was still sitting on her kitchen table. She was dead for over a day before anyone found her. She and I were in a little argument, so, I thought she was just ignoring me. But she was dead."

"Where did the pie come from?"

"No one knows. And her phone was right there on the kitchen table. She didn't even attempt to call 9-1-1. Her EpiPen was in her purse on the kitchen counter."

"Maybe she wanted to die."

If looks could kill, Ox's look would've given me a fatal heart attack.

"Hell no! She was happy. She just got a big promotion at work. She was excited about the next chapter of her life. I was going to marry her."

"Well, maybe…"

I decided to keep my thoughts to myself.

Hell, maybe Shanice killed her.

I wouldn't be surprised.

And I wondered if the thought had crossed Ox's mind.

"I guess love ain't in the cards for me either."

"Don't say that. You'll find someone."

"I found you…but you didn't want me," Ox smirked.

"Welp, that didn't last long, huh?" I shook my head.

"Hell, you know me, I had to try."

"As always."

"Shit, maybe I should've given crazy ass Shanice another chance."

"She doesn't like to be called crazy," I sipped my drink.

Ox chuckled. "Oh, trust me, I know."

"What else do you know about her?" I inquired.

"What do you mean?"

"She just seems…I don't know."

"Shanice is a lot of things. She always has been. But one thing I can say is when she loves you…she *loves* you. And there's nothing you can do about it. And there's nothing that she won't do for someone she loves," Ox paused. "Hopefully, she's found someone that can give her the same love in return. That's all a person like Shanice needs. Just someone to truly love her the way she needs to be loved. I didn't know that back then. And I messed things up. If I had loved her more, better, I'm pretty sure she wouldn't have slept with my family." Ox stood up. "Oh, and don't think I didn't notice that band on your finger. I'm still not giving up on us, girl."

"Bye, Ox," I smiled at him. He walked away just as I got a text message on my cell phone.

Reading it, my heart dropped, and leaving more than enough money on the table to pay for my food, I got up and walked as fast as I could out of the restaurant.

I arrived at the hospital all of ten minutes later.

"She had me down as an emergency contact," Emory said, walking towards me in the waiting room. "I'm sure she probably has Rick down too, but…"

"What happened?"

"Christina was in a bad car accident. I don't know all the details, yet, but guess who was driving the car that hit her."

"Who?"

"Cece."

"Cece?"

She must've found out Christina lied about losing the baby and decided to take matters into her own hands.

If I wasn't pregnant, shoot, I might would've done the same thing!

"Is Christina or the baby…"

"The doctor said they are doing an emergency C-section to get the baby out. The baby is far enough along to be just fine. That's if the wreck didn't cause any harm to it."

"And Christina?"

"They don't know. They did say that she'll need surgery, immediately after getting the baby out."

"Are you okay?"

"I'm fine."

Emory has gone through something similar in the past. A wreck wasn't involved, but he lost both his fiancée and the baby, so, no matter what he says, I know he's far from being fine.

"You don't have to be here."

"And neither do you…maybe. But here we are."

We both took a seat.

"Cece hit Christina's car on purpose."

"Of course, she did."

"But Rick will find a way to get her out of this."

"Of course, he will," Emory said.

I was expecting a little more time to have to face this reality, but Cece hasn't left any of us a choice in the matter.

Almost an hour later, Emory stood as the nurse approach him.

"The baby is fine," the nurse said. "The mom is in surgery."

"Can we see the baby?" I asked.

Maybe we can try and see who the baby looks like, if it looks like anyone at all.

"We're getting him cleaned up now. We'll let you know when he's in the nursery."

"Him?" Emory questioned.

Christina told us she was having a girl.

"Yes. It's a boy."

A son.

Emory could have a son.

The nurse walked away. I could tell that Emory was afraid to look at me.

"Wow. It's a boy. This little boy could be yours."

Emory didn't respond.

I felt nervous.

Angry.

But I kept reminding myself of what I already had in progress. There's no doubt in my mind that Shanice was telling the truth. If she said she found out that my baby is Kojo's, then, I'm sure she meant it.

But I'm going to keep the truth from Kojo, forever.

And give another man the pleasure of raising and loving the child he put inside of me.

I want to feel bad about it, but I don't.

I deserve this.

Emory.

A family.

Happiness.

And, goddamn it! I'm going to have it!

By any means necessary!

Finally, the nurse came to walk us to the nursery. Emory held my hand the entire way.

I felt fear.

Anxiety.

This isn't how things were supposed to be.

Emory and I were supposed to be having a baby; together. And now, we're both having a baby with someone else.

Maybe.

The nurse said only Emory could go inside the nursery. I stood outside the window and waited to see which baby they would approach.

I held my breath as Emory looked down at the baby boy lying in front of him. I waited. And waited.

Finally, Emory looked at me.

His face was hard to read.

I couldn't tell if he was sad, happy, or confused.

He picked up the baby, and slowly walked towards the window.

Looking into my eyes, Emory held the baby up to the window for me to see him and...

~***~

"Nova?"

"Surprise, bitch!"

I didn't wait for Yana to invite me into the semi-mansion she was living in about an hour and a half away from home.

"So, what is this? Your new place?"

"No," she closed the door. "I'm just renting it for a little while."

I turned to face the woman who used to be my best-friend.

"What in the hell is your problem?"

The whole drive there, I thought about what I wanted to say to her. And after the weekend I've had, Yana was about to get a piece of my mind, and it isn't going to be pretty!

Christina's baby is Emory's.

And we don't need a blood test to know it.

The little boy has Emory's entire face...literally.

His eyes, his nose, lips and even his forehead.

He looks just like him.

And Emory, though he tried to hide his love for the baby in front of me, he's madly in love with his son already.

I'm furious!

Angry! Angry enough to kill somebody!

I didn't sign up for any of this shit!

But because of the decisions of Emory, Christina, Cece and Rick, this is now my life! I'm married to a man who has a baby with someone else!

Christina is going to survive, which means, her and her baby are going to be a part of our lives forever.

It would've been nice to have my best-friend to lean on during this time. But here we are!

"You don't show up for my wedding day! You don't call me on my birthday for the first time---ever!"

"I left you some great gifts!"

"Fuck those gifts, Yana!" I yelled at her. "I needed my friend! My sister. Yet, you've been running around the world like a crazy person and acting strange as hell for the past few months. What in the hell is going on?"

"I remembered where I saw Shanice."

"What?"

"I knew I recognized her," Yana took a seat on the black leather sofa. "She was in the same mental institution as Josiah for a while."

"What?"

"Josiah had an episode a while ago. He was going to go to prison behind it, but I paid the judge. I paid him to order Josiah to get a mental health evaluation. From the things you told me about your mom, I knew that something was there. He was too unpredictable, and at the time, I was in love with him and wanted to help him. He didn't deserve to be in prison. He needed help," Yana paused.

I knew about the trouble Josiah had been in, and he told me about the judge ordering him to get help.

"I was right. He's results showed bipolar disorder. It was uncontrolled, so, the judge ordered him to eight months in a mental institution. That's where he was. When you used to tell me you hadn't heard from him, I knew exactly where he was. And Shanice was there too. I only went to see him three times. And two of the times, I saw Shanice. I remember her because I thought about how she somewhat reminded me of you."

Josiah was in a mental hospital?

And I can't say I'm surprised by the news about Shanice. That's why she hates to be called crazy because she actually is.

"She didn't seem like the others though. It was almost as though she was there at her own free will. As though she didn't really belong. I can't explain it. She would just be sitting there, unbothered as though she was on vacation or something."

"Maybe she was there voluntarily."

"Maybe. But she was definitely there. The last time I went to see Josiah, he told me not to come back. I was already talking to Hanz. I flew in from Brazil just to visit him. Just to check on him. That day, Josiah told me that if he ever got better, he would come and find me, and if he didn't, to go on with my life. We weren't exclusive or anything, but I did love him. And I knew he loved me. He just couldn't be who I wanted him to be," Yana paused. "I left that day, knowing that we had to end things. It was the best thing to do for both of us. We had so many secrets between the two of us and being around each other just reminded us of the bad things we'd done."

"What secrets?"

Yana looked at me. "I never told you about Josiah and I because I was hoping I wouldn't have to. It started out as just a little fun and somehow, it became pain."

"What secrets?" I repeated, finally taking a seat.

"Nova, if I tell you…"

"What secrets?"

Yana exhaled. "Josiah killed your father and I helped him cover it up."

I swallowed the lump in my throat. "Daddy died in his sleep."

"I paid for that. It was the first time I really found out just how much money could buy. Your father actually died because Josiah smothered him with a pillow."

I shook my head.

"Yes. He did. He went by the house one night, drunk, and he wanted to talk about the things that happened to you guys when you were kids. Things that still bothered him. Things that he blamed your parents for. Your father was asleep when he got there. Josiah told me that he stood over him, hating him, and that he took a pillow…and he killed him. After he realized what he'd done, Josiah called me hysterical. I told him I would be there to help. And I did. I had to throw money all over the place to get Josiah off the hook, but I did it. For him and for you."

Josiah was a lot of things, but I never thought a killer was one of them. I guess I was wrong. I hated our parents too, but I never would've been able to hurt them.

"That was only the beginning…" Yana continued. "One night, we were talking about it, and just so happens, my parents called after not returning any of my calls for months. Josiah was with me. He saw how little and unimportant they made me feel. All they talked about was themselves and asked if I needed more money. I told them I was in love but they couldn't have cared any less. Once I hung up the phone, without really thinking about what I was saying, I said I wish they were dead. I told Josiah that I hated them and that I wish they would just go away…for good. And…" Yana took a deep breath. "Josiah said he would help me do it. And he did. He helped me kill my parents, Nova."

What!

I felt as though I was about to be sick, but Yana kept talking.

"I knew I couldn't be anywhere near them when they went missing, so, after we made a plan, I sent Josiah halfway across the world to where they were. As you know, I usually knew where they were, and just so happens this time they had a little bungalow by the beach out in Majorca. That's a Balearic Island in Spain. Nice, rich, and secluded." Yana looked off into the distance.

Here I was, thinking I was just a little off with my ways and way of thinking, yet, I've been surrounded by actual killers…for years!

"I told them that I was bringing my boyfriend to meet them. They were surprised that I actually wanted to come all the way across the world just to introduce him, but they were okay with it. I sent Josiah. He arrived and told them we took two different flights and that I gave him everything he needed to find them. They called me, I confirmed Josiah's story and told them my flight was delayed, but that I was on my way. Long story short, they sat around drinking with Josiah. Once they were too drunk to move, Josiah strangled them both. He called me from my father's cell phone once it was done. And for three days, he continued to post on their social media like they were still alive. And then late night, on the third night, Josiah tied them down with heavy rocks and put them in the water."

"Oh, my God!"

Yana didn't react to my comment. "I waited for three months to report them missing. It wasn't hard to prove to the police that not hearing from them for five, or six months at a time was normal. I knew by then their bodies would be long gone. Eaten by the sharks mama had mentioned or rotting away at the bottom of the ocean. Josiah was long gone from the scene. I made sure that he cleaned everything he touched before he left. And if someone did spot him going into my parents place, they never came forward. Of course, I had to pretend to be the concerned daughter and perform the searches. I went to make sure I could oversee the process, just in case something came up about Josiah. It never did. There didn't appear to be any foul play. And the people there barely even cared about what was going on. My parents were never found, and Josiah had gotten away with murder...again."

"Why would you let him do something like that?"

"Josiah had no real remorse when he killed your father. He was only worried about going to jail, but he wasn't sorry for what he did. I didn't ask him to do it. He wanted to do it. But then, I guess the guilt of it all finally caught up to him. He started getting into trouble again, having his mood swings, flipping out on me to the point that I was starting to become afraid of him. And then, that assault, and attempted murder charge he was about to face for nearly beating a man half to death at the bar, I stepped in and saved him. Just like he'd saved me," Yana exhaled. "While he was in the mental hospital, he started going to therapy. Josiah said the pain and the secrets were just too much for him. He said he wasn't sure if he could ever get over it. And with his newfound mental illness, I knew that us not being together was best for the both of us. So, I went away. I fell in love with Hanz. I got married. And then, here comes Josiah saying that he was ready for us to be together again. At the time, I didn't know Hanz was playing me for my money. I thought he truly loved me, because I truly loved him. He made me feel so special. He really pretended to love me. And yes, my love for him, at the time, outweighed what I felt for Josiah. I loved Josiah, but I just didn't think we needed to be anything more, anymore. He didn't see it that way."

"That's why the two of you were arguing the day I saw you?"

"Yes. He said he deserved another chance, after what he did for me. I had to remind him that I'd done something for him too. He didn't care about that. He didn't care that I'd helped him cover up killing your father or that I'd kept him out of prison. All Josiah cared about was us. He wanted me to get a divorce and be with him. He even wanted me to move to California with him and start fresh."

The baby kicked, causing me to change the way I was sitting.

"The day he was supposed to leave…" Yana looked at me. "I pulled up to him leaving the note on my front porch. Again, he asked me to be with him. He asked me to get a divorce. Hanz was inside the house, but because Josiah was starting to get loud, I asked him to come inside. Hanz barely spoke or understood English anyway, so, I tried to have a peacefully conversation with Josiah. He just wouldn't listen. He kept telling me that he was better. And that he loved me. And that he would never hurt me. I believed him. It was just too late. Oh, if I could turn back the hands of time," Yana mumbled.

"So, what happened after that?" I questioned. "Are you saying that Josiah killed himself because he couldn't have you?"

"No," Yana shook her head. "I'm saying…I'm saying…" Yana paused.

Impatiently, I waited for her to finish her sentence.

"Nova, I'm saying…I'm saying that I killed Josiah, because I didn't have a choice."

My heart skipped a beat.

I couldn't have heard her correctly.

Yana must've meant something else.

"Wait. Did you just say…"

"I killed Josiah. Nova, I killed your brother."

I opened my mouth, but nothing came out of it. I could literally hear my heart breaking.

"Josiah said that he would tell. He would tell that it was my idea to kill my parents and that he helped me. He said he would tell everything."

I could hear Yana speaking through my pain and rage.

"He even bragged about being sick and said that he didn't care if he got into trouble. He knew he would most likely just spend the rest of his life in some mental hospital. But me...I would go to prison. And I..." Yana paused, but she forced herself to keep going. "Josiah literally tried to make me be with him in order to keep my secret. We got into a huge argument. I tried to convince him of an alternative. Hell, I even tried to bribe him. I told him I would give him whatever he wanted if he would just leave me alone. Josiah didn't want anything...except for me. He kept saying he loved me and that he only did what he did for me, because he loved me. And if he couldn't have me, then it was all for nothing. I could see it in his eyes, Nova. He was going to tell. He meant it. He was going to confess to killing my folks for me," Yana started to cry. "Hanz walked into the living room that day. Josiah started to yell at him, and even tried to fight him, but Hanz took the first swing. He knocked Josiah out cold," Yana reminisced. "And with Josiah knocked out, on the floor, quiet, I tried to pull my thoughts together. I started to panic. Scream. Cry. And Hanz asked me what was wrong. I wasn't sure of what he would think of me, but I told him the truth. I told him what Josiah and I did to my parents. Surprisingly, Hanz simply told me what I already knew. He told me what had to be done. Josiah had to die. Unless I wanted to spend the rest of my life behind bars. Or I could just be with Josiah, full of resentment, just for him to keep our secret. Neither were options that I wanted to do. So, I did what I thought I had to do. I didn't know how I wanted to do it. I just knew it had to be done. I remembered Josiah's explanation of how he smothered your father. He said it didn't last long. So, I took a pillow off the couch. Hanz offered to do it, but it was my mess to clean up. And with Hanz holding Josiah down, just in case he woke up, I took the pillow and…"

I started to cry. "Are you really telling me that you killed…that you killed…" I couldn't finish my sentence.

"I didn't have a choice, Nova. I just didn't have a choice. Josiah didn't struggle. He just laid there, unaware of what I was doing to him. I cried so hard and so loud, but I pressed that pillow down over his face for what felt like forever. Hanz actually had to bring me back to reality and tell me to stop after he checked his pulse. Josiah was dead. I killed him. I killed the only man that ever truly loved me, as it turns out," Yana and I both cried loudly, but she kept talking.

"Hanz and I put Josiah's body inside my trunk, and we drove all the way to Houston. We got there during the wee hours of the morning. I still had my key to his condo, so, we took Josiah inside and set the scene. I crushed up pills in his mouth. Poured scotch down his throat. Hanz set up the camera. I wanted to know the exact moment someone found him, so I could call in the same favor I did with your father's death. I needed the cause of death to be ruled a suicide. And it was. Leaving Josiah there, dead, was the hardest thing I've ever had to do. Nova, it broke something inside of me. I knew I would never be the same. And I haven't been. I didn't want to be here. I didn't want to live. I didn't want to be around you, so, that I didn't have to be reminded of Josiah. Whether I was in Rome, Brazil, Africa, wherever, as long as I was away from you, I felt like I didn't have to face what I'd done. And having Hanz with me, made it easier. He held me through the nights that I was crying. He told me everything was going to be okay. And once I finally started to believe that things would get better, Hanz used what he knew against me. He told me that his girl-friend was about to have their child, and that I was just a long con. All those trips home for his sick mother was actually to check on his girl-friend. I always wondered why he wouldn't let me go to the hospital with him. It was never about his mother. Hell, the woman he'd told me was his mother, isn't his real mother at all. She was in on it too. And she's still alive. It was all a lie. I found out that Hanz isn't his real name and that all he wanted was my money. He knew two of my secrets, and he charged me one million dollars for each of them. He said he would never bother me again. He was an accessory to Josiah's murder, but being that I didn't even know his real name...I just paid him to go away. I got played for a fool. Had I known that..."

"Had you known what, huh? Had you known you were Hanz's fool, you wouldn't have killed my brother? Is that what you're going to say, Yana? Is that what you're going to say?" I stood up so fast that it made me dizzy.

"Yes," she admitted. "I would've just went with Josiah. At least for the time being. At least I knew he loved me."

Yana stood up.

"Nova, I love you. And I know you'll never forgive me. And I don't expect you to. But you wanted the truth, and now you have it. Now, I'm free."

"Free? Bitch what makes you think you're going to be free?"

"Because you aren't going to turn me into the police. But I also know that you aren't just going to let this go."

"You're goddamn right! You killed my brother! I'll never just let this go! I swear to God, if I wasn't pregnant, I would kill you, right here, right now!" I yelled at her. "You took my baby from me! Josiah was one of my babies! And you took him from me," I sobbed. "No. You're going to pay for what you've done. I promise you. You're going to pay!" I yelled as I wobbled towards the front door. "The way I see it…one of us has to die---and it ain't going to be me!" I spat at Yana just as I walked onto the porch.

"I know," she stood in front of the door. "I know you'll want to get even. I know that, because I know you," Yana started to cry again. "I know you hate me. And I know you'll never forgive me. So, I guess this is goodbye, my sister. My friend. Catch me if you can."

And with that, Yana closed the door in my face.

I started to cry as I kicked the front door over and over again. I kicked as hard as I could, and for as long as I could, until my stomach started to hurt.

I felt like I was about to explode!

I felt like I was in shock.

The things that Yana revealed to me…

I just can't believe it.

She killed Josiah?

I knew he didn't kill himself! I knew it!

Josiah killed our father.

And Yana's parents, with her help and instruction.

Oh, God!

I wish she hadn't told me! I wish I hadn't come here!

Shanice told me I wouldn't be able to forgive Yana if I went looking for answers.

Does that mean that she knows Yana killed Josiah?

Then why didn't she tell me?

For the first time, I wish I had Shanice's number.

And she was right.

I will never forgive Yana.

Never!

I was bawling, uncontrollably, as I got into my car.

I glanced up at the big house to see Yana looking out of an upstairs window.

My sister.

My brother's killer.

And I loved her.

I still love her.

But I want her dead!

I want Yana to die!

And I want her to die right now!

Speeding out of the driveway, I knew that I would never, ever, see Yana again.

And I don't want to.

Unless she's dead; wearing her expensive clothes, in one of her good wigs, in a casket, being loaded six-feet into the ground.

Goddamn you, Yana! Goddamn you!

******

CHAPTER TEN

"I told you. But now you have the proof."

Kojo asked to meet up to discuss the results of the DNA test.

"I just had to be sure."

I didn't comment.

The results are a lie; just like almost everything else in my life. Yana's contact at the laboratory told me the real test results when I went to pick up the papers.

Kojo is the father of my daughter; just like Shanice said he was.

"Well, thanks," Kojo said. "The good thing out of this is that it reminds me of what I want. A family. Something Shanice can't give me."

"You do know she doesn't want to be with you, right?"

"That's what her mouth says," Kojo chuckled. "But that's fine by me. I'm looking for someone to settle down with, maybe have a kid or two. That's what I've been missing."

"I'll be praying for that unlucky lady's vagina," I shivered, remembering how painful sex with Kojo was.

Kojo laughed. And then, he shook the papers in my direction before turning to walk away.

I feel worse than I thought I would about lying to him.

And I know it's because of Yana and all the lies that she's told me over these last few years, when I thought she was one of the only people in the world that I could trust.

I went back by the rental property.

Yana is gone.

"Catch me if you can," she'd said.

She'll never come back here.

Who knows where she'll end up.

I'll never see her again.

I'll never get my revenge.

She was right. Despite everything she said, and everything she's done, I have no intention on turning her into the police.

It won't bring Josiah back.

But Yana doesn't deserve to live the good-life after what she did.

I walked out of the ice cream shop.

"What is he doing with her?" I questioned aloud seeing Emory holding the door for Christina and their son, at a clothing store across the street.

He told me he was going to the shop.

Emory was smiling. They looked like a family.

No!

He's *my* family…not hers!

I called Emory's cell phone.

When he didn't answer, I wobbled across the street with my ice cream cone still in my hand.

Christina noticed me as soon I entered the store.

She had a guilty look on her face.

"Hey, baby," Emory rubbed my stomach once I approached him.

"You told me you were going to the shop."

"I was. And then, Christina called and asked if I wanted to go shopping with her and E.J."

Of course, Christina named her son after Emory.

"Don't think for a minute that you're going to take him from me," I snarled. "He's my husband! He's my family!"

"Whoa! Baby, wait. Chill. No one is going to take me from you," Emory assured me. "I'm all yours, okay? Trust me," Emory kissed my lips. "You've been acting all angry these past few days. Is everything okay?"

"I'm fine."

I haven't told Emory about Yana and all her secrets, and I don't think I ever will.

Christina didn't say a word.

And the smile that she'd been wearing was gone.

I concluded that I did what I had to do about my baby.

I've lost Josiah.

I've lost Yana.

Losing Emory just isn't an option.

So, poor Kojo will just have to go have a baby with someone else.

~***~

"Did you know?"

Shanice looked at me confused.

"You knew Yana killed my brother, didn't you?"

Shanice shrugged. "I figured as much. Either she did it or she had someone else to do it."

The things Yana told me are always on my mind.

I can barely sleep. And I'm angry with myself. Because no matter how mad I am at her and no matter how much I want her to pay for what she did to Josiah, somehow, I still care about her.

And I hate it!

This damn baby is making me a sucker!

"Why didn't you tell me?"

"I didn't know I was supposed to."

"A person with a heart would've."

Shanice chuckled.

"You were in the mental hospital with Josiah. That's where Yana recognized you from."

"Yep," surprisingly, Shanice admitted.

"Did you know Josiah?"

"Yep."

Interesting.

So, this whole time, Shanice knew my brother.

"And?"

Shanice looked at me. "And I loved him."

Did she just say she loved Josiah?

"We loved each other as much as we could, being that both of us were still in love with other people. Ox and Yana."

A car passed by a little too close to me.

I'd spotted Shanice sitting across the street from my house and approached her car.

"Can we take this conversation to my porch?"

"Oh, you're inviting me to the porch? Before long, we'll be best friends. Since that position in your life now has a vacancy." Shanice laughed as she got out of her car.

I didn't see anything funny.

Once we were seated on the front porch, I waited for her to speak.

"After the rape, embarrassment, not being believed by my parents, being paid off to keep quiet, having an abortion and not being able to ever have kids, naturally, I started to have some issues. I felt unloved in every way. I suffered from manic depression, suicidal thoughts, all of that. I even tried once. To kill myself. That was a complete disaster. Anyway, after talking to my doctor, and therapists, I tried a few different prescriptions before finally realizing that I needed a little extra help. So, some months, I would disappear for a while, and check myself into mental facilities in different cities. I was always self-admitted, but with my history, and my money, I guess they trusted my judgment. Almost two years ago, I ended up in Texas for a while. After a while, I started to feel depressed. I checked into the hospital. And I met Josiah..."

Mid-sentence, Shanice started to hum.

"Shanice?"

"Huh? Oh, yeah. Like I said. Josiah and I became close. And I do mean close. Emotionally. Mentally. And, if you haven't guessed it by now, physically. Yes, we found a way to have a little sex a few times while in the hospital. I paid a lot of money for "special" treatment. Anyway, Josiah told me what he did. He told me he killed your father and Yana's parents for her. He told me everything. We trusted each other. I told him some of my deepest, darkest secrets too. We knew everything about each other, and still saw each other as beautiful. Josiah is the one who convinced me to come back and try to get Ox back, since I was clearly still in love with him. And I helped him come to terms with his illness. I helped him accept it. I told him that it wasn't the end of the world. I assured him that if he took his medication, he could live a happy, normal life."

"Let me guess…you often miss a pill or two," I said.

"Mind your business," Shanice smirked. "Anyway, Josiah talked about you and Jacob all the time. He loved you more than anything in this world. He said you always protected him. Always looked out for him. We discovered through conversation that you worked for my husband. It's a small world. At the time, Josiah had no plans on coming to Mississippi. But he did tell me to get to know you when I got here. He said you were a good person and he thought we could be good friends. He told me that you had a dark side, just like me. He said I would like that about you."

I shook my head.

Shanice and Josiah knew each other this whole time.

They loved each other.

And they had sex.

I'm speechless!

"I left the hospital a little while before he did. But I told him how to find me if he ever needed me when he got out. And he did. Josiah contacted me while he was here. He told me that Yana had gotten married and that he couldn't accept it. He couldn't accept her being with someone else. Hell, I understood what he was feeling since it was clear to me that Ox was in love with you. The feeling of rejection can be overwhelming for someone like me and for someone like Josiah. The last time I saw Josiah, he gave me the note that I left on your porch. He told me that he was going to give Yana an ultimatum and that he wasn't sure how it would all play out. He talked about how powerful Yana felt once she inherited all of her parent's money. Josiah figured there was a possibility he might end up dead and he wanted you to know that Yana had something to do with it if he did. He was right. And he also made me make him a promise."

"What promise?"

"He made me promise to look out for you, if something happened to him. He asked me to be your friend because he knew once everything came out, about him and Yana, you would need one. He made me promise to help you when or if I could. And like I said, I loved him. So, I agreed. And there's nothing I won't do for someone I love," Shanice stared into the distance.

"So, all this time, you've been bothering me and hanging around because you promised Josiah to be there for me?"

"I keep my promises. I always keep my word. You and I had a conflict of interest, Ox. So, my evil side would take over, sometimes, but I always remembered my promise to Josiah. In my way, most of the time, I was just trying to help you. Most of the time."

Well, I didn't see this coming!

Quietly, Shanice and I stared at Rick and Cece as they walked their dog down the street.

Cece told the police that she was blinded by the sun momentarily and that's how she ended up slamming into Christina's car.

It was a lie.

Of course.

Cece tried to kill Christina, or at least she tried to kill the baby. But she's going to get away with it. And now, since the baby is Emory's and not Rick's, she never has to worry about Christina again.

But I do.

"Remember how you said for a wedding gift you thought about killing Kojo for me?"

Shanice didn't respond.

"Do you have a package for killing lying, murdering ex-best-friends? What about unwanted, sneaky baby mamas? I'm asking for a friend…"

~***~

"She said your baby is Kojo's. And to tell you to stop looking for her. She said don't bother her and she won't bother you. I don't know what the fuck that means, but what does she mean by your baby is Kojo's?"

It's been over two months since I last saw or spoke to Yana.

Shanice and I have been trying to figure out where she might be. Shanice never said she was going to kill her for me, but she has been entertaining me by trying to help me find her. We must've gotten close.

Yana called Emory and told him that my baby isn't his. She told him that I'm carrying Kojo's baby and to leave her the hell alone.

"She's your best-friend, so, whatever the fuck is going on, I know she knows!" Emory yelled. "Is the baby Kojo's baby? My friend, Kojo?" Emory's voice broke. "That night you were over there, is that what the two of you were talking about? Huh? Were y'all fucking?" Emory screamed.

I'm going to kill Yana!

I went to get my copy of the fake DNA test results.

I'm going to have to admit to having sex with Kojo, thanks to Yana, but I can attempt to prove her wrong and show Emory the altered results.

Emory followed me.

"The baby isn't Kojo's. It's yours, like I said."

I reached Emory the papers.

Speedily, he read them.

"But it could've been? The baby could've been Kojo's. You fucked my friend, Nova?"

"Two for two. You fucked two women. I fucked two men, too."

"But my goddamn friend!" Emory yelled. "And y'all hid it from me? He was working at my shop, smiling in my goddamn face and..." Emory hissed. "You disgust me!" Emory threw down the papers and stormed out the front door.

My stomach started to hurt, so I took a seat.

I can only assume that Emory is headed to Kojo's house for answers...or for blood.

I'm surprised that Yana played this card.

She didn't tell Emory about the fake DNA results, so, she purposely left room for me to savage my relationship.

She just wanted to make her point.

Our friendship is over.

And to leave her the fuck alone!

I finally had Shanice's phone number, so I texted her.

I told her that I was done looking for Yana.

I don't care where she is anymore.

Yana is gone.

And after telling Emory the one thing I never wanted him to know, she can stay gone.

Forever.

Yana is dead to me.

I called Emory for hours, but he never answered his cell phone. The sun went down, and I figured he wasn't coming home, so, I showered and just as I got into bed, my phone started to ring.

"You have a collect call from…"

"Me." Emory said.

"An inmate in the Marshall County jail. Press …"

"Hello? Emory?"

"Come get me," is all he said, and disconnected the call.

After calling the jail to get more information, it took a while for me to find a bondsman, but I found one and made my way to the jail.

Just as I headed up the steps, Kojo and Shanice came out of the jail.

Kojo's face looked horrible.

He and Emory must've gotten into a fight.

"I'm sorry, Kojo. My best-friend told him about us. Not me. Well, she used to be my best friend," I corrected myself. "I told him the baby wasn't yours. I'm sorry."

Kojo didn't say anything.

I looked at Shanice.

"And what in the hell are you doing here?"

She shrugged. "He called me to come get him out. I wasn't doing anything, so, here I am."

Kojo remained quiet.

"I'm sorry, Kojo."

I put him in this mess. Hell, I practically forced him to fuck me in the first place.

I walked away from them, rushing to set Emory free.

It took almost an hour, but finally, Emory headed towards me.

His left eye was swollen shut.

"Baby, what happened?"

"Don't touch me," he blocked my hand from touching his face.

"Emory?" I walked as fast as I could behind him. "Emory? Are you going to stay mad at me forever? You're the reason it happened in the first place."

Emory stopped walking and turned around to face me. He growled and balled up his fist.

"I would've never cheated on you if you hadn't cheated on me. But I forgave you. I married you. You have a baby by someone else. Or did you forget that? A son by the woman you cheated on me with. A son that I have to look at for the rest of my life. Your first son. Your Junior. Something a son that we may or may not have in the future could never be. But I forgave you, and I stayed even after the baby turned out to be yours. I have to look at you with that child and know that he's here to stay. All because you cheated on me. All because I wasn't enough!"

Emory's face softened.

"So, you know what, fuck you! You wanna' be mad? Fine! Stay mad! I don't care! You started this war, and yes, your friend was collateral damage! But fuck how you feel! I have to feel like shit every, single day!"

I stormed down the steps. At some point, my ankle twisted and I fell.

"Nova!"

"Is my baby going to be okay?" I asked listening to the sound of her heartbeat.

After falling down the steps, Emory got me to the hospital as fast as he could.

The baby moved around on the monitor as though she didn't have a care in the world.

"Yes. She's fine," the doctor said. wiping the gel off my belly.

"Oowww!" I said just as he'd said the words.

"What? What is it?" Emory asked.

The doctor ordered a nurse into the room as he put on gloves.

"I thought you said she was fine?" I questioned.

Hurriedly, the doctor did a pelvic exam.

"Doctor?"

"Well, she's still fine. But a few weeks early…here she comes! We're having a baby tonight! Well, if not tonight, maybe tomorrow!"

I looked at Emory.

"What? I'm not ready!"

"You better get ready, because she sure is!"

The doctor gave the nurse instructions, and they both left the room.

"This is my fault," Emory said. "If I hadn't gotten into a fight with Kojo, and arguing with you at the jail, you would've been at home in bed…"

"Emory, it's no one's fault, okay? But we're about to have this baby, whether we're ready or not. I don't want to bring her in this world with us a mess."

"I'm sorry. You're right. We will be fine, baby. I'm sorry," Emory said. "I'm sorry. I didn't think about what you have to deal with. And how much you've forgiven me."

"I'm sorry for having sex with Kojo. And Ox. I wanted to hurt you, because you hurt me. I know it's bad to say, but you really hurt me, and I just wanted you to feel the same pain. I'm sorry."

Emory exhaled loudly. "Okay. Let's stop talking about that. We're having a baby."

I forced myself to smile. "Yes. We're having a baby."

~***~

Thank God, she looks like me!

Emerald Skye is perfect.

Yes. I changed her middle name. I refused to name her after Yana, though these days, I'm not as angry anymore.

All I want is to live for as long as I can, making memories with the most beautiful little girl in the world.

Nothing else matters anymore.

I no longer want to know where Yana is.

I don't care.

What's done, is done.

There doesn't need to be any more drama, death or pain. Besides, I'm no better than Yana is, in a way.

I mean sure, I've never killed anyone.

But hurt is hurt.

And pain is still pain.

And I've caused my share of pain throughout the years. I guess karma finally had her way with me.

And now…we're even.

Would you like to hold her?" I asked Shanice.

She nodded her head.

Surprisingly, since I've had the baby, she hasn't been around much. I found it amazing that she'd kept her promise to Josiah after he died. Although she was a pain in my ass, and not to mention that she pulled a gun out on me;

but if it wasn't for her ruining my abortion appointments, I wouldn't have my beautiful, precious baby girl.

Shanice held my daughter in her arms, for the first time.

"This may seem like a crazy question…but…would you like to be her godmother?"

Hell, she's been around, watching over me the entire pregnancy. And I have a strange feeling that she doesn't plan on going anywhere, anytime soon.

Shanice swayed back and forth, smiling at Emerald.

Finally, she looked at me. "No," she said.

"No? Well, I'm surprised."

Shanice grinned as she laid the baby in the basinet.

"No. I don't want to be her godmother because…I want to be her mother."

Before I could say a word, Shanice reached for the statue on the table, and with one blow to the head, suddenly…

~***~

SHANICE SPEAKS…

Love can be a strange, crazy, and sometimes scary thing. But when you get a second chance at it…take it!

Honey, sometimes you gotta' do what you gotta' do!

Even if it's a felony.

"Ox, hold Emma for a minute."

Ox dried himself off, before grabbing the baby and kissing her face.

"Hi, *Daddy's* baby."

Yes.

I stole Nova's baby.

And now, Ox and I are raising her as our own.

Okay, so, no, this wasn't the plan.

Not at first. It just sort of happened.

I was just watching after Nova because of my promise to Josiah. I loved him almost as much as I love Ox.

That part was the truth.

But things changed one night when I ran into Ox at a bar. I saw an opening for a second chance, and I took it.

It was two or three months before Nova had her baby.

Ox looked horrible and sad.

He was mourning the death of his little girl-friend; whom I killed.

Yep. It was me.

Ox doesn't know that though.

Ox's girl-friend had no idea who I really was when she invited me into her house that day. I'd told her I was new to the neighborhood and that I was making my rounds and baking pies to give out as a friendly gesture.

She asked me if there were nuts in the pie. I lied and said no. After following her to a doctor's appointment one day, I found out about her little nut allergy and made the pie especially for her. I watched her take bite after bite, and then I held her phone and her purse away from her once she started to panic because she couldn't breathe.

She had to die.

Ox was going to ask her to marry him.

I'd followed him to the jewelry store days before I killed her. I wasn't ready for him to have a new wife.

So, I did what I had to do.

Anyway, the night Ox and I ran into each other at the bar, instead of being mean to me, Ox actually asked to buy me a drink.

For the first time, in years, we were civilized with each other. We talked like adults. We talked about the past and about love. We talked about second chances.

And Ox talked about Nova.

He talked about how he'd chased her for years, fell in love with her, and how she used him just to get back at Emory. It bothered him that she had sex with him, knowing how he felt about her, and then dropped him like a bad habit once she and Emory were back on good terms.

Ox was jealous of Emory.

I knew Ox loved Nova, but that night, I realized just how much. He said he would've given her the world.

So, I asked him what if he could have the world with me instead. I told him that I was still in love with him and if he was that angry at Nova, let's do something about it.

Let's show her what getting even is truly all about.

I told Ox that I was going to take Nova's baby and I asked him to run away with me. Start our own little family. Fall in love with me, again, on a tropical island underneath the sun.

Ox called me crazy…at first.

But the more I talked, the more he listened.

Ox knows how much I loved him. He knows that no one will ever love him more than I do. He said it. He was sure of it. And he said maybe it was time to give us another chance.

I told Ox about the island where Josiah killed Yana's parents. I told him we could hide out here for years, or forever if we wanted to and raise the baby.

Between the two of us, there's plenty of money, and Ox could still come back to the States because I would make sure that no one ever knew he was involved.

Ox and I had sex that night.

Well, actually, I think we made love.

He took his time with me, stared deep into my eyes, knowing that I had some issues, but in that moment, he saw past them all.

And to my surprise, the next morning, Ox told me if I could pull it off…he was in.

He would run away with me and Nova's baby.

We would have a chance at a family.

So, right under Nova's nose, I started to prepare.

With help from Ox, and a few of my resources, I had things in place, and ready to go a whole two weeks before Nova fell and accidentally put herself into labor.

Everything was ready.

I just had to wait on the right time, the right moment, to set everything in motion.

Nova asked me to come over a few times to see the baby before I finally agreed to come by.

I was waiting on the right day.

The right opportunity.

I waited for weeks for everything to line up just right. And one day, Nova told me that Emory had to run to one of his other shops in another city for the day.

That was the day.

It was perfect.

It was enough time for me to do what I needed to do.

Holding the baby that day, I didn't try to talk myself out of it at all. Taking the baby was my only chance at love and happiness with Ox again.

I had to take that chance.

So, I hit Nova over the head with a statue from the coffee table.

With her knocked out, I got to work.

After dragging Nova to her bedroom, I handcuffed her to the bed. That way, even if she woke up, she wouldn't be able to get to a phone, and it would probably be hours before Emory came home. I placed a sock in her mouth and then I locked the bedroom door before shutting it behind me.

To keep Emory from worrying, pretending to be Nova, I texted him from Nova's phone and told him that she and the baby were taking a nap. Emory replied that he would be home no later than eight. I told him not to rush and to take his time.

It was only one o'clock in the afternoon.

That left me more time than I'd expected.

With the baby asleep in a blanket, I placed her inside my oversized purse that I'd worn on purpose. And then, I walked outside as though nothing was wrong, locking the front door behind me.

Cece was walking her dog that day.

I smiled at her as I got into my car. She turned her nose up at me, just as I drove away.

Without hesitating, and because I was already prepared, I drove to the building that Kojo had purchased for his new shop. Behind it, I'd purchased a used car that was just sitting there waiting for me. I knew Kojo wouldn't be at the building because he was out of town…with Christina.

Kojo was pissed about Emory attacking him.

Giving Kojo something to keep him entertained, I encouraged him to get back at Emory by fooling around with Christina. I already knew that Nova's baby was really his, but I figured he could go play step-daddy with Emory's son, because this baby, *his* baby, was going with me!

There was a thirty-day tag on the used car, and a car seat for the baby inside.

I switched cars, and then I headed towards the highway. Two and a half hours later, I made it to Alabama from Mississippi, just as the baby woke up and started to cry.

There, I'd prepared a small storage.

I changed my clothes, darkened my face and hands with makeup, put on a wig and glasses, stuffed my bra, fed the baby, picked up the fake ID and passports I'd purchased, and then I made my way to the airport.

I still had plenty of time.

At that point, if Nova was awake, she was gagged and handcuffed to the bed. There was nothing she could do and there was still four to five hours before Emory would get home.

I made it to the airport twenty minutes before our plane was scheduled to take off. No one was looking for me or the baby, yet, so, everything went smoothly.

Our first stop was Freeport, Bahamas.

Things were already set in place for us to hide out there for two or three weeks. They would be looking for me soon, so, I felt hiding out for a few weeks, versus trying to make it to Spain, all in the same day, was the safer option.

Me and baby Emerald, at the time, landed in the Bahamas just a little after seven.

I had to get to where I was going and stay put because things were about to get interesting.

And they did.

Every day, I followed the story online.

Nova and Emory begged me to bring their baby back. Nova blamed herself. She said she knew that she shouldn't have trusted me and that she basically put her child in harm's way.

That's not true.

I would never hurt the baby. And honestly, I wouldn't hurt Nova either; at least, not physically. Not unless I have to.

Cece did interviews saying she saw me leave the house that day, but that she didn't see me with the baby.

That alone sparked a ton of questions.

Ox got on T.V. and told the world I was crazy and that he's not surprised by what I did. He told them that I wanted a baby so bad, that he was surprised that I didn't do something like this sooner.

I wasn't angry at him for saying those things.

He had to. I told him to. I didn't want anyone to think that he was involved in any way.

Even my parents and my sister got on T.V. and begged me to return the baby. I barely recognized them. I hadn't seen them in years.

Fuck them!

No matter what was said about me, no matter how much of my history was exposed, I stayed put.

Me and baby Emerald; who I'd started to call Emma, were just fine. We had everything we needed in the little condo that Ox had gotten ready for us a week before, while in the Bahamas on business. He paid for everything in cash, and he used Josiah's name after I'd gotten Ox's photo added to a copy of Josiah's license.

Josiah is dead.

I knew no one would be looking for him.

Using his name was perfect.

After three weeks, things started to calm down.

No one knew of my whereabouts and I knew it was time for us to go to our next and final destination.

I was waiting on the signal from Ox to know if it was safe. And I was waiting on him to let me know if it was time to catch the private jet that he was supposed to be sending my way.

I knew I couldn't contact him, so I waited, and I waited. Finally, a whole additional month later, the signal came.

By then, I was so in love with the baby that I didn't care if I had to spend the rest of my life locked away inside the tiny condo. I was just happy to finally have a baby in my arms.

Nevertheless, the time came for me to put baby Emerald in my purse again. I prepared my disguise. A cab waited outside that night to take me to catch the private plane.

I made sure to get the baby nice and full so that she would sleep comfortably in my bag, making as little noise as possible.

I remember feeling anxious once the jet was in my sight. And honestly, I had a few negative thoughts.

What if Ox was setting me up?

What if he changed his mind?

What if I was about to be arrested?

I wasn't sure what to expect, but I got out of that cab and walked towards the plane with baby Emma.

Needless to say...

Everything went smoothly.

I got on the jet and the pilot flew me to Spain.

That was six months ago.

I've been on this beautiful island for six months, and I've never been happier.

Ox stayed in the states for months while I made a home for us in Majorca.

And guess who else was on the island; the same island where she'd sent Josiah to kill her parents.

Yep, Ms. Yana.

I guess she decided to come hide out, in Majorca too, as far away from Nova as possible.

I saw her on the beach one day.

I stayed out of sight. I had the baby, so there wasn't much I could do. But once Ox finally came for a visit, finally, I kept my eyes open for almost a week, hoping to spot her again.

Finally, I did.

One evening, I followed Yana.

And while she was relaxing in the back of her bungalow, in her hot tub underneath the stars...

I pushed her head underneath the water.

I drowned Yana that night.

Since Nova told me that Yana left everything to her in her will, I figured it was the least I could do.

Nova can't have her baby back; but now she has millions, and she can thank me for that.

Killing Yana was for the both of us.

She deserved to die after what she'd done to *my* Josiah!

Yana was number five.

She was the fifth person that I've killed and gotten away with it.

The first time, I killed someone was on accident.

Sort of.

I'd gone to some crazy, wild party in my early twenties. I wasn't supposed to be there. I wasn't even invited. I just happened to come across the beach house, and being that I was already drunk, I wanted to party too.

I wandered inside the house.

There were so many people.

Needless to say, I joined in on the fun.

I had tons of drinks. And I danced the night away.

I remember feeling sick, so, I wandered into one of the many bedrooms. I remember plopping down on a huge bed and closing my eyes.

After only a few minutes, I heard the door open.

A man.

He was just as drunk as I was.

He noticed me, and immediately started to flirt.

I'll be honest; usually, I would've slept with him.

I was wild and crazy like that.

But that night, I wasn't in the mood.

I just wanted to sober up.

And he wouldn't let me.

He started to grab on me, and touch all over me.

I told him to stop, but he wouldn't.

And that's when I started to get flashbacks of the rape.

Needless to say, I lost my cool.

I started to fight him off, and once I was finally free from his grip, I grabbed the beer bottle that he'd sat on the table beside the bed.

I broke the bottle, and I pointed the sharp, broken piece at him. I told him to stay away from me.

He didn't.

So, with all my might, I pushed the broken beer bottle into his stomach. After doing it once, I did it again and again.

Blood was everywhere.

And once he fell down to the floor, still holding the piece of bottle in my hand, I ran out of the room.

People were everywhere.

Drinking, laughing, and dancing.

No one cared about me running through the house with blood all over me. If they even noticed.

Finally, I made it outside and ran towards the beach.

I remember feeling…

Shit, I felt good!

I felt powerful!

And walking into the cool beach water, I finally let go of the broken bottle, and stared at the blood on my hands.

I knew at that very moment that my sister's husband, one day, would be the next.

My sister's husband, my rapist was the second person I killed. I left that part out when telling Nova the story.

Only a few years ago, after forcing myself to take a look at my sister's social media pages, I saw that her husband was going on a business trip to New York.

So, I followed him there.

On the second night, my rapist left a bar and as he headed down a dark alley, after almost two decades…I got my revenge.

I stabbed him.

I made it look like a mugging.

Unfortunately, I had to kill the homeless person that was lurking in the shadows watching me too.

I didn't want to, but I had to.

Ox's girl-friend and Yana were my last.

I don't ever want to kill anyone again.

I made sure Yana's body was found so that there wasn't some kind of delay in Nova getting Yana's money.

It's the least I could do.

Josiah was right.

I did come to like Nova.

Nova and I were more alike than she wanted us to be. And it would've been nice to finally have a friend.

But I had to choose between love or a friend.

In my book, love always wins.

"I'm tired of going back and forth," Ox interrupted my thoughts. "I think I'm going to start talking about selling my half of the company, retire, and I'll be here with you and *our* daughter, for good," Ox smiled.

"How is Nova?"

"Last time I saw her, she was better. They're moving out of their house. With the millions and all she got from her friend's death," Ox eyed me, knowing what I'd done to Yana, because I told him. I'd wanted to see if it would scare him away. It didn't.

I told him I did it for Nova.

I told him *we* owed her that much.

He said he understood.

"They're buying a mansion out in Oxford. Oh, and she's pregnant again."

"What?"

"Yep. She told me she'd just found out. She said it wasn't planned, but she seemed happy about it."

"So, Emory and her are okay?"

"It looks that way. Emory is going through a lot with his son's mother though. Apparently, she married his friend, and wants Emory to sign over his rights."

"So, Kojo and Christina got married?"

"You knew about them?"

"I set it up," I smirked. "Emory isn't going to sign over his rights though. That'll never happen."

"That's what Nova said. She's hopeful that her baby will be a boy this time."

I smiled. "See. It all worked out. We're going to love and take good care of this baby. Nova is having another baby and she can have as many babies as she wants. It all worked out. And this time, her baby is actually Emory's, I hope, so, that's even better. This is how it was supposed to be."

Ox didn't respond.

"Do you regret what we did? Do you regret it at all?"

Ox kissed the baby. "What's life without regrets?" He answered. "But I can live with regrets. Can't you?"

"Hell, yeah, I can!"

I never intended on doing this to Nova, but this is what it took to get my life back; to get Ox back.

And for that reason alone, I'd do it all over again.

I needed someone to love me.

I wouldn't have survived much longer otherwise.

I understand why Josiah was willing to ruin his life if he couldn't have Yana in it. He was willing to be locked up for the rest of his life for love. He was willing to die for love.

And he did.

And I know I would be willing to do the same.

But finally, I have love again.

I have Ox and Emma to love and to be loved by.

And if I ever get caught, it'll all be worth it.

I smiled as Ox carried the baby towards the water.

It's so beautiful here.

Josiah always said he'd wanted to come back here and now, I know why.

Here, you can live, breathe, and fly.

Here…for the rest of your life…you can live a lie.

And that's exactly what I plan to do!

*****

THE END

www.ingramcontent.com/pod-product-compliance
Lightning Source LLC
Chambersburg PA
CBHW031701170626
46808CB00005B/1550